SPECI[AL]

THE U[LVERSCROFT FOUNDATION]
(registered UK cha[rity])
was established in 1972 to p[rovide funds for]
research, diagnosis and treatment of eye disease.
Examples of major projects funded by
the Ulverscroft Foundation are:-

- The Children's Eye Unit at Moorfields Eye Hospital, London
- The Ulverscroft Children's Eye Unit at Great Ormond Street Hospital for Sick Children
- Funding research into eye diseases and treatment at the Department of Ophthalmology, University of Leicester
- The Ulverscroft Vision Research Group, Institute of Child Health
- Twin operating theatres at the Western Ophthalmic Hospital, London
- The Chair of Ophthalmology at the Royal Australian College of Ophthalmologists

You can help further the work of the Foundation by making a donation or leaving a legacy.
Every contribution is gratefully received. If you would like to help support the Foundation or require further information, please contact:

THE ULVERSCROFT FOUNDATION
The Green, Bradgate Road, Anstey
Leicester LE7 7FU, England
Tel: (0116) 236 4325

website: www.foundation.ulverscroft.com

740009836156

HEART OF THE GRASS TREE

When Pearl's grandmother Nell dies unexpectedly, she and her family — mother Diana, sister Lucy — return to Kangaroo Island to mourn and say farewell to her. Each of them knew Nell intimately, and each woman must reckon with Nell's passing in her own way. But Nell had secrets, too; and as the family reflect on their feelings about the island, Pearl starts to pull together the scraps Nell left behind — her stories, poems, paintings — and unearths a connection to the island's early history, of the European sealers and their first contact with the Ngarrindjeri people. As the three women are pulled apart from each other in grief, Pearl's deepening connection to the generations before them, who formed the foundation of the island, grounds her, and will ultimately bring the women back to each other.

First published in Australia in 2019 by
Vintage Australia
Penguin Random House Australia

First Aurora Edition
published 2019
by arrangement with
Penguin Random House Australia
and Curtis Brown

A catalogue record for this book is available
from the British Library.

ISBN 978–1–78782–194–1

Published by
F. A. Thorpe (Publishing)
Anstey, Leicestershire

Set by Words & Graphics Ltd.
Anstey, Leicestershire
Printed and bound in Great Britain by
T. J. International Ltd., Padstow, Cornwall

This book is printed on acid-free paper

MOLLY MURN

◆

HEART OF THE GRASS TREE

Complete and Unabridged

AURORA
Leicester

For Sally

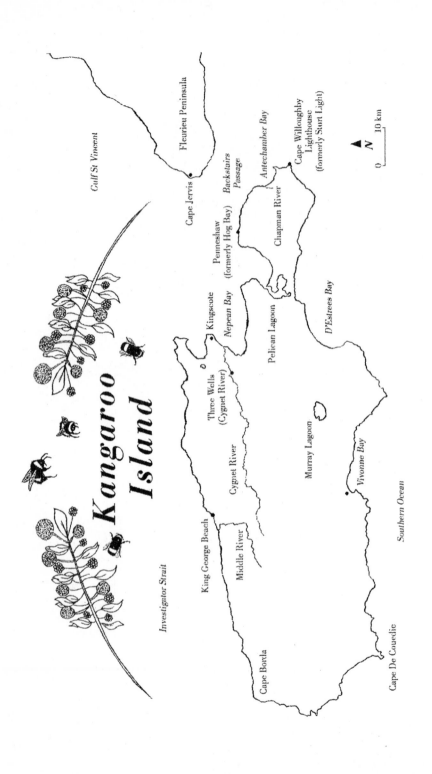

Kangaroo Island

Gulf St Vincent

Fleurieu Peninsula

Cape Jervis

Backstairs Passage

Penneshaw (formerly Hog Bay)

Antechamber Bay

Cape Willoughby Lighthouse (formerly Sturt Light)

Chapman River

Kingscote

Nepean Bay

Three Wells (Cygnet River)

Pelican Lagoon

D'Estrees Bay

Cygnet River

Murray Lagoon

King George Beach

Middle River

Vivonne Bay

Southern Ocean

Investigator Strait

Cape Bortla

Cape De Couedic

N   10 km

0

Grass Tree

if fire could renew my heart
as it does yours

seeds polished shiny as hope
would transform within me

the sweep and rage of flame
cracking open each hidden tendril

flowering with possibility
birds supping from this alchemy

but your heart grows and swells
to an ancient wildfire rhythm

and mine is renewed simply
by the strange architecture

of your beauty

Each island represents a victory and defeat: it had either pulled itself free or pulled too hard and found itself alone. Later, as these islands grew older, they turned their misfortune into virtue, learned to accept their cragginess, their misshapen coasts, ragged where they'd been torn. They acquired grace — some grass, a beach smoothed by tides.

Anne Michaels, Fugitive Pieces

Saw the gigantic rollers that set in, which, when they break, cause the very earth to vibrate. Perhaps some of those grand undulations had come from the South Pole, and, like the lives of many, finished their career upon a wild, barren and unknown spot.

William Cawthorne, 'Journal of a Trip to Kangaroo Island', *Observer*, January 1853

The weaving pattern represents life.
Stitch by stitch, circle by circle.
The lands, waters and all living things are connected like family.

Aunty Ellen Trevorrow,
Kungun Ngarrindjeri Miminar Yunnan

Glossary of Ngarrindjeri Terms

brugi fire coals
dawuldi crow
kalari coastal wattle
kalathami native currant; coastal bearded-heath
kateraiperi echidna
kildjeri grass tree
kinyeri heart of the grass tree
kondoli whale
kringkari spirit people; whitefella; corpse; under layer of skin
kukaki kookaburra (laughing)
kuti cockles
Maringani Autumn, when the Maringani stars appear in the sky
minka bird (most probably a stone curlew) messenger of death
munthari wild apple; muntrie
Muntjingarr Seven Sisters constellation; Pleiades
narambi period of initiation; sacred; dangerous; forbidden; taboo
ngalaii honey from the flowers of the grass tree stem
nganangi fruit of pigface plant
ngatji totem; friend; countryman; protector
nginbulun run(ning) away

Ngurunderi the Creator
Ngurungaui Kangaroo Island (from Ngurunderi)
nori Australian pelican
panpandi native cherry; wild cherry
plonggi fighting club
ruwalruwar body
ruwilruwelruwee land; country; ground; birthplace
taralyi throwing stick; spear-holder; woomera
tawari basket made of rushes
tiyawi goanna; iguano
wakaldi shield
wiloki winter yam
wiltjeri native cherry
wolokaii sponge for collecting honey
wurlie shelter
yalkari old man's beard; reeds; rushes
yunnan speaking; talking; yarning

Nell

King George Beach (Sandy), Kangaroo Island, South Australia

My mother kept bees: *Apis mellifera ligustica*, the Ligurian bee, which exists in its purest strain here on Kangaroo Island. The bees were born in the Ligurian Alps in the days of the Roman Empire and were introduced to the island in the early 1880s by a certain August Fiebig. Because of the island's isolation from the mainland, it is its own protected entity, and here the Ligurian bees have found a sanctuary in which to build their pristine citadels. My mother used to say that the honey of her bees was the island transmuted, that in its viscous gold you could taste hints of salty coastal heath and white mallee and sugar gum and ti-tree and the very tang of the sharp midnight air, or the midday sun, robust and concentrated. And I liked to think, because of the Italian heritage, a hint of something alpine, windswept, exotic.

Once upon a time I was in love. I was only fifteen, so what did I know of love, except that when it rained it was the fecund smell of our love-making, and when the sun shone it was his warm hand on my breast. And I thought it a private, secret thing, our love. Schoolgirls were not to know what men and women really did together. But I knew. I knew, and I didn't want it taken away from me. I also knew what the terrible consequences would be if we were to be discovered. Not just for me, but for him, too. In his family, there were complex laws that governed who belonged to whom, which were far beyond my naïve understanding. Yet we were beautiful together; we fitted. I remember our fingers entwined — mine luminous pale, his velvet dark — a perfect chiaroscuro.

I was only a girl. I didn't realise then that when two people make love together, impassioned concentrated love, there is a contract made. Call it a spiritual vow. What I mean to say is that one can only truly give of themselves to another if they are willing to bear the fruit of that union. And I don't just mean in the biological sense (although I learnt about that only too well); I mean that something is made by and between lovers so precious that they are rendered vulnerable, completely vulnerable, to that precious thing breaking. I knew nothing of this when I loved Sol. I was just being carried on the wings of something much larger than myself. Loving Sol felt right. Now that my body is softer — like worn velvet — more slow, less mine, more mine, I look back and know that we were only learning. We were novices — at sex, at love, at being ourselves — but we were gentle and kind and reverent with each other. And we laughed. We were innocent to the consequences of our being together, of being drawn to each other's honey.

Mother started beekeeping when Father got ill — a bout of influenza that left him so depleted it

2

was months before he could get through a day's work without shaking, without stopping to sit down every half hour — so Sol and I must've been about thirteen years old. For a good while, Mother's honey was in high demand, and it helped tide things over while Father was recovering. Her Hog Bay Honey was not sold in the Hog Bay Store; our neighbours would come to the house directly to buy honey. Soon enough, Mother was also selling honey biscuits, honey cake and honey apple tarts from the kitchen door, just about as soon as they came out of the oven. She became known simply as 'the honey lady'.

In my memory of the honey harvest of late summer, Sol is always there. He'd wander over from his family's farm, which neighboured ours, but was a good hour's walk away, in his bare feet, and with his skinny yellow dog, Gem-Gem, in tow. I remember Sol as a streak of blue. I don't know why. Perhaps because his shirt was always blue. Or perhaps I have gazed out at this ocean for so many years that somehow the glinting blue out there and Sol, dear Sol, have become one and the same. He is always moving, always mercurial, always on the edge of things, and blue blue blue.

It is the later beekeeping years that I remember most clearly. I would find Sol waiting on the back doorstep in the shade of morning, drawing in the dirt with a piece of fencing wire which had a small loop at one end and was bent into a curve so that when he wasn't using it, he could hang it around his neck for safekeeping. I would bring him a steaming cup of tea, which he gulped down in three big slurps before springing to his feet, and saying something like, Thank ya, gorgeous, while winking at me in my long sleeves and baggy trousers, and then smoothing over his inscriptions on the ground with his heel. Sol never wore anything but his regular clothes when bee-handling, his frayed straw hat pulled down so low as to almost cover his eyes. And I only saw him get stung once. It was right on the chest, under his shirt, and I remember that all morning before the sting, Sol had been in a particularly bad mood. The bees were cross that day, too — butting against us angrily, their drone a higher pitch than I was used to, and Sol frowning and cursing. I wish I could remember more clearly what he told me later that afternoon, but all I can recall is holding a cool flannel against his left chest, and his agitation, and his eyes of a darker colour than I was used to. But that was a harvesting day out of the ordinary.

Mother thought Sol made the bees calm, which is why he became known as Smoky in our house. She thought he didn't need to use the smoking canister to subdue the bees, but of course he did need it. I'm not that crazy, he would say. He was fearless, and the bees knew it, but he was also sensible. I never called him Smoky; to me he was always Sol. Sol of the bees. Sol of my heart. And of course, he has another name too.

It is time to write of him. Time to write of us. But how? I'm afraid. I'm afraid of words. And what unloosing them will bring. Once written,

4

they are so set down, so finite. I'd sooner paint. I know how to speak in pictures. When I paint it is heart to brush to canvas. Nothing in between. Beyond thought; beyond feeling. Beyond words. But now, I'm afraid. I'm afraid that if I don't utter these words they will be lost. And I want them released. I want them found.

★ ★ ★

The house is swept, dusted, mopped, scrubbed. I've started another sculpture. A thing of bones. I've walked and swum and scraped a new supply of salt from the rocks for the pantry. I've been in to Kingscote for groceries, and I've phoned my granddaughter, Pearl. I heard something in her voice — a catch, a holding back. We must talk again soon. She thinks my cough sounds serious. From paint fumes and smoking, she says. She worries too much. I've been to the doctor about my chest, but she just says that I need to rest. Stress. It's more than that, though. If I don't set these words down, this tightness around my heart will only get worse. The stuck words will stop me from breathing. Please help me. Today the sea is glassy flat. A blank page. So bright it throws the sun right back at your eyes.

I take down Sol's story-wire from its place on the ledge above the window. I haven't touched it in years. The wire is thick, heavy, slightly rusted. I place it in the centre of the kitchen table (my mother's oak table) that has seen so much. I walk tentatively to my bedroom. Slow, like I'm performing a Japanese tea ceremony. I find the pale-green shoebox, stashed away at the back of the wardrobe, and carry it carefully back to my writing place. I am uncertain. When I paint, I fly. When I write, I might break.

A white-bellied sea eagle skims the water, dipping into a mirror. I think of my daughter, Diana. I don't want to be angry with her anymore. She is too much like me. A mirror. And Pearl's turned out fine. More than fine. Stronger than all of us.

I arrange the contents of the box in a semicircle around my notepad, with Sol's wire at the centre. The periwinkle necklaces spread out on one side, and the black glass scraper and woollen caps on the other. The smell of the patchouli leaves I've scattered through the box is pungent, grounding, overpowering.

And I have a jar of Ligurian honey beside me. The island transmuted. I will eat spoonfuls as I write. I take up my pen — fine-tipped, felt — and I smooth my hand along the page. I begin with trepidation because I am afraid of what it is I have to say. Until this very moment, the words were taken from me, fossilised, so that now as I turn them in my palm or line them up beneath the glass (my own exhibition), I am forced to see again, but worse, to feel again that long-ago moment frozen in time. I carry this fossil of memory.

★ ★ ★

Sol and I worked together to collect the honey, while Mother worked alone on the opposite row

6

of bee boxes. I would puff the smoke into the entrance of the hive, just two puffs, and then wait until Sol let me know that the bees were ready. Nothing was more harmonious than those suspended minutes. We hardly spoke, but what passed between us as we stood listening to the changing pitch of the bees felt something like relief, something like excitement, and something like an incredible descending grace, light as the smoke that encircled us. The bees — those little drops of light — taught me to listen. And Sol taught me to listen, too. I couldn't exactly meet his eyes, veiled as I was by my apiary hat, but I felt him. I followed his lead. He knew exactly when to pry open the lid of the box, and I would be ready with the smoker, three puffs, while Sol whispered to the bees, Shh, shh, busy ones, show us what you've been up to.

Once he'd removed the inner cover, and more smoke had sent the bees clinging like little clusters of raisins to the bottom of the hive, Sol would gently lift out the wooden frame, brushing away the bees with a branch of dry leaves, making soft crooning noises as he did so.

Nell, is it sealed enough?

I would quickly scan the combs checking for holes or gaps or fissures. No gaps.

Sol, glancing around to check that Mother wasn't looking, would press the side of his hip against mine, That's right, Nell, no gaps at all, and then together we would carry the honeycomb carefully to the collecting shed, giggling quietly to ourselves.

I still remember his fingers, quick and sure, as he sliced through the wax caps of the honeycomb with a knife warmed in hot water. Even now, when I heat a knife to cut through my neighbour Marian's famous chocolate mud cake, I think of those days in the shed. I would wait, holding the wide uncapped jar beneath the honeycomb, ready to catch the honey as it flowed out thick and slow — Sol and I locked together in concentrated stillness, guided only by the fall and glug of honey. Afterwards we would lick the drips from each other's fingers, but only if Mother was elsewhere. The smell of fresh honey — subtle, spreading, spiced — has never left me, not to this day; it is the smell of vulnerability.

At the end of the honey harvest, there would be at our house a meal shared by Sol's family and mine. While Father scored and basted the leg of ham, poking cloves into each of the diamond-shaped spaces, I would stand at the kitchen bench rolling beeswax into balls, running them up and down my warm cheeks remembering Sol and the way our teeth sometimes tapped together when we kissed.

Out of my way, Nell, hot saucepan coming through, Mother would say, and she would bustle past with honey and ginger syrup for drenching the semolina cake.

Father would interrupt my reverie somehow, flicking me on the legs with the tea towel, or blowing sharply down the back of my neck, Make yourself useful, Nell. Stop daydreaming and chop some carrots or something.

The meal was always the same, even if the day had been a scorcher, and often we ate on the wide verandah because the kitchen was airless. Sol's aunties smoked, and Mother didn't approve — mostly because Father would end up having three or four as well, but also because she didn't want the kitchen all smoked up. The women puffed away on roll-up after roll-up all evening, the glowing ends of their cigarettes sometimes all you could see in the blackness, like the roving eyes of night animals. I preferred it when we ate under the stars, because Sol and I could grin away at each other in the shadows, Gem-Gem trotting between us, with no one to give a thought to my blazing cheeks. Or so I thought.

Looking back, I guess I had it all wrong. As I understood it, my family got on well with the Walcotts and I thought Mother had a particular soft spot for her bee-whisperer, Smoky. She was always praising him and slipping him bags of biscotti and fresh apples to take home to his little cousins. One evening, after the honey harvest meal, and after the Walcotts had left — though we could still hear their voices carrying across the nearby paddocks — Mother grabbed my wrist as I stood drying dishes for her. Never before or after did she look at me in quite that way. She was holding back tears but holding back fury and despair also. Her words, however, she did not hold back — The Walcotts are our neighbours, but they will never be our kin, so you better stop making eyes at Smoky. It will come to no good. I will say no more.

9

I was so shocked and embarrassed that I ran from the kitchen, rubbing my wet and soapy wrist where she'd gripped me vice-like, and sobbed until I was wrung completely empty.

I heard Mother and Father squabbling in the kitchen, Leave her be, she's just a child.

My point exactly. She doesn't know what she's getting herself into.

They're just good friends —

Don't be so naïve, you want a black for a son-in-law?

Mother really got him on that one. He was silenced. And after that Sol and I were hardly ever alone. Father was attuned to my whereabouts like Gem-Gem was to the sheep.

But had they not noticed my swollen breasts? Did they not know it was already too late? After that night, Mother and I hardly spoke, and I kept my friendship with Sol a firm secret. I was stopped, shuttered, silenced. Only Sol could make me cry out. And now that the something new and fragile growing between us had been disturbed, everything turned for the worse.

I have hexagon-shaped holes in my memory. Where did the details go? I don't remember now whether the last time I saw Sol before everything went wrong was down by the creek at the bottom of the paddock, where we sat together on an uneven rock, my body leaning deliberately against his, as he trickled creek water over my bare legs. Or if it was the day he was stung on the chest. I don't remember because everything is out of order now. So how do I tell my story? I have a beginning and an end, but the middle leaves me lost for words. How do I spiral into the heart? Aunty Hettie would say, Begin in the centre.

The sea is bruising; the sky is monochrome. I can't stop now. I gather the strings of periwinkles and place them around my neck. Dear Aunties, give me words. I take a spoonful of honey.

★   ★   ★

They took the baby away. But first they took me away. To the mainland, to a place where girls like me were sent. I had no idea what was going to happen once the baby came. Not where the baby and I would go, and certainly not what would happen to my body. The policy was to tell us nothing, to protect us from what they knew would tear us apart, I suppose. But we should have been given warning. I was meant to feel ashamed of my swelling body like Mother and Father were, but I spoke to that baby every minute, and I was beautiful. If only Sol could see me now — and why won't he write — I remember thinking. My darkening nipples, my glossy hair and my heat my heat. I had never felt so isolated; I had never even left the island, but now there were two of us, and that gave me some comfort, and with Sol we were going to be three. I imagined that once the baby was born, Father would come and take us home, and that when he laid eyes upon the child, he would forgive me everything, and somehow Sol and I would be allowed to make things work, and that we wouldn't have to give the baby away to a good Christian family.

I don't remember much of the birth at all, except the incredible bearing down pain and crying out, and putting my hands down there, to try to hold myself together, and the blood on my fingers, and the nurses holding a strong-smelling rag under my nose, shoving it in my face, and the waking up in an empty room with hard full breasts and a burning between my legs and no baby no baby and somebody screaming. Now, as I write this, I know that it was my own scream that I heard. There I've said it! This is the centre of all that's been petrified. An impression of grief hidden in strata.

They took the baby away immediately. I never even saw a glimpse of it.

I look up and realise it's been hours. My shoulders ache. There is a sailboat right in the centre of the bay — it is a distraction — like a prickle caught underfoot. Something in the way. I feel nauseous. And I'm burning hot. My body remembers even though I've tried to forget. Sol. Cellular memory. I should eat something more than honey. But I can't move. All I can do is keep sitting here. Write this.

I was seasick, like now, the entire journey home from the mainland back to the island. The ketch reeled from side to side and I scraped the dried blood out from under my fingernails in between retching. My breasts dripped milk; I was hearing my baby faraway hungry. We needed each other. Tears and blood and milk and my words, just all leaked away. Wasted. Til now, til now, til now. At least give me back the words. Mother rocked me like a baby on that long journey home, realising the gravity of what she'd made me do, crooning and whispering in my ear, crying into my hair, but my heart was closed to her. My heart was closed full stop. Brittle as dry honeycomb. When we arrived back at the farm the first thing I noticed was that the bee boxes were ruined. There's been a terrible storm, my mother explained. Oh, don't I know it, I thought to myself.

I hold this moment gently. I want to be unstopped. I've never spoken of this. Not to my husband, Reg — he came years later, darling Reg — not to my daughter, Diana, not even to Pearl. And not to myself. But lately that child comes to me in dreams. Brown eyes and pursed lips. And Sol, my streak of blue. My sun. They've come to give me back my voice again. I trace the length of the story-wire. There is a residue left on my finger. Dirt from our farm, from Sol's hands, or am I imagining that?

My mother never kept bees again. Never repaired the broken hives. After that it was yaccas — grass trees. Extracting resin from grass trees for explosives, and for burning in churches — an Antipodean frankincense — and for polishing floors. My mother, stealer of the essence of things. Honey and sap. I weep now for my stolen baby — Samuel, I call him — and for my mother, whom I wasn't able to let in again. Now these shuddering tears leave me as if without skin. There's nothing between me and the air, the light, the sound, the heat. Nothing between me and then. Sol.

And now I remember — deeper still — the last time I saw Sol before Samuel must have been down at the creek, and I would have been pregnant, though we had no idea. He said he'd never seen me look more beautiful. Something's changed, he said. It was too hot, even for kissing. He took out his pocket knife and gouged our names into the rough bark of a grass tree. A tall one leaning like an old man towards us, its trunk naked, bare-chested. Our names an open wound. I traced my finger gently over the letters knowing even then that this would be the only place those markings would sit together. Nell + Sol. Our tree. Later, after I'd come back home and everything had gone wrong, I found Sol's name bleeding bright sap. And I remember something else: the day he was stung was the morning after the very last time we made love, beside that tree, though we couldn't have known it then. That day, covering my hand that held the flannel to his heart, Sol said, The bees are worried for us, Nell.

And so you see, I was only fifteen. What did I know of love? Only, that in the place where beauty grows and swells, something hard and brittle can also form. To break apart the layers of bedrock, I must go even further back, to a time long before me. And now that I'm finding my way — without skin — I must tell a story. It's not my story, and it's not exactly Sol's, either; it is greater than ourselves, but it belongs to this island and beyond and it belongs in our hearts. This is the vow. Sol, it is our precious thing.

1822
Encounter Bay, South Australia

Anderson knows he has picked an ideal night for the Sabine expedition. Calm, mild, black. With only a scrap of moon up above, he and the men will be able to move under the cover of darkness. A child's cough punctures the silence as they near the edge of the camp, and Anderson feels a lurch of adrenaline. He spreads his coat on the ground and eases himself down as precisely as a cat stalking prey; the only guiding light is the distant smoulder of campfire. Here he will lie in wait, not sleeping, until the milk-blue dawn finds him crouching on his haunches, spying on the husbands and fathers and brothers who are preparing for their hunt. Anderson's senses are sharp, honed; he's never felt so alert. A well-oiled musket, he thinks to himself. He spreads apart the fanned leaves of a grass tree and, peering through, he makes his choice. He wants the woman with the elegant neck and wide, strong shoulders. But his legs are cramping. They must wait so long for the men to disappear through the gaps in the trees. When the mothers and children are finally alone, Anderson gives the signal — an exaggerated nod of the head — and all six men rush in, to drag away their bucking spoils.

A small boy makes a skittish run from the camp. He is caught. Anderson snaps his arm like a twig across his knee and casts him aside. When Anderson seizes his prize from

15

behind he is surprised at her strength. She clamps her mouth on the fleshy mound below Anderson's thumb and draws blood. A small girl wraps herself around the woman's legs and Anderson has to use all of his force to kick her off. He quietens the woman with a punch to her mouth. As he hauls her away from the camp, the girl flings herself around the woman again and Anderson drags them both in the direction of the vessel. At the water's edge, Anderson slips his hold momentarily and the woman and child make to escape, but he lurches after them and strikes the woman across the back of the neck. He slings her over his shoulder like she's a seal, and throws her into the cutter along with the other stolen women who claw and bite their attackers. The child follows, too stunned to make a sound, and flails her way to the side of the boat. The woman leans as much as she can over the edge of the boat while being restrained by Everitt, and somehow drags the girl aboard, her mouth bleeding into the child's hair. Propelling the cutter away from the shore, the sealers jump aboard with expert timing. The women moan and beat at their chests as if their cries alone could bring down the sky. Anderson is irritated that they have a child with them, but he decides to keep her aboard for now because her presence placates the woman with the bruised and delicate neck. Anderson looks back to the shoreline. The women's people stand along it, weapons raised, wailing their grief.

Chapman River, Antechamber Bay, Kangaroo Island

William watches the negotiations between his father and the other sealers, Munro, Everitt, and Piebald, from atop an upturned dinghy about twenty metres away from the huddle of women. He is particularly fascinated by the small girl, who seems to be as interested in lizards as he is.

She is crouching beside the women, swapping a tiny, reddish salamander from hand to hand as it crawls over the edge of one palm into the other. William flicks a small piece of quartz with his thumb and forefinger that skids near her feet. She looks up quickly, and he grins at her as he balances on the hull.

William, get here, Anderson shouts.

William slides down the edge of the boat and, as he walks past the girl, drops a trochus shell his father collected from King Sound into her lap.

He turns around and she's staring at the shell. He wonders if she has ever seen such a shell, with its smooth and lustrous inner lining and its spiralling exterior. The girl kneels up and lets it slide from her lap onto the ground and then edges away from it. The woman who bit his father's hand yesterday picks it up and turns it over, talking to the other women in a lilting, low voice. The shell is passed around the group, each of the women examining it carefully, whispering. When Anderson and Piebald yank the women to their feet suddenly, the shell thuds to the ground. William can't help but notice the boiled-meat colour of the men's hands against

17

the polished black of the women's skin. They've even been given names — Emue, Poll, Mooney, Puss. He mouths the names to try to remember them. Picking up the abandoned shell, he wonders what the women said about it, before running to keep up with his father, who calls for him like he's one of the dogs. The girl runs in and out from between the women — restless shadow — as they are herded to the beach.

She can't come with us, Anderson announces as he blocks the girl from getting into the cutter. The women are frightened and exhausted and beyond protest, and they gesture for the girl to wait behind. William tries to smile at her, he wants to tell her that they will be back before nightfall, but she won't look at him. He hopes that she will not spend the whole day crouching on the shore staring past the headland to where the boat has disappeared. The sun could eat you alive on a day like this.

★ ★ ★

Maringani watches the child from a distance. Kringkari kop, her brothers call the pale men. Spirit people. Noses come first. Sniffing out the women. The pale boy is crouching by the fire, resting his elbows on his knees and cupping his chin in his hands. The kringkari looks solid, real, like he would be warm if she touched him. He looks kind. She wonders what his skin feels like. The pale men are around, too. One of them sits beside the boy and appears to be making something in the fire. Some of them are walking

18

about tearing off chunks of what looks like meat with their teeth and chewing noisily. Others are smoking or talking loudly over piles of skins. The man by the fire hands the boy something to eat and ruffles his hair. The kringkari eats like he is alive, not like he is a spirit. He glances up and meets her gaze and she ducks behind a ti-tree. Maringani's heart quivers, like that of a caught bird.

She watches the kringkari approach with an offering of food. He says something to her, but she can't make out the words; they are stones rattling in a basket, but his voice is gentle.

Maringani is surprised when he somehow wriggles out of his shirt, drops it in front of himself and places the food on top of it. She turns away from his smile and she hears him make his way back to the fire.

The smell of the offering, which looks a bit like wiloki, makes Maringani's stomach lurch and growl. She snatches up the morsel and runs to the women. Maringani shows it to Emue, who smells it, takes a small bite of the roasted potato, nods, and then passes it on to share with the other women. Emue gestures Maringani to stay close, and holds her gently under the wing of her arm. Maringani feels that she holds her too tightly, but she leans in, hoping that if she is still enough, Emue will stop whimpering.

King George Beach (Sandy)

There is a moment between sleeping and waking where everything is silver. Before orientation. A threshold of possibility. Calm. Then slowly Pearl remembers who she is, what time it is, what day it is, what must be done. She remembers that Nell has died. She tries to lengthen the silver moments by keeping her mind as empty as a stone. But then awakeness rushes in and it hurts. An avalanche.

Lucy — little sister — is beside her on the bed. She is holding Pearl's hand, running her thumbs over the tops of chipped fingernails.

You need to file your nails, Lucy says. Let's paint them later, too.

How long have I been asleep?

Oh, quite a while now. I came in to see if you wanted some lunch, and you were whimpering in your sleep, so I lay down with you.

God! I am so tired. From —

I know. I know. Ssshhh.

There is the jolting thud of children running in the hallway. There is the clatter of dishes. There is the voice of her brother-in-law, Joe, in the kitchen — a soothing bass note, Pearl thinks. There is the clack of Diana's ridiculous heels. There is the pleasurable static of ocean. The keen of gulls.

20

When Pearl arrived a few hours ago, Marian and Red, Nell's dear neighbours, had steered her through to the lean-to sunroom that Pearl always stayed in, and tucked her up in bed. The room, neat and uncluttered, with its small desk, dresser and bookshelf, and patchwork quilt folded neatly on the end of the bed, always made Pearl think she was somewhere quaint like Anne Shirley's bedroom at Green Gables. All it needed was a washstand and jug and a vase of waxy flowers, and she could be an orphan grateful for sanctuary. Pearl had closed her eyes to the smell of laundered sheets and wished for no dreams.

Can you see that face up there on the ceiling? In the knot of wood? Lucy asks.

Rumpelstiltskin? Yes! He's always been there. I used to be so afraid of him, sleeping in here. He's snarling at us, even now. And there's the maiden spinning gold. Can you see her long floaty hair? How I wished for her hair.

No, that's a woman's naked body. See the curve of her back?

They laugh, their heads tipping together. Pearl wonders if it's just sisters that know how to hold skin together. And to stick fingers deep into wounds as well. Pearl would cry except that she's all dried up. She turns away from Lucy. *All in the same room.* We need to cry together all in the same room, Lucy had said on the phone the day before. She was right, of course, Pearl thought. But she was a husk, just an outer covering with no moisture, let alone tears.

Pearl, you know that Marian and Red found Nell?

21

Through the window there is just the sea, the scrubby headlands at either end of the small, curved bay and the outcrop of rocks not far from the shoreline that look like a wallaby lying on its side. Nell called it Wallaby Rock and sometimes when the tide is low you can walk right along the tip of the wallaby's ear and fish for whiting.

Yeah.

Pearl thinks of the clot that killed Nell. A piece of grit rushing through channels of blood. Caught in a snag. Damming up the flow. Burst river. That's all it takes, just one little snag.

Alfie calls for Lucy and, hot-wired to his demands, she lets go of Pearl's hand and then pads out of the room. I'll make you a gin and tonic, she says as she leaves.

Pearl sits up and pulls off her clothes, tossing them in the corner of the room. She is suddenly hot from sleep and worry. Sweaty from travel — an early flight from Melbourne to Adelaide and then a bus to Cape Jervis to catch the ferry — she wants to start over. Wash this day away in the ocean. Rummaging in her suitcase for her bathers, she catches a glimpse in the dresser mirror and straightens to look properly: smooth white and golden-freckled. Dark around the eyes. Small high breasts. Plum nipples. Stomach not as flat as it used to be, she thinks. And pubic hair wilder and scragglier. She smooths her hands over her bottom as if to press it into a more held-together shape. The light catches occasional strands of silver in her already pale hair and she winces. Pearl snatches her bathers and quickly pulls them on, wiggling to stretch the fabric over her hips. She ties her hair in a knot at the base of her neck and has a final glimpse in the mirror as she slips on her sandals without doing them up. She wonders at her face sometimes. She thinks, It's me but so much older.

In the living room, things are calmer than when she first arrived. Marian and Red were baking all afternoon in Nell's kitchen, but now they've gone back home. Ginger muffins, Marian's specialty, cool on a wire rack. Ariel is playing with Nell's collection of sea treasures, making families out of shells and sorting smooth stones from jagged ones, and clear ones from opaque ones. Ariel has divided the glass into piles by colour. Turquoise, navy, green, black, amber, milky. And she has built a barricade of cushions around herself to deter Alfie from interrupting, but he is happy enough playing with his animal figurines. Joe is juicing limes and whistling and Lucy is at the table scribbling things down.

I'm making a list of things we still need to do, she says.

Like what?

Like, ring the funeral home about flowers. They have to be native. Um, borrow more wine glasses from Red and Marian; work out running order. That kind of thing.

Right. We should pick our own flowers. And what about Uncle Jim, did you get in touch?

Is Uncle here now? Joe asks, holding a bunch of mint leaves under the tap and spraying water everywhere. Turn the tap down a bit, Pearl thinks.

23

He's staying with his niece Caroline over near Murray Lagoon. Arrived yesterday, says Lucy.

He's agreed to read the eulogy? Pearl asks, straightening the mat on the floor with her heel.

Yep.

Diana is smoking on the verandah outside. Even from a distance Pearl can see the slight shake of her mother's fingers. When she was a child she would take Diana's hand in hers to make it more still. She desperately wanted her mother to be more solid. From behind, Diana could be mistaken for a young girl. Slim and narrow-waisted. Thick hair. Straight-backed. A delicate heroine. People were always falling in love with her — even if just for a moment. In shops and in cafes and on the street, admirers would keep her engaged in conversation just that little bit longer than usual. She would brighten under their attention. Later, when Pearl or Lucy called her on it, she seemed oblivious in some way. Surprised. Oh no, that's how people talk to everyone, she would argue. Her beauty was a given.

And Dad called. He wants you to ring him back, says Lucy.

Pearl thinks that if she were to see David walk into the room she would not be able to hold herself together. She would howl, swear and fall into his arms. But she's sure he won't come. Diana would give him too much of a hard time. When they separated, Diana became unhooked. She needed him to soften things for her: the spikiness of the world, her tendency to overthink everything, her lack of confidence in parenting

24

and her fears that she wasn't a good enough artist. And if she wasn't a good lover, parent, teacher, artist, then what was she, she used to scream down the phone to David after he'd moved out.

How is he?

He's good. Sad. He's going to come. Just for a day or so.

Does Diana know?

Um, maybe. She'll be pissed off if he does. Pissed off if he doesn't.

Hmm.

As if she knows they're talking about her, Diana turns towards the window and flattens down her dark bounce of hair. She is incongruous here in this wild place, with her buttoned shirts and bangles and make-up. Pearl smiles at her, but Diana doesn't see anything past her own reflection.

I'm going for a quick swim. I'll be back soon.

I want to come, says Ariel.

No, you've just been for a swim. Pearl won't be long, Lucy says firmly.

Pearl kisses Ariel's sweaty hairline. We can go for a morning swim together tomorrow, okay, darling?

Okay, she says with a pout and slumped shoulders.

Good girl. And Joe, I'll have that gin and tonic when I get back. Pearl grins at him as he carefully slices lemons. She knows that Joe's painstaking slowness to complete simple domestic tasks drives Lucy wild but what would they all do without him? He is unflappable.

Sometimes he reminds Pearl of the cows she and Lucy passed on the streets of Rajasthan — lumberingly calm, gentle-eyed, slow to blink, long muscles on fine bones. I must be delirious, she thinks.

The best and longest to make gin and tonic ever, Joe calls after her.

Can't wait.

Once outside, Pearl takes a quick inventory as she bends to do up her sandals. Nell's sandshoes by the back door. A pile of cuttlefish and tiny bones and stones in the wheelbarrow — perhaps the beginning of a project? The peg basket tipped over on the concrete. A spill of buckets and spades and plastic animals. A skirt of Nell's wrapped impossibly around the clothesline. Pearl wonders if she should unhook it. She doesn't.

It is warm and still. The sky billows: a vast blue tent pegged down at the horizon, saturated with colour. No wind at all. It is so bright today that Pearl is panicked. Since hearing the news four days ago, she's been all curled up inside, relishing darkness, seeking small rooms, Nico's tight embrace, finding little shells of protection in everything. Now she's exposed, shrinking in the heat and beneath the endless unforgiving sky. Pearl takes a deep breath, wraps her red cotton shawl around her head and takes the path at the back of the house that goes through the scrub and along the inlet — mostly to avoid Diana, who's rummaging in the shed, and because she and Nell walked this path many times together. Our path. She follows the wallaby scats, the native grasses crackling under her sandals. She

26

thinks of Nell and how her feet were always bare. How the skin on her heels was thick and callused, so that she could walk along these tracks and along the beach unfettered and without flinching as she stepped over prickles and rough stones. Nell was terrified of coming across a snake, though, so she used to bang the ground with a long stick to frighten them away.

Stomp, Pearl, when you walk. Let the snakes know you're here.

Pearl remembers Nell's feet stretched towards the camp-fires on the beach, her fourth toe curled in and nestled against the middle toe like a small prawn. They all have a curled fourth toe — Diana, Lucy, Pearl. But not Ariel, she has fine, long, just slightly crooked toes like Joe's. And not Alfie.

Pearl, a curly toe is very useful for climbing trees and picking things up with your feet. Prehensile. It makes you special, my dear, Nell used to tell Pearl. As a teenager Pearl thought her feet very ugly. Hated wearing sandals that showed her ungainly toes. Nell used to give the children a dollar to pull gently on her toe to lengthen it and hold it straight, loving the sensation of straightening out a kink. Pearl has started paying Ariel to do the same.

As she nears the inlet, she can smell the brine. It is the end of summer and with no rain in months the creek has narrowed to a brown, stagnant ribbon, snaking through the gully. Tomorrow she will bring Ariel down to lay some nets, she thinks. The water could be just deep enough and brackish enough for catching yabbies and marron. There are flies and midges trying to get to the moisture of her mouth and she spits them away. Nell used to swim in this creek when she was a girl, but now it's really no more than a boggy puddle. Pearl remembers paddling in the mouth of the inlet at certain times of the year when it would swell out to the sea, but she hasn't seen it flowing like that since she was a child.

She thinks of the Ngarrindjeri sisters that once camped along here. Nell used to tell it like a love story. They ran away from the sealers' camp and lived here for a time with the white son of a sealer. He'd run away, too. She wonders how the inlet looked to them, how much has altered. The she-oaks with their timeless whispering, what did they say? She remembers yesterday morning with Nico, she astride him, moving relentlessly until he came. They'd had to. Right day, right hour, Pearl the correct basal temperature: small window of fertility. But the look on Nico's face was of worry and not of desire: and then he had wept, his face turned away from her, hiding quiet tears.

The sun is getting so fierce that her walking ambles to a stop. I'm sorry for all this, Nico, she whispers. He and Lewis, her stepson, are coming on Thursday and she hates to admit that while Nico isn't around, there is relief from having to worry about the labyrinth of her body — its core temperature and hormone levels. She knows he doesn't want to think about those things, either. Ever. And that is part of the problem. She kicks at an abandoned, broken beehive, splintering the wood further along one of its seams, and then sits herself down beside it, wiping at her temples to stop the sweat from running into her ears, and brushing away twigs at the back of her thighs. She wiggles one of the trays from the beehive, and there is the sudden smell of dust and candles and honey. Desiccated bees entombed in wax drop around her feet like dead, curled leaves as she pulls out the tray. It is achingly quiet. So quiet she can feel the wings in her chest spread just a little. And there's a warm hum behind her navel. She tries to shove the tray of old honeycomb back into the box but it jams, catching on something. Giving up, she tosses it to the ground and dust mites whirl and eddy. Pearl picks at the layers of peeling white paint. The drooping whispering she-oaks and the stillness of the creek water and the hot wind and the smell of honey coax something out of her. A tiny rasp of tension.

The inlet, stained brown from gum leaves and shallow warm (*like wee*, she and Lucy used to say), peters out. She takes off her sandals and then carefully picks her way through the spinifex and saltbush at the edge of the dune. Nell's beach. Our beach. Heart place. The wind picks up and she makes her way to the rocky outcrop that skirts the curving trace of the inlet. Here, the sheer edge of a hill blocks the wind. The stony face of it looms shadowy. Later, lit by the sun, it will glow gold. She jumps from rock to rock, like she and Lucy used to do as girls. They would try to walk all the way around the edge of the outcrop without touching the sand. A slanting foothold gives way beneath her step and, as she catches herself, she jags the edge of her foot on a point of slate. The pain is instant and searing. She clamps her hand over the cut and manoeuvres onto a flattish bit of sand.

Nell is everywhere: standing on the verandah waving them in for dinner, walking slow at the water's edge and bending at the hips to pick up shells, walking brisk in the morning to warm the chill in her knees, picking her way over these rocks to scrape salt, sitting here contemplating the silver line of the horizon. A person leaves so many traces, yet no trace at all. Pearl wishes she could just retrace the seams and tracks she's made since she last saw Nell — the lines that led her away — and follow them back like gathering in a roll of skein. It would take her to their last moment together, at the ferry terminal, and the feel of the warmth of her hand would not be a memory that disappeared the more she tried to snatch at it, but solid and material — their hands a furnace together. Those paths are ghostly corridors of something else now. Closer to dreams. She gropes at them.

So, I left that day, thinks Pearl. I should have stayed.

She takes her hand from the cut on her foot and licks the spot of blood from her fingers before walking carefully towards the shoreline, letting the ridges of sand massage her arches, the cut foot stinging. At the threshold of water and shore she is very still. And then she walks in, gasping as the water reaches her thighs, the cold shock of it making her cross her arms over her breasts protectively. The waves break forcefully against her and she lets herself be taken. Pearl opens her eyes underwater and it is grey and emerald. It is so cold it's like being slapped all over. Everything sharpens.

She swims in long, slow strokes, stretching into her fingertips, flexing her toes, and for just a moment she can't be sure whether the brine taste is the water or tears as she slips under. The taste of olives. But she won't cry yet. She always makes a wish when she swims in the ocean. Lately, it's the same wish. She resurfaces and there's a sea eagle with an elegantly hooked neck diving for fish, neat as a dancer. It sits on the surface of the water carried back and forth by the swell and then dips below. She thinks of Nell's sea eagle feathers lined up on the windowsill, and turns and floats on her back, her arms outstretched. She squeezes her eyes tight. Sometimes in the periphery she sees the children she can't have. Wisps of blonde and light dancing at the edges of things. Please. Can you see them too, Nell? she whispers.

* * *

Diana wonders where Nell hid her marijuana. She knows it will be here somewhere and, now that she's had the thought, she wants to smoke her mother's weed in her mother's shed. The task gives her something tangible. It occupies her. She's never really spent any time in here. This was Nell's sanctuary and Diana had not felt welcome. She scans the space indulgently and feels like a trespasser. Tools hang neatly on the wall at one end. There are shelves of Vegemite jars containing nails and screws and hooks and every small part you might ever need, carefully labelled in Nell's jerky hand. The cream Morris Minor, long in automobile-repose, is shrouded in a thick and dusty canvas sail. But the other end, the light end, is where Nell spent most of her afternoons priming canvases, selecting colours — an act of divination, and then marking out the broad outline of her compositions before the intricate labour of the detail. Beside the easel on an old beehive box sit her paintbrushes and mixing palette.

Diana takes in a deep breath of the dry smell of dust and paint. And she is reminded not of her mother, but of her father, Reg. Nell had been the one to have a shed after Reg died and something in her seemed to flower. She threw herself into painting, and as Diana had become more and more amorphous, insubstantial, upon Reg's death, Nell's outlines had deepened, strengthened. It was like she gave off solar flares and Diana thought her mother's fire would burn her up like dross. When Pearl was a baby Diana missed the grounding presence of her father even more. Every time Pearl cried, or even when she pawed her tiny scratchy fingernails at Diana's breast, Diana felt she was being scattered. She imagined finding parts of herself flapping like a rag on the barbed-wire fence that edged the paddock behind the house, or flung against the hill and pinned down by the wind. She was only seventeen then, and yet Nell expected her to

32

know what to do with the baby. She could never have guessed at how much babies needed to be held. They did not lie in baskets all day purring with sleep. And so she concentrated on becoming nothing more than vapour; she imagined herself a wisp of blue flame so that nothing could break her, so that no sound could penetrate her, until eventually Nell had sent her away to study in Adelaide. And Pearl became Nell's.

Diana had been glad to give her up. Glad to flee the chaos of that house, baby toys scattered everywhere, dishes teetering in the sink, piles of tiny clean jumpsuits on the kitchen table never making it back into drawers after being washed. Glad to leave the sweet smell of milk and powder and washing detergent. And glad to leave Nell, who paid Diana no attention, so consumed she was with fussing over Pearl. Her body could belong to her now, as though the pregnancy and birth were an illness she'd had to endure and from which she'd now recovered. Diana decided that she would concentrate on filling herself in again. She imagined the thin blue flame that she was expanding outwards until she was a ball of golden light spreading in all directions, spreading right to the edges of the universe. She imagined she was a bird with a puffed-up chest, her feathers rustling and gleaming.

Walking into the grounds of the University of Adelaide for the first time, Diana remembers, she was struck by the lush green lawns, the pretty arches of the Cloisters, the students with their flares and satchels and open handsome faces. How important it all looked. She felt ridiculously out of place and was sure everyone could tell that she was not from the city. Surely her dusty steel-toed boots gave it away. But David had been gentle with her and he seemed to adore her, so she'd started hanging out with him on Mondays, catching a bus from the Teachers Training College to the university, where David studied. That first time on the lawns, waiting for David, she'd pulled off her boots and shoved them into a bin. He'd been unfazed by her bare feet, there were plenty of others with bare feet, and later when her soles ached, he'd carried her to the pub on his back. They sat outside because she had no shoes.

The next day she'd bought a pair of long brown boots with an insert of olive green suede from John Martin's. She used up her monthly allowance from Nell in one go and so had to rely on David 'to put her in the way of food'. They went to exhibition openings and ate the cheese and gulped the wine, they went to the Hare Krishna place where they gave out free sloppy yellow dhal at lunchtime and copies of *Bhagavad Gita*, they went to parties and ate dope cake, and sometimes they shoved packets of rice and pasta down their fronts when they were in the deli and hurried out without paying. But her boots, her lovely boots that softened and crinkled with fine beautiful lines as they aged, made her feel at last like she knew who she was. The brown of the leather matched the brown curtain of her hair and she loved the way her legs rose out of them, golden and shapely like the legs of a dancer. She was taller in them, more beautiful; no longer a country girl in work boots whose breasts leaked great alarming circles of milk whenever her baby cried.

Diana sidles between the trestle and a stack of cardboard boxes lining the wall. Fuck, she says, as a button from her blouse catches on the edge of a dusty box and pings off. She brushes the dirt from her top. Bloody Nell, what is all this junk? How will we pack this up, she thinks to herself. The concrete floor is cool and gritty with sand, and as she rounds the trestle to stand in front of the easel, her skirt snags on a splinter of wood. Oh for god's sake! Diana unhooks herself carefully, straightens her top and moves towards the easel. She stares at the unfinished painting. The shapes begin to make sense, like watching a Polaroid photograph taking form. A grass tree — long strokes of green and brown and gold and black — and in the red middle, a baby perhaps. Around the edge is a circle of tiny periwinkles stuck to the canvas. And there is a layer of background Nell hasn't filled in yet. Madonna blue, thinks Diana. The paintbrush sits stiffly in a pool of dried paint. Diana runs her fingers over the shells, gently, lovingly, fleetingly, and then yanks her hand away as if she's been stung. It's the thought of Nell's fingers touching those same shells, assembling them into place. She sees her sorting through the shells on the trestle, picking out the ones that are just the right size. She lowers herself down onto the stool and pictures herself filling in the rest of the painting with the blue. Would that be wrong?

And then she sees it, not even hidden away.

On top of the beehive is a round silver tin. She pries it open and the smell is sweet and damp and thick. She takes out the Tally Ho papers and licks two together, placing them flat down on the beehive top. Then pinching a little morsel off the bud she sprinkles it along the papers, scraping pieces from her fingers sticky with resin. She takes her time rolling, her tongue nipping deftly along the seam, and then turning it over in her hands, marvelling at its symmetry. David had taught her to roll an expert joint — one of his many talents, like polishing shoes and selecting the perfect avocado, that he undertook with relish. She narrows her eyes to watch the blue flame as she lights. The paper sizzles, and she sucks in deep, and her throat burns. But she holds the smoke down in her lungs and it's like she's filling up with bubbles of honey. She coughs and the smoke expels suddenly, the lighter skidding across the beehive box as she flicks it away. Her eyes water and she stares at the painting again and coughs. The leaves of the grass tree seem to shudder slightly, as if there's a breeze coming under the gap in the door. And the red of the centre pulsates, like every atom of the painting is jostling and spinning in its own small universe. Diana takes another puff of the joint and blows the smoke forcefully at the painting, stirring the baby.

★ ★ ★

Lucy fills up the sink with hot soapy water, and beside her Joe slices onions for dinner. Alfie is napping on the couch and, through the bay windows, she can see Ariel turning cartwheels down on the beach with Pearl. As she swishes the first of the glasses through the suds, her kimono sleeves flop into the water.

Oh shit. Joe, help. She stands back from the sink and holds out her arms, the points of her sleeves wet.

What do you want me to do, he laughs.

Take it off!

Joe puts down his knife, wipes his hands on his jeans, and slips behind her, standing close.

This isn't a sexual thing, Joe, just take it off.

Okay. Okay. Joe puts his hands on her shoulders and drapes the kimono off, nuzzling her on the back of the neck.

Have you told Pearl yet? His hands rest on the small curve of her belly, the kimono dropping to the floor.

Lucy rolls the glasses around in the bottom of the sink. No, I haven't. Can't bear to yet. Lucy chews her bottom lip.

You better tell her soon, Joe says, picking the kimono up from the floor and slinging it over his forearm.

I know, I know, but I spoke to Nico on the phone yesterday, and he's really worried about her.

You are allowed to be pregnant, Lucy.

I know. Soon, I promise.

Lucy remembers that even when they'd had Alfie, it was difficult. Not just because of Pearl, but because Ariel was still so little, too, and it was exhausting. She'd swayed and jiggled Alfie in a continuous state of motion to become the tiniest version of her. A streak of moonlight, Joe called her. When Pearl came to stay she'd held Alfie in the bathroom while Lucy showered, the steam and the white noise sending him off to sleep — the only thing that sent him off to sleep — and Lucy had wished, while the water drummed over her tired body, that they could have shared becoming mothers together. But Pearl was such a help to Lucy and the kids back then that she was also guiltily relieved for the time Pearl was able to devote to them all, unencumbered by children of her own. Beautiful aunty.

Where's Di? Joe asks, scraping the onions vigorously into heating oil.

Um. In the shed?

What does she do out there all day?

Lucy has been wondering this herself. Between Diana and Pearl she is the only one keeping things humming along. Because of the children she cannot stray too far from the order of the day. It is comforting to know that things will largely unfold in the same way — Ariel will have toast for breakfast, Alfie will nap in the afternoon, they both will have stories at bedtime — but sometimes she thinks she is unravelling. She is like one of those silkworm cocoons that Ariel brought home from kindy. The family will start unwinding her silken layers, and eventually she will be revealed, exposed and translucent. Her mother and sister keep threatening to upset the fabric — last night Diana had clattered dishes away just as she'd taken Alfie off to bed,

38

and he had taken more than an hour to fall asleep, and this morning Pearl clomped down the hall to go to the toilet and woke Ariel before dawn. She is just so tired. Too tired to be sad about Nell. She wonders whether she has it in her to handle the next few days.

Lucy peers out the window to the shed. She's probably sulking. Smoking, Lucy adds.

I might go check on her, Joe says, tipping the chopped tomatoes into the frying pan. Take her a drink.

Don't smoke, though.

I won't. And then in a bit, I'm gonna go fishing.

What! Now?

In a bit. Just a quick sunset fish. He runs his hands through his dark sticking-up hair. Massages his stubbly jaw.

What about dinner and the kids?

If I don't go now, I'll miss the light, Joe says, grinning.

Lucy rolls her eyes. Right. Yep, just go. She leans on the sink and pulls off the gloves.

After he leaves, the screen door banging shut behind him, Lucy looks around her. Every bench surface is cluttered with knives and chopping boards and plates and pans and wooden spoons. She sighs and begins piling the debris up by the sink. Joe can do these later, she thinks. His turn. Fucking fishing! She pulls the plug from the sink and the water groans away. It was Nell who taught her the order in which to wash the dishes. She was methodical about it. Glasses first, followed by the cups, and then the bread and

39

butter plates. Lucy used to stand beside her on a stool and pass her the dishes. She slides the breakfast bowls into the water.

Lucy loved to clean Nell's paintbrushes for her, dipping them in turpentine and then blotting the colours out onto paper towelling. Vermilion, verdigris, madder. She would form the strange and delicious names with her tongue, and she would dip and blot until the stiff, smooth bristles left no stain. Indigo, cyan, cinnabar. Nell mostly painted birds. Close-up birds in bright, bold colours that took up the whole frame so that you could see them only in parts.

She turns the heat for the sauce down to a simmer and puts the lid on the pot. Peeling off her damp socks, she wanders over to the couch to check on Alfie. His arm is flung over his head and his cheeks are flushed. She nestles in beside him and Alfie takes a deep shuddery breath and rolls towards her, plugging his little thumb into her ear. She falls into the quiet. The kimono hangs over the arm of the couch and she stares at the patterned flowers blooming. It is strange to be here without Nell. She has never really been alone in this room. The saucepan lid rattles on the pot, but she can't move. Mustn't wake Alfie. She dares not even shift a muscle and he rolls more towards her, so very warm and yielding. I've been such a good daughter, she thinks. Keeping everyone happy. Sometimes Lucy felt so outside of Pearl and Nell that she would deliberately play up. She remembers the upset and confusion at having to go home from the island a week before Pearl, back to Diana and David to spend half of the holidays with them. She remembers painting an angry red splotch in the corner of one of Nell's paintings right before she was due to go back. Lucy never did understand why she had to leave without Pearl. This arrangement was just part of the strange deal between Nell and Diana.

Nell didn't ever notice the glary blotch. Either that or she never said anything about it. Lucy closes her eyes, fatigue descending heavily and swiftly — she'd forgotten the black tiredness of early pregnancy — and she is falling through Nell's painted birds flashing and winging past her in silent busy flurries.

★ ★ ★

Ariel is turning cartwheels on the beach. Having just mastered how to do them over and over in a row, she reminds Pearl of Lucy at the same age. Eight. Ariel's been practising pointing her toes and stretching into her legs like a starfish, as Pearl has shown her. And she puffs out her chest in preparation to propel forward just like Lucy used to. Pearl remembers Lucy's spangly little green leotard that she insisted on wearing everywhere for a couple of months. Even to school. She remembers Lucy on this very beach in that too big leotard, cheeks tear-streaked, asking Nell if she could stay for as long as her sister. Pearl had felt so much older than Lucy in that moment, even though they were only three years apart. Lucy understood nothing. Your mother needs you, Nell had responded matter-of-factly. And Pearl knew she was betraying her little sister somehow, but did not want to go home. She would have lived here if she could. Poor Luce, she thinks.

Soon Ariel collapses in a heap, and rests her chin on her hands, lying flat in the sand. The sea lapping behind her is a clear unruffled blue. The sky is feathered with milky clouds. Ariel leaps up and runs towards Pearl, kicking sand behind her. Come on, Pearl, let's see which one of us can do the most cartwheels in a row.

Oh, sweetheart. I'm not sure I can do one right now. Pearl leans back on her elbows and stretches out her legs. Her skin is luminous in the sun — never goes brown.

You can you can you can. Come on, Pearl.

Ariel grabs Pearl's hand and tries to pull Pearl up, puffing out her cheeks with the effort. Please Pearlie, I'm begging ya. I promise to be your slave when we go up to the house.

Pearl smiles at her and stands slowly, hitching up her dress into her bather bottoms. Okay, Ariel, let's do some cartwheels and then we really better be going back.

Yay. *Lots* of cartwheels. So we're going to start here. Ariel draws a line in the sand with her toe. And then whoever gets the furthest without falling over, wins. Got it?

Got it. Pearl sucks in her stomach.

Together they spread their arms long and place their right foot forward. Ariel tries to make herself as long as Pearl, her little face serious with effort. She swallows and juts out her chin.

42

Ready, set, go, she shouts.

Together they start turning over — one slow, one quick; one graceful, one gangly; one lagging, the other light — a sprite — veering sharply towards the shoreline. Pearl stops after a couple of rounds and kneels to massage her wrists. Her arms are heavy; her ears thud. Ariel falls into the shallows and turns quickly to make sure Pearl is watching.

How many, Ariel? Pearl stands.

Twenty-three, Pearl, twenty-three! How many for you?

Erm . . . five, I think, calls Pearl.

I win then. And she flips up into a handstand.

You win, Ariel.

Ariel collapses down, arms and legs everywhere. But Pearlie, what's that?

Pearl follows after Ariel, who is loping towards something small and grey in the distance, lying just above the shoreline. Ariel's bathers are blue with a white frill around the bottom, and as Pearl hurries to catch up with her, she feels like she is chasing the tail feather of an exotic bird. Wait, Ariel. Slow down, let me catch up with you, she says, as Pearl realises that the clump they're approaching is not seaweed or a large rock, but seems to be moving slightly. Ariel stops suddenly and stoops forward from the hips. From the little clump a small head peers round in an awkward judder to look at them.

A baby seal, whispers Pearl, cupping Ariel's thin fingers in her own.

Its breathing is laboured and Pearl notices the unsteady rise and fall of its breath, the skin hanging loosely over jutting ribs. Pearl coaxes Ariel to kneel down where they are and Ariel leans into Pearl, subdued by the wildness they can both sense in its sharp twist of neck and the shudder of its flipper. Is it okay, Pearl?

It looks deep into them with its brown eyes. Pearl reaches out and strokes its damp and sandy fur. It is too weak to protest, and for a moment it reminds her of a trusting puppy.

What's the matter with it, Pearl? Is it sick?

Pearl rests her hand on its back lightly. I think it's lost its mother. Not sick. Hungry and heartbroken, possibly. Sad.

Sad? Why?

Um. I've seen this before with Nell. Exactly here, too. When a baby seal gets a bit older, its mother leaves it to fend for itself, Pearl says, gently flicking sand away from its lashes.

Is it going to die?

Pearl looks out to the water. I don't think so, darling. Eventually it will make its way back into the water. It'll be sad for a bit and then really brave.

But it has a broken heart, says Ariel, matter-of-factly.

Pearl nods. If grief is tangible, it is in the sheen and glimmer of those vulnerable eyes — so glassy and brown and knowing.

Water whooshes over the seal's tail, and it lurches up on its flippers and propels itself forward with a lumbered strain. Pearl and Ariel drop hands and move back to give it space. The seal turns to look at them again, beseechingly almost, as if to say, You have seen my sorrow, please do not use it against me. And then it disappears.

Poor little thing, says Ariel. Can we come and check it in the morning?

Yes, we can.

It was so lonely, wasn't it?

Yes. But it will know what to do. It will just keep swimming until it feels better or hungry. I'm sure its mother taught it well.

Pearl?

Yes, darling.

Do you think Nell knows where to go?

Pearl turns to Ariel. What do you mean?

Now that she's dead does she know where to go? Because I think she's still here.

The wind picks up as if to take hold and shake them. Ariel squints against the flurries of sand. Before Pearl can answer, Ariel's on her feet and running up the dune towards the house.

It's cold, she calls out, and I'll beat you home, Pearl. Easy.

Pearl stays kneeling in the sand. The sky is darkening, the sharp lines of the day softening. The beach has never felt so mute, so unable to give her anything. She looks for the seal, but it is gone.

Nell

When Pearl came she was a scrunched red thing. Her tiny crinkled eyelids dewy and luminous. Tulip petals. And her little mouth sucked and mewled even when she was resting. Pearl's fingers were long and grasping, and those fingernails — so perfect and small like periwinkles. I kissed them. She was the exact size and weight of my grief. She was hope. I held her in my lap when she was just hours old and looked at her for a long time wondering where she'd come from and marvelling at her. My own daughter, Diana, lay on the bed, pale and beautiful and utterly transformed by childbirth — heightened, other-worldly, exhausted and ecstatic both. Only a little older than I was when my own first child was severed from me. I was determined that Diana would never feel that terror, and this was the one thing I could give her. I could support her so that she could be a mother — a very young mother, an accidental mother even, but a mother who would not be taken from her child, for the severance goes both ways. But Pearl was the lost child returned. I could see her in no other way. It pains me deeply to write it, but Diana was not that; she could never have been that to me simply because she was not Samuel. That first one, Samuel, whom I whispered to every night in the girls' home while he grew inside me, oh how I needed him. Samuel — my only solace in that strange place of limbo. He was a dream, a promise, a prayer. He was my invisible thread to Sol, or so I hoped.

The pregnancy with Diana had been some kind of awful re-enactment of grief. My body could not forget. All I could think of was that first one. Who was he? Did he think of me? What was he doing now? He was the first one and I had lost him. I lost Sol, too. And so, I was not ready for Diana, this new being, this new gift that wouldn't be taken away and whom I should have loved more generously. But I could not understand her. It is my own fault, but both my children are burning stars that char the inmost heart of me.

With Pearl, I could rise from the ashes.

1822
Antechamber Bay

William leaves out damper in the same place for the little girl each morning. Sometimes he leaves a piece of driftwood for her as well, or a tiny hollow eggshell from a fairy wren, or a shard of smoothed green glass, or a length of string. He watches her approach his offerings from a distance, on top of a splintered wooden crate that once held supplies from a ship his father had bartered skins for. William knows that she is aware of his presence, but somehow the gap between them puts her at ease. Always she comes softly down the track, deliberately not looking in his direction. William thinks she is like a bird — small-boned and agile. She makes herself quite invisible from the sealers. He thinks she is very clever. He can tell by her large, shiny eyes that she notices everything, and that she might even know more than him about hunting for lizards.

She kneels, undoes her basket and handles his presents with a delicacy that makes him reel, before placing each gift carefully in her woven bag. Without acknowledging his presence she stands up, remaining perfectly still for a moment before flitting down the track.

On the morning that William likes to remember as the day of the scrimshaw, he leaves out a whale's tooth — carved into a scrimshaw. He had found it a few days before, wedged into a split in a sugar gum near the camp. It is polished and engraved with a woman's face. Fine mouth, sad eyes, high forehead, and hair twisted and pinned loosely back. Not like any of the faces that William knows. He had decided not to show his father, but to keep the carefully hidden treasure a secret. On this morning, the girl picks up the smooth bone and fingers the intricate design. She seems to consider it with both fascination and dread. And while he is thinking that the next thing he wants to find for her is one of the splendid blue feathers of the tiny wren, she turns towards him. She is half-smiling, but with her lips pursed together out of shyness. Not wanting to frighten her he stays where he is and nods in her direction.

From then on, William and Maringani always exchange a silent greeting that William knows to be louder than any talking he has with his father.

★   ★   ★

Anderson likes the way his son rests the full weight of his palm on the side of his face, almost lovingly, without shrinking away from him. William holds the knife firmly with his other hand and is carefully removing the bristle from the dip just below Anderson's right cheekbone. He is slow but precise. Anderson leans his head back and shuts his eyes to the glare. The red that thumps beneath his eyelids makes him think of seal blood mixing with seawater. The blade against his stubborn hair makes a scraping sound that Anderson finds strangely comforting. Anderson jumps as the boy nicks him under his jawbone.

Watch it, says Anderson, and sits up straight, knocking the boy back a few steps with the swing of his arm.

William doesn't say anything, just takes a slow breath and lifts his father's hand down from where it is rubbing at the cut, spits on his own thumb and presses it against the wound to staunch the bleeding.

Concentrate or yer'll slit me throat, Anderson mutters as he allows William to take his head in his hands, lean him back and swap his thumb for a damp piece of rag that William holds firm against his neck.

William's steady pressure to the wound eases

the sting. Anderson likes the feel of someone taking care of him.

You needin' practice before I let yer at me again, he blurts out to William when it is all done.

I'm sorry. I —

Anderson fingers the clean lines of his beard before interjecting, It's yer hands, they shake like a gerl's.

William examines his hands and Anderson looks at them as well. They are nothing like his own thick-palmed and square ones, Anderson thinks to himself. William's are brown and scratched, and the fingers are finer than Anderson's, tapering at the ends like William's mother's fingers. Beatrice spoke with her hands. They fluttered and danced about her. Sea fronds in the current. When Anderson thinks of those days back in the old country before she died — her lungs hacked with tuberculosis — they seem so distant that it's like he is remembering a life that he was never a part of. Like he was there, but only as a bystander. Perhaps it was all a dream? He can no longer picture himself in those narrow streets — the damp, the stink, the filth — with the sky hanging so low you could almost pull it down. But Beatrice is a visceral memory beyond the limits of time. The physical absence of Beatrice makes her everywhere around him. Sometimes, burying his face into handfuls of saltbush with its faint crystalline spice, he feels as though Beatrice is there and it is the hollow at the base of her throat that he smells. It is not to Him that he prays, but to

Beatrice. Anderson reaches out and tousles the boy's hair, causing him to stumble.

Dry the knife. Wrap it. It'll rust, Anderson says as he splashes handfuls of water against his face, snorting forcefully as he does so to stop water going up his nose. I'll make a man of yer yet, he whispers to himself.

★　★　★

William scrapes silver from the fish with his knife, and the scales eddy around his feet in the shallows. He has caught five whiting, which he handles tenderly, thinking them the most beautiful of fish, the way they streak and glide under water, beautiful even as they lie motionless in his hands. They are clever, too. Fast. So hard to catch.

It is late afternoon, the time of day when the seals like to rest on the rocks. Emue and Poll walk to the water's edge and splash water up their arms, over their heads, down their chest and backs until they are wet all over. William crouches, leaning back onto his heels, and watches the women as he runs his hands over the silken fish, smoothing them underwater. Slowly, Emue and Poll walk along the shore until they are opposite the outcrop where the seals are basking. The women swim out to the rocks — knives in their mouths. William has not seen this before. Usually, they are armed with a club, or some kind of stick. In the water, Emue and Poll are strong — sleek-headed, they bob out from waves. Once they reach the rocks, Emue

51

and Poll lie gently down beside the seals. From this distance William finds it difficult to distinguish the women, shiny and dark, from the seals. If a seal lifts its head and sniffs, the women also lift their heads. If a seal props itself up with its left flipper, then the women prop themselves up with their left elbow, scratch themselves and then lie back down again. They are perfect mimics. Occasionally the water washes over the women, but they remain there as hushed and languorous as the seals. William watches Emue and Poll for about an hour and it's almost as if they are making peace with the lumpish animals. The men have come down to the beach, and are also watching the women with great interest.

Prepare the boat. We is goin' out, Anderson shouts.

Just wait, Father, let's see what they do.

I know what they up ter and I want ter be ready.

Without any warning at all, Emue and Poll jump up, raise their knives and bring them down on the seals' noses, striking them with such force that they crumple instantly. The seals have no time to scream. Once half a dozen have been struck in this way, William watches the men rush in to collect the spoils.

King George Beach (Sandy)

Diana sits on the verandah and begins a list.
  Things my mother has taught me.
  How to live alone.
  To love the taste of salt.
  To light a fire.
  Sorrow.
  Everything about the island.
  What to do with babies.
  What to do with bees.
  Grandmothers are nicer than mothers.
She stretches out her legs to catch the sun. The others are down on the beach and she can just make them out, clumped together like a little deposit of discarded shells. Alfie is asleep inside. To *wade in water.* Being here again is like stepping into a river. She's up to her knees in it. When Diana was a child she had recurring dreams of being engulfed in water. Of a tsunami flattening their home, or even the whole of the island. Nell had taught her that thousands of years ago the island was connected to the mainland by a land bridge, but that the sea level kept rising, until the island became separated. But the explanation that Diana preferred belonged to Nell's *things about the island* category. The island's severance was due to Ngurunderi, the Creator and spiritual ancestor of the Ngarrindjeri, whose

country extends to Kangaroo Island. Ngurunderi was chasing his two wives, who'd broken taboo — eating fish forbidden to women. Near the end of the chase, Ngurunderi's wives ran across the land bridge that connected the island to Cape Jervis. Ngurunderi made the waters rise and drowned his wives. The women became the rocks known as the Page Islands in Backstairs Passage. Or Rhunjullang — two sisters. The Ngarrindjeri speak of Kangaroo Island as the land of the dead. Uncle Jim has told Diana this many times. We are close to our dead here, he says. Land of souls. Ngurunderi crossed to Kangaroo Island when he knew it was time to leave. He threw his spears into the water, dived in, and then rose in his canoe to become part of the Milky Way. A bright star watching over.

You see, Diana, Nell used to say, those women had agency — they are at the heart of the story. The lands of the Ngarrindjeri could not have been formed without them. But Diana could only worry for them — their anguished flight. To *flee*. Diana liked to imagine the land bridge back into being — the sea cleaving open to reveal a muddy slippery passageway that she could run or slide along, the water closing in behind her, like it did for Ngurunderi's wives as they tried to escape their raging husband. Sometimes this was the only thought that calmed her dread. Especially once Pearl came along. Came along! She laughs at that. That was a cleaving open, too. Nell didn't warn her about the pain, the blood, the burning, the wanting to flee right out of her own body.

And now here she is, back again, wading deep. She might at least corral her thoughts by not drowning in them — write this list. Yet she approaches the exercise with an unusual detachment for someone whose mother has just died. *Detachment*. To step out of the river, to reach higher ground, back to Adelaide, is at least a ferry trip away and nearly two hours' drive. It's at least a whole funeral away. Days away.

The last time she was here was three years ago. It had been a mistake to come, although not at first. Nell was so ill with the flu that she needed Diana to hold her glass to her lips so she could gulp down paracetamol. And Marian and Red, the neighbours, were away. When Nell got better enough to boss Diana around, they began to fight. Not about anything much but because Nell was resentful of her incapacity and Diana felt a kind of guilty satisfaction in Nell's need of her. *Not to be afraid of snakes.* While Diana was there, a king brown snake visited daily to drink from a leaking seam in the water tank. Nell's house squats high on an enormous concrete-encased water tank — half of the tank protrudes in a semicircle in front of the house to form the wide exposed verandah. The water tank and the snake was, of course, not the only thing Nell and Diana fought over, but the memory of that snake was burnt cruelly on Diana's mind.

Diana puts down her list and crawls to the edge of the tank and peers over, the rough surface scratchy on her knees. It's still there, the trickle of water at the base of the tank, darkening the sand. The snake lay on the cool side — it was

February and startlingly hot, like now — and flicked its tongue at the water. The first time Diana saw it she screamed. The unearthliness of it. The shock of it pressed tight along the bottom of the tank. Its proximity, like it brought the scrub and all its dark secrets right up to the house. She was horrified that Nell didn't mind it being there.

Why would I mind? It's not bothering me.

What about the children — when they're here?

They're not here.

But when they are here?

Then I'll teach them not to be afraid of snakes.

This is the kind of conversation Diana remembers having with Nell, where Nell would set her mouth into a line and not ever relent. Diana had slammed the glass doors and gone inside to pack her things. It wasn't that she was overreacting, it was that this stand-off about the snake came after so many other small grievances, like gravel collecting in shoes. When she came outside to get her cigarettes and her sunglasses, Nell was down on the sand holding the shovel, shaky with exertion and illness. Diana remembers Nell's hair blowing the wrong way revealing a pink line of scalp. She remembers Nell's eyes wide and hard. She remembers the snake in two raggedy pieces and blood seeping into the sand.

Snakes should be scared of *us*, Nell said.

She's mad, Diana thought. And now that brown snake haunts Diana. Its glinting skin. Its emblematic death. *Not to be afraid of snakes.* Nell's awful lesson. But what was the lesson?

Alfie cries from the bedroom, and Diana shivers. She folds the list up and slips it into her book, steps through the glass doors. Closes them gently behind her. Walks down the hallway to the spare room and tries not to think of Nell following ghostly behind her, hands gripping her shoulders, vice-like.

Shh shh, darling, I'm coming now.

Alfie is getting almost too heavy to lift, but she leans down and he scrambles up, nestling into her neck.

Mummy, mummy.

Mummy's at the beach. She'll be back soon.

He begins to protest, his little body stiffens, and she staggers under the weight of him until the two of them plop heavily backwards onto the double bed. He laughs.

Do it again, Nanny Di.

I can't, I can't. My back.

Alfie rolls off Diana, and they lie together, his warm head squashing her arm. Diana rubs her thumb over the back of his chubby hand and breathes him in. She feels stranded, pinned down in a boat with Alfie. *I am half-sick of shadows,* said the Lady of Shalott. Tucked into the dresser mirror opposite the end of the bed is a postcard. It's a reproduction of a painting of her namesake, Diana. The figure of Diana is turned away, looking over an expanse from a great height, to a glimpse of moon or sun breaking through impasto clouds. Her calf and shoulder and cheek sheen with light. Her clothes fall in Grecian folds like the clouds. It's almost as if she holds on to the side of a mountain — tenacious like an olive tree. Diana loves the strength of her. The hanging on. The quality of the light as if lit from within. Nell had bought her the postcard at the National Gallery in Adelaide when Diana was ten. It was the only way Nell had been able to get Diana out of there. She hasn't seen the postcard in years. When she was a child she'd stuck it on the wall next to her pillow. She would gaze at it and wonder how to sketch light so that a moon on a canvas shone back at you more alive and visceral than actual light.

On that first visit to the gallery she'd been alone. She remembers thinking that her dress was embarrassingly rumpled and her plaits loose and scrappy after spending all night on the ferry from Kingscote with Nell. She hadn't slept at all, and she has never been able to sleep in a room full of strangers — their coughing and their wriggling and the close smell of them. It sharpened her into a fine vigilant point of light that could not sleep. It is still that way — she has to take Valium now whenever she goes on a plane. When they finally arrived in Glenelg, Diana was so relieved for the stinging fresh air and the firm ground underfoot that she practically tripped out of the MV *Troubridge* like a little lamb disembarking. She was hoping for an ice-cream and a stroll along the foreshore, as if she was all cultured and from the city and not an untidy, thick-in-the-head island girl. This was the *seaside*, not an unruly deserted beach. But she realised as Nell steered her through the crowds that she didn't really know why they were here and what they were doing. Visiting friends,

Nell had said. So why then was she put on a tram all by herself? Nell had dropped a pouch of coins in her hand, along with hand-drawn instructions of how to get to the gallery once she reached the city, and when the tram trundled away from Nell, Diana hated her. Nell hadn't even watched her go, but stalked off towards the bus stop for Brighton with her shoulders all hunched. Bitch, thought Diana, but then felt immediately like weeping. She pressed her face up to the oily glass and looked at her own lips in the reflection until the pricks of tears disappeared back inside her skull.

Looking beyond her reflection, into backyards and vacant lots and railway sidings, she felt sorry for all of those people whose lives backed onto the tramline. Their flappy sheets strewn on lines, their broken swing sets, their weedy gardens, their crumbling chimneys, the furtive smoking on back porches, the trampolining in just underwear — all of it, exposed. So Diana stared straight ahead at the wooden panelling for a while, and then counted how many bald heads there were on the tram. Twenty-three. As they got closer to the city, the back gardens became prettier and thicker, and Diana didn't feel embarrassed anymore about being a voyeur. In fact, she made a promise to herself then that one day she would leave the island and one of those shapely gardens in Adelaide would be hers.

In the city she was frightened. The buildings hunched over her, and Nell's map made no sense, especially when people kept knocking into her. In the end, she asked a mother with a daughter about her own age for directions. The mother held Diana's elbow kindly while she explained how to get to the gallery, and Diana admired the woman's heavy eyelashes and brown knitted skirt. She wished that the woman was her own mother. She bought an ice-cream on the way for lunch and realised she was ravenous — the ice-cream settling in her belly like a cold stone sinking. Nell had instructed her to buy a sandwich at a particular location marked on the map, but she couldn't find the spot, and she didn't give a stuff about Nell's silly plans. I don't give a stuff, she said aloud, throwing the map satisfyingly into the gutter.

Sitting on the steps below the imposing porticos of the art gallery, she finally did weep. She felt like a scrap of paper, like the discarded map, blowing about in the wind. Who even cared where she was? Nell certainly didn't. The thing she longed for most in all the world, the thing she wished for on every birthday cake, the thing she wanted right now, was a sibling — preferably a brother who was older than she was and could pick her up. It was lonely bearing Nell all on her own. But it was a secret wish. And so in all of her little games, she played alone, her dolls lined up in a row with their static faces standing in for the characters and siblings she needed them to be. Diana took a long time to go inside the gallery because she didn't want anyone to notice her. Not only because of the shabby dress and her red nose from crying, but also because surely she must be the only child here. She was a beacon. But it was still hours until Nell said she would meet her here, so she bit the inside of her cheek until she tasted blood and entered.

She remembers now the emerald green walls, the shining parquet floors, the leather chesterfields, the high ornate ceilings, the concertinaed rooms, but mostly the peacefulness, like walking into a cool pocket of air. And so she wandered. Imagining that she was there with an older brother who was just over in the next room kept her from blubbering shamefully.

She scanned the first room and the paintings were flat and old and offered no allure. There was nothing to pull her towards them, so she decided to stand in front of every single painting for the slow count of five. At least then she would look like someone who was supposed to be in an art gallery. But this made her dizzy, and the only thing that steadied her was staring into the beautiful mirror silver of a waterhole. Its edges seeping pink from the sunset, the trees reflecting back, creating a black and silver chiaroscuro effect. At the edge of the waterhole, an Aboriginal woman stood with a baby secured to her back in a sling. She carried a basket. Her feet were bare. The mood of the painting, so peaceful that Diana could almost feel the mist between the trees, the smoke curling from a little fire on the other side of the painting. A second woman knelt beside a wurlie, making the fire. And a man sat with a blanket around his shoulders gazing at Diana knowingly. She read the inscription, *Evening Shadows, backwater of the Murray, South Australia*. She knows now that the painting, as arresting as it is, depicts one of the most insidious colonial romantic notions, that the first Australians would die out. It's meditative scene, a lament for a lost idyll. Yet this painting did something to that young Diana. It slowed her down and made her see. Even now, she thinks of that painting when flying in an aeroplane and looking down to expanses of water — the way they soak light, or can be the darkest bodies, the only part of the country that cannot be strewn with electricity. Dark portals. She was first shown this in *Evening Shadows*.

When Nell found Diana she was curled up asleep in a chesterfield, the light through the skylights, subdued. Nell spoke softly and kindly, Diana, are you all right? To Diana her mother looked smudged out. Exhausted. The security guard looked on with pursed lips. Diana did not want to leave then. She felt wanted finally — it was the way Nell looked at her. And she felt scrubbed through with light.

The young woman in the postcard was the Diana she hoped to grow into. Agile. Beautiful. Strong. *Art. To acknowledge the creative self.*

Alfie pulls Diana from the bed. I'm hungry, Nanny Di. It was nice to be wanted. To be pulled along. *The trick of the light.*

★ ★ ★

Later that night Pearl cannot sleep. This is something that has been happening lately. Even with the hush of the sea. Even with sheets so clean and comfortable. Even with wine making her body loose. She'd hoped it might be better without Nico in the bed — his swift descent into sleep leaves her stranded nowadays — but it was no better sleeping alone. In fact she wishes she could back herself against him, skin to skin, and drape his arm over her hips. She wishes she could take back their last conversation. Too often lately, they cannot understand each other. The sky, lit by the almost full moon, glares back at her, and she burrows into the covers so she won't leak away brightly out the window. When she was about twelve she had gone nearly a year without being able to fall asleep easily. Especially at Diana's. But she thinks it all started one night here — at Nell's. And it's a similar feeling. Like she has no edges, no skin, and her skull is light but too open, and everything is pouring out. Or in. And her chest hammers wildly. And she digs her nails into her ribs until the skin tears and the physical sensation of this braces her. It is not quite so severe as that now. Tonight it's just that her thoughts are bright and glary like the moon. Her body is taut and will not yield. Reminders of Nell surge then drift. She follows them.

When the sleeplessness began, when Pearl thinks back to its beginning, the realisation she could not switch off came suddenly. She was in this very room, the sea surging outside, Nell busy somewhere in the shed, and she was aware not that the bed enclosed her, protected her, but that it could spit her out. She fussed with the bedclothes. Pulled her socks off then back on; plaited her hair and then unplaited it. Turned her pillow over. She bit her lip hard. She prayed to

Jesus because she knew of other girls that did that. It was a feeling of being engulfed. Of not knowing her place in the universe. And once she submitted to the rising sense of panic, she could not control it. Her mind raced in an effort to calm down. *You are okay. Yes, you are. You are a baby in your cradle. You are being sung to sleep.* She sang, but her voice clanged. *You are in the womb of the world. The rain is soft on your cheeks. The sun is warm on your back. You are cloaked in a sealskin.* But the more she tried to reassure herself the more untethered she became. Next morning she was ragged and her body ached. Nell had noticed something was off.

You look worried.

No, I'm just . . .

Nell smiled. Sleep in my bed tonight. If you want to.

Pearl wondered how she knew. Did she know?

Take your book down to the dunes. It's perfectly still. It'll do you good to get outside.

And that was how she recovered from each night's terrible struggle to be in her skin. Every morning after breakfast, she took her book, a hat, an apple and a bottle of water down to a little sheltered valley in the dunes. The warm sand took the ache from her spine. The upturned dinghy, long abandoned, was a windbreak and a shelf for her things. She buried her feet and she was safe. A hawk circled every day and she imagined it was watching out for her. Protecting her from snakes. She imagined the snakes lying undisturbed nearby, like dark jewels. And Pearl would get so thirsty lying there with the sun

64

massaging the long bones of her limbs and drying out her lips, but she just kept reading and reading until her eyes were heavy. She slept in small sun-melting moments. It was enough to make up for the nights.

One afternoon Nell joined her and when Pearl woke, Nell had placed a small stone on each vertebra of Pearl's spine. Pearl was lying on her tummy, using her book for a pillow, and the stones radiated such heat into her sleep-deprived joints that she wanted to weep. But that was a kind of letting go that she wouldn't allow. She was becoming reptilian. She craved only warm sand.

Nell leant back on her elbows. What are you reading?

Pearl had plucked the book from Nell's own shelf. She still has the book now. An old friend.

The Bone People, she said. Pearl rolled onto her side and the stones slid off. She fished the sand from the crevices between the pages of the book.

Nell nodded slowly. You can keep it. Do you like it?

Pearl wasn't sure. She was only reading it to keep anchored, the words on the page a life rope that she inched along. I'm worried about the little boy, she said.

Yes. Well it only gets worse.

Pearl knows now she loves the book, and is able to recall vividly certain scenes from it even twenty years later. What is it about some tracts of writing that are able to seep into our cellular memory that way, she wonders. And then she

65

pulls the thought back, letting it diffuse into a blue expanding flame — a getting to sleep technique that sometimes works. But the thoughts roll in. Every few years she reads the book again, each time finding something she hasn't noticed before. She found the insight into Maori culture and resistance revelatory and the writing candescent. But really the book is associated now with the incredible and terrifying openness of her mind during that sleepless year, and the little rafts she clung to. Reading was one of them. Lying whole body to the earth or sand or creek bed was another. Do you remember, Nell, when you used to tell the selkie story? Seal Brother. All because of this dinghy. Pearl picked at its flaking paint.

Nell threw her head back and laughed. Oh, yes. Of course. Been telling it for years. True story that one. She winked at Pearl.

Pearl knew that it was sort of true in the sense that Nell needed the story. Diana needed it. Even Pearl did. Why that was she didn't know. But Nell was their storyteller, and she made things alive for them. Her stories inhabited the island. And Nell told the Seal Brother story again as they sat there in the dip of sand with the cliff in the distance like a great hunched shoulder reddening in the sun, as their own shoulders were. And the story was a raft that day, so that when the desolate night came on, she would try to take herself back there to the spreading sun, and Nell's slow voice and the hulk of the dinghy hard on her wing bones, and the croon of the wind in the she-oaks. She was practising visualisation.

The dinghy belonged to a brother and sister who were very close and lived on an island with their parents, who were fisherfolk. The children were excellent swimmers, especially the boy, who could swim like a seal and wanted so badly to be one. Every day the brother and sister would play on the beach and swim off the rocks and the sister teased the brother about his crooked toe. It really is ugly that toe, she would say. And he would dive into the water and disappear and then come back up, and say, Oh well, I'll just have to live with it, seeing as it's what I've been given.

One day the father thought that he'd take the children out fishing, but the sister didn't want to go as she was happy enough rambling and playing on the rocks. She didn't feel much like going out in the dinghy this day. But the father and the son went and it was such good fishing that they kept going further and further out, until they realised the weather was turning and they were much too far out to turn back easily. The father was worried and he said to the boy, We're going to try and turn back but the storm is coming. And then they were caught in the storm and the boat overturned and the father said to the boy, We're going to have to swim back, but you're a strong swimmer so I know you'll be fine. Forget the boat, forget everything. Let's save ourselves. And the father was a great swimmer himself being a seaman. And he swam. When he came into the beach he stood up and looked all around. There was no sign of his son.

67

His son was gone . . . his heart was broken.

They searched the next day. And they searched far and wide. But the boy never turned up. He was lost at sea. A week passed. Two weeks passed. And then a strange thing began to happen to the girl.

She would not look at her parents. She would not eat. She would pick at her food. She lost weight. She would not go to the town. All she would do was walk along the beach when she had spare time, staring into the sea. And of course her parents were very worried about her. Their hearts were broken for their little son but they knew he was gone. As for the sister, she became a changed girl. She could hardly go on without her brother. Years passed this way.

One day, many years later, she took a walk along the beach. The tide was out. She walked the beach with her hair straying behind her, staring into the sea. The tide was full out; the gulls were crying. She walked where she had walked many times before with her little brother. By this time she was sixteen years old. The beach was very clear and the sand was very soft along it. Nestled into a cliff was a cave where the sister had played many times with her little brother, but she never visited it anymore. Then walking along the beach this evening she saw an odd thing. She saw flipper marks coming out, as if a seal had come up onto the land. But then there was something uncanny. The flipper marks gave way to footprints.

She followed the tracks. But there was something unusual about them as she looked.

She followed them as they were quite plain in the soft sand. And just for curiosity she counted — one, two, three, four. On the right foot there were only four toes. Then she counted the left foot. And she saw one, two, three, four, five. She followed the footprints gradually along the beach. And she felt excitement in her heart. Something was taking place. Then she walked along the shore and came to the rocks. And she climbed up over the rocks, and followed the wet prints to the cave. When she entered she was in for the biggest surprise of her life, for sitting in the cave was a boy. She looked, and she saw, she stared. He stood up. He threw his arms around her.

Tell me, she said, where have you been?

He had grown tall; he had grown stout. His eyes were dark and glinting. And his dark hair was streaming down his back. And she looked at his hands, and she saw that in between his fingers were like a duck's foot, with webbed fingers. Then she looked at his foot. She said, What's happened to your foot? For his crooked toe was gone.

When the seal people rescued me, I had to give them something of myself. Before I became one of them. And I knew you hated my crooked toe. So I gave them my toe, the only thing you didn't like about me.

I didn't mean it. I didn't mean it, she said.

It didn't hurt. They took it off. It didn't hurt! I feel fine without it.

Brother, please come home. Mummy and Daddy are dying to see you.

I can't come home to Mummy and Daddy tonight or any other night. And I want you to make me a promise. You will never tell them that you've seen me. Promise me right here and now you'll never tell you've seen me.

I promise. But will I see you again?

You'll see me many more times. But you must never, never tell our parents. Because you see I'm happy. This is the life I want. I must go now. But I'll see you again. You know where to find me. And then they walked to the sea. He bade her goodbye and dived in.

But she stood there and watched. About ten metres out, up came the head of a great big seal. It shook its head and then was gone.

This was the happiest moment of the sister's life. She was completely changed. And for many, many years the sister would go off on her long trips along the beach at night-time. Every time she came back from her walks on the beach she was brighter and chattier. Her brother told her about his life among the seal people. He told her how they transformed and how they walked on the land, and how no one could recognise a seal person. But they always returned to the sea. And the sister, she just wrote everything her brother said down in a little red book, so that she wouldn't forget. This was her secret. She never told a soul.

The years were to pass by, and the sister kept her own reclusive way of life. When she was an old lady and came to die, her wishes were carried out by her neighbour, and she left the neighbour her little red book. She was laid to rest in a grave not far from her parents'. And the neighbour got a small stone carved in the shape of a heart. And on it were the names of the brother and sister, forever marked together.

There were always wildflowers on the grave. Sometimes people visiting the cemetery saw something strange in the dirt — the mark of two bare feet. The strange thing was one of the toes was missing from the footprint. People wondered where the marks had come from. Only one person knew, and that was the neighbour who read the little red book. She read that book many times. And one evening she could not keep it to herself. So she told some friends in the town the story. She had to before she died — otherwise the story would be lost forever.

And this story was passed along and passed along and passed along, and now, Pearl, I give it to you. The strange and true tale of Seal Brother.

Pearl stood up on the hump of the dinghy, the wind flapping at her clothing. This day the waves were small and whipped like meringue. She could just make out the pitted shadows between the peaks — mercurial shadows like seal faces appearing and disappearing.

Darling, if it ever gets too much, coming here. Travelling back and forth. I'll understand. It might be harder when you get further into high school. Nell rubbed her shins vigorously. Unfolded her brown dry legs — shapely from all her clifftop walking.

Pearl didn't answer. She couldn't imagine not being here, but felt herself getting stretched into long tenuous threads between Nell's and the mainland. Lucy had stopped coming and Pearl wondered if this was the beginning of a kind of fracturing. And from then on, she only had to think of that first night of being shipwrecked in her bed, sleepless, at Nell's and her body would remember and she couldn't make the panic stop.

I don't want to stop coming, Nell.

Tonight, though, her restlessness is something else. Not panic. She's learnt to head that off. Tonight, she is honed to a diamond point. Alert. Aroused. So sad. She is not so much too awake as too alive. She thinks of those seal pup eyes, luminous and wild, that she and Ariel had witnessed on the beach earlier, and the longing those eyes revealed was the same as any human's. She thinks of Nico and how he is so quiet with her now. Even when they argue, he clasps his hands and nods sagely. His heart breaks, she knows. He would protect her if he could. She would love him better if she could.

Nell

And so it has been more than a week now — I think. I am becoming lighter. There is a strange kind of absence of hunger, of need, but I'm making myself eat. Just now, a sandwich of wild rocket — it grows everywhere — and it is so weedy and bitter it keeps me sharp. Followed by a spoonful of honey. That one's for Sol. Perhaps even for Mother. Poor Mother. The days run into each other as they do here in late summer. So much daylight. Too much. Long silver evenings, early lilac dawns. This is my daily practice now: wake, coffee, walk, write, lunch, write, coffee, paint, smoke, snack, sleep. I won't be able to keep it up when the girls, Lucy and Pearl, and their fellas and urchins, come for the end of the holidays. And so this is fevered. Writing against time. I will finish it. I'm so very very close. William and Maringani are in my dreams now. I've asked Red and Marian not to disturb me. I've switched off my phone. But of course, Marian leaves me little packages by the door. Muffins, cakes, and last night a serve of risotto, even. She watches over me, and that is enough sometimes to hold the seams of me together. I am so very grateful to her for that.

But as I write this story other memories — even closer to home — break me open, and

73

here I am spiralling back to the centre. I know now, it was a very wrong thing to keep Sol and Samuel so deep inside. I grew strange and hard around the hurt of them. It is only possible to write of love, even love grown strange, with a heart wide open — this I know — so I gather everything in now.

There was a time when I was unbelievably unkind to Reg. Diana was little and it was just after Mother passed away. I hadn't expected to feel so bereft with her gone. But she knew my deepest secret, and it was like she took it with her when she died. Theft upon theft. And when I sobbed in the bath, remembering Mother washing my hair, combing it, braiding it, and remembering all those little things she did — looking down my top to check I was wearing a singlet, putting a hot-water bottle under the covers an hour before bedtime, picking jasmine flowers and putting them next to me in the day cot when I had bronchitis, letting me lick the spoon when she baked, teaching me about the bees — Reg came in and knelt by the bath and made soothing sounds and embraced me with his shirt on. You are not a handsome man, I said to him then.

He didn't turn away; he didn't flinch. Well I know that, Nell, he said, and kissed my forehead. But you love me all the same, don't you? I did not answer but I let him help me out of the bath and dry my hair and comb it and put me to bed. Diana made me a picture and I heard the two of them in the kitchen playing cards, and thought to myself, I do love you Reg I did love you. What

I know now is that it was because I *did* love Reg so much that I couldn't say. I couldn't tell because what if, afterwards, I was so changed, I was no longer recognisable? It was myself I was afraid of. Not Reg, not Reg at all. Without the slow burn of our marriage, I may have given up on everything long ago.

And another thing. Reg and I made a life together. It was real and we lived it. Whereas my love for Sol was a solar flare seared into my line of vision. For all time. It was a lost opportunity. A broken vow. It's funny what a coveted thing memory becomes after so much time, and it's funny how enduringly a path not taken becomes a kind of haunting. And so, of course, it is Sol's body that I crave, always craved, and it is all that growing together we never did that leaves the widest gap. No one else knew my body in that brief and incandescent threshold between girl and woman. We were just saplings. Just little seeds of hope. First love. And Samuel, I can barely utter his name. I worry for him every day of my life.

1823
Chapman River

William is picking tiny purple pigface flowers for the girl when he notices something strung from a low branch nearby that glints in the sunlight. All the presents William has left for her — stones, shells, glass, eggs, wood, flowers, feathers, the piece of whalebone and a dried snakeskin — are bound with a piece of twine into a kind of ornamental hanging. He runs his fingers over the decoration and examines how skilfully all the small knots have been tied. Beneath the hanging on a round woven mat is a pile of red currant-like berries of a kind that he has never seen before and about half a dozen seedpods that are split open to reveal shiny, black seeds. William puts down the flowers and rolls one of the red berries in his fingers. It is slightly firm and looks like the miniature rosehips he has seen growing at the Wallens' farm. Henry Wallen is the self-appointed 'governor' of the island and William hopes to one day have a garden such as his with flowers and vegetables and real live hogs wandering about the place. The idea of it is something precious to hold.

Maringani walks noiselessly towards him. He sees her coming along the edge of the river and the river brightens. She is holding a knot of damper, which she breaks in two, handing half to him. They crouch in front of the crate and eat the damper together. She giggles every time he glances at her, which makes him laugh as well. He doesn't want to frighten her. She has never sat this close to him before, so he utters not a word.

Maringani fingers the pigface flowers and among the leaves she finds a small tear-shaped succulent fruit. She plucks it and takes a bite, placing the remaining piece in William's palm. Nganangi.

He feels lit up inside, like she's blown on a flame to make it catch. And for a moment he is very still, to cradle the warmth spreading through him.

William turns the fruit in his hands, brushes it along his lips and takes a small taste. It is sweet and sticky like a fig. Wallen has those, too. He smiles at her and attempts the word for it. She laughs and he notices for the first time how large and white her front teeth are.

Nga . . . na . . . ngi. She mouths the word slowly and deliberately.

Watching carefully the way she puts her tongue right at the back of her mouth to make the 'ng' sound, William tries to pronounce the word again — Na . . . na . . . nee.

She giggles again, and this time gestures for him to copy each sound with her. The way he has to move his tongue feels very strange. He is used to talking at the front of his mouth, not with his tongue back near his throat. It is a useless slab, his tongue, but he likes the sound of her voice when she speaks. It is just as he imagined it, uneven and song-like.

He keeps practising the word for pigface until, finally, the two of them say together, nganangi.

The girl nods vigorously with approval and they try more words together. She teaches him how to say her name, Maringani, and he shows her how to say William and damper. He likes the lilting way she says his name. Weellum.

Anderson's voice comes cracking through the scrub, William — get here, scattering the delicate covering, William imagines they've built around themselves.

Scrambling to his feet, William hides the

77

berries and seeds Maringani left him, putting them under the crate, aside from one berry, which he pops into his mouth with a flourish.

Munthari, she whispers to him.

Moontaree, moontaree, Maringani. Maringani, Maringani, nananee, William repeats as he speeds recklessly through the scrub, knowing he has probably spent too much time away from the camp and that his father will be stalking back and forth, irritated and long ready to go out sealing again.

★ ★ ★

Maringani sits with the weaving in her lap, stitching quietly — a sitting mat, knowing that soon she will help Emue and Poll to scrape the sealskins. The older women are spreading out the new skins and shooing away the festoons of flies with leafy branches. Maringani still cannot get used to the sharp flesh smell. She traces her finger around the spiral of her weaving and then tucks in the end of one rush and gets up to place the weaving inside the wurlie. She'll work in the next rush later — after the scraping is done. The mat she's weaving is for the kringkari boy. He seems to not have all that he needs, something for himself, like the men do. Maringani squats in front of a skin and rummages for the flint scraper in her sister basket. Emue presses something cold to Maringani's arm and smiles so wide the bridge of her nose crinkles. Maringani laughs. She knows Emue is very pleased with her new scraper. Maringani holds it up to the light. Even though it's black the light gets through, like when you're swimming and looking up to the surface. The day before, Emue smashed one of Anderson's ale bottles and fashioned its heavy base, keeping most of it smooth to sit comfortably in her palm, but chipping the ragged edge until it was knife-sharp. Emue points with her lips. Try it.

Maringani looks to the bloody skin, its two sides unfolded like great wings. She scrapes down from the rent where the fin used to be with Emue's new tool, cutting through to the underlayer with the sharp edge. The fat and sinew and blood clots pull away easily. She keeps going and can get just the right angle so as not to tear the skin. The scraper is so sharp and solid. Soon Emue folds her hand around Maringani's sticky slippery one and pries the scraper from her. Maringani giggles and gently nudges against Emue's upper arm until she unbalances and they both fall over. Poll shakes her head and giggles too. With her own scraper, Maringani has to work much more slowly to protect the skin. Poll and Emue whisper between themselves. And Maringani agrees, they can seal better without the men and their loud voices and loud boats because the seals are not frightened of Emue and Poll. But the men need many more skins out of one haul.

The flies sit thickly on the mess of blood clots and thready sinew, and Maringani drops a branch over the whole lot. The three skins the women are working on start to show their fragile pink undersides and the sun warms the skins as if they are alive. In the distance, Maringani sees the boy crouching at the shoreline. The water shines silver behind him. Is he digging for kuti? She cannot tell. She wonders again who he belongs to. He seems to be of both the sea and the land like the seals. Seal brother. He is bright to look at and bright in her thoughts.

★   ★   ★

William finds himself down at the women's spot most evenings. There is a well-trodden track running between the camps. The women have set up their wurlies just on the other side of the shallow part of the river to be out of sight from the men. He thinks this clever. His father and Everitt have tried every which way to keep the women permanently at their own huts, but the women will do their own thing. He likes listening to their voices collide and overlap and then fall abruptly away into silence; he has noticed a kind of stop-start rhythm to their stories that is hypnotic. When Anderson isn't around it is Emue who quietly presses native cherry, panpandi, into William's hands, or puts aside mutton bird eggs for him, or gives him the best piece of meat from the cook up, or doubles in laughter when he attempts to learn their words, and then strokes her hand over his face in one motion when his cheeks are all aflame.

If the women are with the men, then it is just he and Maringani and half a dozen skinny dogs lazing by the fire. William and Maringani compare words for everything, and to William it feels like his world is being renamed in colour, and sound, and texture, more vivid than it ever was before. And not just the tangible elements that make up his world, but all the quivers of things unseen, that have lately come to settle and fly apart, then resettle in the spaces between everything he thought he knew and Maringani's way of seeing. William knows that the stars serve a similar purpose for him as they do for Maringani, as a navigational tool and a way of measuring time, but some stars seem vastly more significant to her than others. In particular the Pleiades, which Maringani calls Muntjingarr, seem to be very important. Maringani won't swim until the cluster has started to rise in the night sky in summer. William can tell, by the quietness in her voice when she talks of the story of Muntjingarr, that it isn't just the stars themselves but it is the story of the stars that is precious.

Maringani has a story for everything. She has stories about the kuti, nuts and berries she finds, as well as about the birds, lizards and whales. She has explained that the grass tree, or blackboy, or yacca, with its long, jutting stem and cascading leaves is the whale spurting water from its blowhole. It seems there is symmetry between things on the land and things in the ocean or rivers. There is a connection between the whale — kondoli, and the echidna — kateraiperi, because they both take their food with their tongue. Whale is law of the sea. Echidna is law of the land. William has always thought of stories as something fanciful, something you told to pass the time out at sea or by the fire after drinking rum like the men did. For Maringani, he realises, stories are how she understands.

*　*　*

Anderson watches as Emue makes an incision at the bottom of the wallaby's tail, slicing the skin along its length, over its belly and to the head. She then cuts the underpart of the wallaby across its body from one inner leg to the other and again from inner arm to inner arm and then across its neck. Once the cuts have been made, Poll helps Emue scrape the skin from the wallaby's flesh. He notices Emue's new scraper. Resourceful, he thinks.

Emue separates the skin into two smaller squares and then stretches and pegs out the skin with the fur side down. She scoops hot ash onto a flat stone that is taken from a smouldering fire attended by Poll, who is rolling the glowing coals to one side to uncover the ash. Emue smothers the pegged-out skins with the ash to dry out all the moisture.

Maringani, calls out Emue, the sound of her voice flat against the wind.

In the shallow banks on the opposite side from Emue and Anderson, the sleek, wet heads of Maringani and William poke out of the water like seals. They lie on their stomachs, churning up the sand with their restless feet, keeping their shoulders submerged. The ease with which William frolics with the native child unsettles

Anderson, not only because he feels William is behaving more and more like a black, and what would Beatrice think, but because just sometimes he wishes Emue would smile at him the way Maringani smiles at William.

Son, stop yer cavortin' now and get yer jobs done. Yer been shirkin' of late. There's wood that needs choppin' and the cutter needs to be made ready for tomorrah, Anderson says as he sharpens his knife with long, swift strokes against a large piece of flint.

Comin', William replies, before taking in a big lungful of air and going under.

Emue calls out again to Maringani, who at that moment dips her head under and doesn't hear. Once she emerges, William nudges her and nods in the direction of Emue and Anderson. Maringani flips over onto her back, breathless. With one swift arm gesture, Emue beckons her daughter to return to camp.

William, stop yer breath-holdin' contest or whatever it is yer doin' and get out of there now. We've a big day tomorrah.

Anderson watches Maringani and William spring out of the water, their feet squeaking in the powdery sand as they race towards him and Emue. Maringani tears ahead and drops herself in beside Emue, who cuffs her gently on the head and frowns at the sizzle of water splashing from Maringani's hair onto the coals. Anderson can't help but notice the way Emue and Maringani move in unison. The same turn of the wrist, the same deliberate step.

See ya tomorrah, Mari, William shouts over his

shoulder, as he pelts past Anderson, flinging him with sand, away to the men's camp.

Will, plenty of wood do yer hear? We is celebratin' this night, Anderson calls after him, thinking with pleasure of the unopened barrel of rum, like molten gold, sitting patiently in the hut.

We did good with the skins this morning, Emue, very good. We be sellin' another 'undred in no time at all at this rate. You gins are mighty fine at this skin venture o' ours, mighty fine, Anderson says as he kisses Emue on the top of the head. This life here, finding our own way, sure does beat life aboard a ship. Enslaved to captains. And lays. Choosing to stay was the best thing I ever did. Sometimes, Anderson feels almost kingly. We're doing just fine, he thinks to himself. No one to bother us. The sky endless, the air sweet as the morning.

Emue murmurs something to Poll as she spreads more ash over the skin, and Anderson grins at them with a sudden rush of appreciation and pride for their quiet diligence.

I'll see you tonight, Emue, my Polecat, he says as he turns and whistles up the tracks, altogether missing Emue and Poll mimicking the swagger in his voice while convulsing with laughter.

Stokes Bay Road

Pearl leans back on the vinyl seat and closes her eyes. The air through the open window is grassy sweet and cool. The sky is beginning to hunker down as bright clouds mass. She can feel the scrub, preparing for rain. She wants to stay put. To keep on arriving here is too hard without Nell, but she also can't bear to go inside. It takes nothing for Pearl to clamber into the driver's seat and start the ute. Nico and Lewis have gone inside, and the keys still hang in the ignition, invitingly. As Pearl drives away from Nell's house there are the first spatters of rain like big dusty coins on the windscreen. Her phone jolts on the dash. A message from Nico: *What the fuck? Where are you going?* She keeps driving on through the paddock gate and out. When she hits the road she feels spacious again — like she can breathe. And then Nico's calling. She doesn't answer, just lets the phone spiral until it hits the floor. She slows the car and reaches down to get it. *Nico's going nuts. What are you even doing?* This is Lucy now. Pearl pulls over and punches out a reply, first to Nico, *I'm sorry. I can't deal with Diana. Or Lucy. The kids. Taking a drive. See you in bed? Won't be long xxx* And then to Lucy: *Can you chill N out pls? Open some wine. Make conversation? I just need an hour P x*

She fiddles with the radio knob again but there's only static, so she switches it off and opens up the heater vents instead. Soon the night will descend purple and complete like a shroud, but now the moon is rising like a shard and only the roads and the paddocks and the sky can hold all that pours from her. She thinks of the Leonard Cohen song about the night coming on, and sings it throatily. I'll have to dig out my box of tapes, she thinks, if I'm going to keep driving this thing everywhere. She could do this. Live on the island and drive utes. *You're nuts! Don't crash* — pings in from Lucy.

You mean can't deal with me? ☹ *Fuck Pearl. Yep, see you in bed then. Worried! Nxxx* Pearl presses the power button off and chucks the phone onto the passenger seat. The rain begins smearing down the windscreen and the trees bend low, and on the silhouette of the hill are the humped backs of kangaroos like sentinels watching the day cross over. She is not really at all sure where she is going, but it is warm in the cabin and the headlights cut a path before her that is clear and purposeful.

She turns off onto the East West road, which cuts across the middle of the island, as she zigzags her way down to the south coast. I guess this is going to be a long drive, she thinks, and reaches into her pocket. Her fingers curl around Nell's black glass scraping tool. She'd swiped it this morning from Nell's green box before driving to pick up Nico and Lewis from the ferry. She didn't really know why she had, except that Diana was hovering around it protectively yesterday, and more importantly, it used to fit Nell's hand perfectly, so absurdly, Pearl feels closer to Nell when she holds it. It is also satisfyingly cool to the touch and she needs these cold sparks of ignition. She had intended to return it today, but here she is driving aimlessly towards the south coast instead. Lightning illuminates the outside world at brief searing intervals. A steady rumble of thunder gathers momentum and Pearl thinks of a slow train trundling alongside the ute. The trees shake their heads in fury as if to say go home go home go home. But still she doesn't turn back.

When the lightning begins cracking in front of the wind-screen she pulls over. The tyres sluice in the dirty water at the edge of the road. The rain is coming fast and the wipers can't keep up. I'll just wait for the rain to ease, she thinks, and then keep going. But where am I going? She reaches for her phone and turns it back on. Eight missed calls from Nico and one from Diana, and barely a cell of reception. *I'm okay. Closer to the south coast now, so not going to turn back. I'll head to Caroline's at Murray Lagoon. Phone nearly dead. Sorry xx* She presses send and hopes Nico will get it. Yes, this is the best plan, she decides. I can't keep sitting here, in this deluge. I'll be hemmed in. Just another half hour and I'll be at Caroline's and Uncle Jim will be there and all this is making sense now. But slowly the road is being swallowed up with water, and all the wipers can manage is to briefly reveal a ghostly way forward. When the trees light up, their naked bright trunks leave an imprint as if pasted on the glass in front of her. But even through the rain she can smell that she's getting closer to the coast. She scours the edge of the road for the turn-off to Murray Lagoon, and realises her heart is racing. I can't miss this. And then as she turns onto the smudged white road, past the row of rusty letterboxes, it is a relief to be off the corrugated track and now that she's not jolting up and down so much that her ears itch, a memory of Nell descends. Or really it's of Diana, and it's something to do with all of this water and the relentless droning sound of it.

She is sitting at the kitchen table, home again with Diana and David, after leaving the island earlier that morning, and the bath is running. And she hates the back and forth. She hates the way Diana throws all Pearl's dusty island things in the washing machine sort of contemptuously, and says, Does Nell not know how to wash clothes? Does she always have to let you ruin your best shoes? Does she ever ever make you wear sunblock? Pearl scratches at her peeling nose.

Don't scratch it.

We went to Red Cliffs yesterday and we covered ourselves completely in mud and pretended we were at a French spa. Marian looked like a hippo, though.

And that's when you got burnt?

No, not then. Have you been there?

Diana sighs and crashes the dishes into the sink. Oh, I can't remember. Go and turn the bath off.

Pearl submerges in the steaming water right to

88

the lobes of her ears. The bathroom here is better than at Nell's; Diana is right about that. The tiles are art-deco green and the sink is curved like a Cadillac. And the red dirt from Red Cliffs starts forming a deliciously startling rim around the edge of the tub. Diana will hate that. Pearl rubs at it with her toe, and can just make out Diana talking to David in the kitchen.

It's impossible, this situation.

Not impossible, just difficult.

You would say that. Fuck.

Do you like this colour on me?

You know I hate maroon. On you. What should I do?

About maroon?

For fuck's sake!

Pearl slides completely under and tries to pin herself down, but her knees bob up, and then her buttocks lift as if pushed from underneath and her flat nipples peek out like little depressions on a white expanse. Her bathers have left an imprint, or the opposite of an imprint, in their exact shape, and she rolls over to inspect her very white bum.

You can't stop the visits.

I can if Nell won't communicate with me.

As long as Pearl wants it, you can't stop it.

Shouldn't I be protecting her?

From what?

David, you've cut the onions too thick again.

Pearl remembers yanking the plug out and slicing her thumb on its metal edge. Blood unfurled in the water like little red butterflies opening and pirouetting. She clenched her thumb and swooned back down in the water, her body becoming heavy and lumpen as the water gurgled away. Diana found her shivering in just a pool of grit from Red Cliffs.

Pearl, what on earth! God, David. David.

★ ★ ★

Pearl drives now as if the rain carries her along. As if she's steering a boat and all she has to do is only what the water suggests. It's a kind of surrender. *From what? What from, David?* And the cabin is so warm and dry and reassuringly cramped in. I really need nothing bigger than this, she thinks, to contain me. On the other side of the road, there is a car pulled over and someone waving her down frantically with a torch. The headlights shining back at her are so bright her eyes want to shrink back into her skull. She slows and a shower of grit sprays the bottom of the ute. It's Uncle Jim and he's dashing across the road, his oilskin gleaming in the high beam. She winds the window down.

Jesus, Pearl, Caroline saw you drive right on past. Turn around and follow me back.

I missed your driveway. How'd you know it was me?

Nico.

near Penneshaw

The first sight of it is a swift kick to the guts. Diana grips the steering wheel tightly and swallows hard. It's not just that the bare bones of her first childhood home are on show, its skeleton, but the olive trees and peach trees have disappeared. The dry stone wall is gone. The bank of geraniums, gone. The slate path, gone. Dad's sprawling corrugated shed, gone. It's all just a building site now, flagged and cordoned off. And somehow with the house so altered from the pristine version of it she carries in her deepest imaginings, and in her very tissue, the location seems wrong, strange, too. She'd never wanted to leave this home after her father died. All the pieces of him were here; his hands had touched everything — each wall, each stone, each plant, each corner — all bore his mark. Diana was worried that she would forget him or, even worse, that no other house would be able to protect her again because it had nothing to do with her father and his shelter. She was angry with Nell for wrenching them away from this place when he died. This had been the only home she'd known and it held remnants of her father. His brushstrokes and his hooks for paintings. His laughter and clomping footsteps. But Nell had other plans. She wanted to move deeper into the island; she wanted a wild beach — or so Diana thought. Nell never explained. One day they just packed up and moved.

Diana slams the car door and ducks under the bunting. She flattens a shell necklace from Nell's green box firm against her throat so it doesn't get caught up. She ignores the warnings not to trespass. There are wooden planks through the mud leading to the frame of what was once the front door. She has to hoist herself up out of the crevasse left by the verandah to cross the threshold. The wide jarrah floorboards of the hallway have been removed. She wonders where they are now. Shiny things. Only the joists remain. Diana steps carefully onto the first joint, steadying herself against the dusty wall. It is dark inside and a corner of tarpaulin secured over the window lifts and slaps and lifts and slaps, like ship sails. And the remains of the house heave and lurch as if at sea. At the far end, the leadlight window holds kaleidoscopic patterns of light. She balances her way along the length of floor beams, and the space seems so narrow now. How did they ever live and dream here, in this tight box, she wonders. There is a trace of blue in the plaster of the hallway arch. She'd squatted on the floor by the ladder stirring the lovely thick paint and passing things up to Reg. Nell didn't like the blue — ostentatious — but Diana had chosen it, and Reg agreed with her that there was something Hellenic about it that really made a dramatic feature of the hallway. Diana slips off the scaffold and her ankle gives way, mud snaking up over the edge of her sandals. She unstraps them and balances them carefully on the joists. Barefoot, she is better at picking her way along the vertebrae of the hallway. Light seeps in at the bottom corners of the foundation, and she remembers Nell complaining endlessly to Reg about bloody draughts and gaping cracks you could stuff with entire books. Entire libraries. There is a crack in the leadlight window. Diana runs her finger along it, and remembers a recurring dream she had as a child that the crack in the glass was from a bullet — the house under siege. This was long before Reg died. A portent, maybe? Sometimes she couldn't tell if it was, in fact, a dream or something that actually happened — preposterous as that may seem — the stress in the stained glass so entangled in her memory.

At the back of the house, the porch is still enclosed, the sleepout — her bedroom — still in place. Standing in the centre of it she can almost touch every wall with her outstretched fingers. A dog box, but she loved it. Her own private ante-chamber. She closes her eyes and there is her bed jammed next to her brown narrow desk, a straight-backed chair and the broom cupboard behind the door, which served as her wardrobe. Nothing much else in there — just a box of pencils on the desk and a row of feathers on the sill. Back then, we didn't own much, she thinks. No one did. There are louvre windows missing like broken teeth. And there is Reg out the back in the workshop. Wood shavings curling at his boots. The whirr of his drill. Diana sinks to her haunches, and scrapes the mud from her feet. There is Reg falling from a ladder.

She wonders whether things would have been better for her and Nell if Reg was around to see Pearl grow. Diana would have had an ally. She was on the outside of Pearl and Nell's intimacy, their colluding, their whispers and raised eyebrows. Their matching eyes. Even now. Nell has taken something from Pearl which means Diana can never be close. She cannot forgive

Nell for this. Cannot forgive Nell for the fuss she made when they took Pearl back again. Just two years old, Pearl could have easily forgotten that she had ever lived with her grandmother. But every month Nell came and got her for a long weekend. And when she was older, every school holidays. It hurt Diana that whenever Nell arrived at their front door, Pearl ran to her and wouldn't let go, in those early months of transition. Even when it was a relief to have a break from looking after Pearl; she was that strung out with new baby Lucy. Even then she knew she had messed everything up.

Diana takes a pencil from her handbag and holds it poised to the wall. Nell smacked her once for drawing on the hallway walls — she'd refused to stop when Nell asked her to, and she just kept on scribbling gloriously, frowning at Nell and terrified. This was one of the reasons they'd had to do a repaint. But Reg made light of it. Those walls have been looking shabby for years, Nell. Let's spruce up. This is a good thing, Nell. She didn't agree.

On the sleepout wall Diana sketches a man's hand curled around a child's. She draws shells, seals, and a heart like a piece of glowing fruit. She draws a woman's secret places. And blood. She writes the names of her parents and daughters and signs her own name and then stands to measure herself against the notches in the door frame. She is a full head and shoulders above the last date marked. The air coming through the rattling louvres is grassy and dry. She won't ever stand in this room again.

Nell

It was almost a full moon and hot when Marian, Red and I saw in the New Year together at Pelican Lagoon. Pearl had gone to live with Diana and David on the mainland just eight weeks earlier, and the house rattled empty without her sweet toddling presence. The days were long and undefined. Unpunctuated. I suppose my little silly heart was breaking. The expedition to Pelican Lagoon was solely my idea — I think Marian was hoping for a night in with Red. A night where Red didn't write and the two of them could just really talk and get a bit drunk. But I was going out of my skin with the heat and loneliness.

We pulled in at the edge of the lagoon, tyres skidding in the shale. The white quartz ground of Pelican Lagoon, pitted and scooped, shone like a moonscape. Red grabbed Marian's hand and I followed them, weaving a path through the spinifex and low-lying clumps of spear grass and saltbush. The air was hot, body temperature, and it made Marian feel like making love, she announced. Twenty years of marriage before Red and she hadn't known at all that sex was her thing, she once confided in me. We found a clear patch between the scratchy rocks. Marian poured more sparkling into the metal cups she kept in her glove box. The cups lent a dusty metallic taste and the champagne was on the verge of too warm, but it was a beautiful amber colour, and I gulped it down. The lagoon riffled slowly and everything seemed so very loud — the oyster-catchers skimming the edge of the water, too hot to sleep, and skinks disturbed the undergrowth. Red laid her head in Marian's lap. And I thought of the weight of little Pearl squirming in my lap, reaching up to twist my necklace in her fingers. I was heartbroken.

So, Nell, plans for the new year? Red asked.

Oh, the usual. I'm going to paint more and drink less.

That's what you said last year, Red pointed out, kicking off her Birkenstocks. I'd given up drinking when Pearl was nearly born, and I'd stopped painting altogether — it still worries me a lot that in order to paint I need to drink.

Actually, I'm going to write more, I said.

There was a pause and no one said anything. I'm writing a story and it's taking everything out of me.

Oh really? Red said.

It's about here — the island. This place.

And I realise, now, that I've been trying to write this story for the whole of Pearl's life. She is the living embodiment of my growing story. But it's only now that the right words will come. This is my hope.

Red was silent for a moment and then levered herself up on her elbows. You're going to have to tell me more about this writing of yours, Nell.

Not much to say. Just gathering my thoughts,

really. This was true.

Red gulped her drink.

Well Marian and I are going to Morocco next month. That's my news.

Marian let out a small sound. What? Red, how? Marian knocked over her cup of champagne. You didn't tell me.

I wanted it to be a surprise. Red stood to avoid the wet seeping across the picnic rug.

But what about your book? You've gotta finish your collection by April.

I'll finish it in Morocco. I've already booked the tickets. Red grinned.

I was so thrilled for them, I sneezed and wet my pants. Just a little. Gosh. Wow. That's wonderful news. So you'll stay with Amelia?

Amelia was Marian's daughter. They hadn't seen each other in four years, and Marian had never met her now two-year-old granddaughter, Aza. Amelia went travelling in Morocco after finishing her degree, fell in love with Abdul, and only came home briefly to pack up her house in Adelaide and break Marian's heart. Morocco of all places, she'd said to Amelia at the time. All those years Marian had been Adam's wife, raising their daughter and son. Sometimes it was as if that former life never existed. Both children lived abroad with families of their own and her marriage was now just a washed-out dream. We often talked about this. It was just an inventory of images, like photographs, Marian told me. And I was sad for her.

Did you speak to Amelia? What if she's busy then?

I've spoken to Amelia, and everything's fine.

Marian was overwhelmed and I went off to pee.

Crouching low, I held my pants out of the way and watched piss clumping in the dirt spectacularly. I was reeling. With all this talk of grandchildren, I felt like I'd lost somehow not only my son, my daughter, but now, my granddaughter? Granddaughter. I mouthed the word and it came out strange. Pearl. Something inside lurched, in my miwi. I wobbled and piss sprayed the ground and my bare feet, splashing them with dirt. Christ, I said, when it finally petered out; I hiked up my trousers and faced the lagoon. The night Pearl was born had been a full moon like this one. Diana held on to me until my upper arms were bruised with her thumbprints. We both cried at the little wet thing that slipped out of her.

In the moonlight, the lichen-smothered rocks pulsed white. And the she-oaks were unusually still — not whispering and whooshing ghostily as they usually did. The lagoon itself pinched the island into a bottleneck, marking its narrowest point — just a kilometre between the north coast where the lagoon spread its great pelican wings, and the furious south coast that faced Antarctica. I've always felt its ancientness — *these islets in a hidden lagoon of an uninhabited island, situate upon an unknown coast* — my favourite words of the explorer Matthew Flinders. Place of bones and souls . . . *nor can any thing be more consonant to the feelings, if pelicans have any, than quietly to resign their breath, whilst surrounded by their progeny, and in the same spot where they first drew it. Alas, for the pelicans! . . . I named this piece of water Pelican Lagoon.* Marked territory. I shivered. Pull yourself together, Nell, I said aloud and, tugging at the amber beads around my wrist, Pearl's teething beads, I meandered my way back to Red and Marian. They were smoking, and the smell was thick and high in the bridge of my nose.

Marian opened up the cake tin, hoping the smell of chilli-laced chocolate would bring her back to herself after taking in such a lungful of marijuana, she explained giggling. She hadn't smoked in years, and it took all her effort to keep her worry down in her groins. I told her it was best to actively resist anxiety. I was an old hat at this. Red passed me the joint and my throat burnt as the smoke went down. Before long all my gestures felt vastly exaggerated like I was a great big flourish of a woman. It was strong dope.

Well this year — after Morocco, of course — I'm going to get some hives. Keep bees, Marian announced and then asked us if she'd spoken too fast. Or too slow.

My mother kept bees, I told them.

Did she? I've never really heard you talk about your mother, Nell. What was she like? Red asked, dismissing Marian's bees.

Mother. Bright eyes. Bright silver hair. A sort of drawn look — pale around the mouth, flushed cheeks. She was the most loving and most ruthless woman I've known, I said.

We gobbled up the brownies, and the chocolate left a film along the roof of the mouth. Spiced. I lay back on the rug, sending out a silent wish to Diana. Please be gentle with me. Red stood over us on a stand of granite and beneath the *cloths of heaven*, read aloud her new poem . . . *seeds polished shiny as hope* . . . and at midnight we stood in the shallows of the lagoon holding on to each other for dear life. I let my feet sink into the sludge and wondered whether it was ever peaceful to be a mother.

Tiny nocturnal creatures scuttled in the undergrowth and unseen things splashed in the water; it was absurd to be a human and so brash in this place of animals. This brightening midnight lagoon. I made a promise, a new year's wish, to not give up on Pearl. I would do better for her sake. I would write Maringani and William one day, not only for Sol, but also for Pearl.

1823
Vivonne Bay

William sits squished against the bulk of his father. The hold is loaded up with sealskins, blood mixing with the swill of water that sloshes around the bottom of the boat. Metallic stench of death. William tucks his feet up under himself to avoid the blood. His feet are already pickled and white from being wet for so long. He begins to pull at the puckered skin on the bottom of his big toe and peels off strips. Emue nudges his hand away and takes his feet into her lap. William turns to see what his father's reaction might be, but Anderson is too busy guiding the cutter in the fading light to notice them. Emue pats the bottom of her shirt against William's feet to dry them and then wraps them in a wallaby skin, which she takes from around her shoulders. It is dry because she does her sealing naked, keeping her clothes and animal skins bundled into a tight ball on the boat. She holds the pelt firmly in place and beneath the pressure of her hands William can feel the blood in his feet starting to circulate and reach his toes again. He is shaky with exhaustion and would close his eyes as he leans against his father but has to remain alert so that he can whisk his feet away from Emue as soon as Anderson turns in their direction. Emue belongs to Anderson.

William looks up at Emue but she is staring out into the distance. He can tell she is tired because her normally very straight shoulders are slumped forward slightly and her bottom lip hangs from her top as if closing her mouth requires too much effort. William can barely make out her features in the encroaching darkness, but he feels calmed by watching her.

About eleven baby sealskins lie on top of the adult ones. William knows that Emue doesn't like killing the pups but Anderson forces her to do it because the fur on the pups is softer than velvet and gets a high price. She shakes her head and clicks her tongue and sings to the seals after she has clubbed a baby or a mother seal.

Emue unwraps William's feet and presses his toe back. He winces a little and she glances at him and lowers her gaze as if to tell him not to touch the skin of his toes now. William grins at her, pulls his feet from her lap and tucks them under himself.

Who is my mother? William addresses the back of Anderson's head.

Anderson doesn't answer. His massive shoulders stiffen. William is used to getting no response to this question but continues to ask it anyway, although today he is too spent to push it any further. He wonders, again, why his father will never speak of her.

He strokes his foot along the fur of one of the seals, thinking how, just hours ago, it was warm, alive, pulsing with blood. As Anderson rows the boat towards land, William wriggles his way past Emue and crouches at the bow, chewing the quick around his nails. The gamey smell of the skins makes him feel like retching. He wonders if he will ever get used to that smell.

Later, back at the hut, William sits with his feet so close by the fire they itch. He feels like nothing will make his feet warm again. The men's voices are loud but strangely comforting as their conversation swells and crashes around him. In the distance he can hear the women singing. He hopes he can fall asleep to the men talking and the women singing and not be interrupted by the grunts and moans of his father with Emue.

★ ★ ★

Anderson lets one of Emue's dogs, the pale one, lick him between his toes as he lies on his side watching Emue. She is making shallow vertical and horizontal cuts in a wallaby skin that has just been scraped clean over a log. The scores make the skin supple so that it can be sewn into a cloak. Emue folds the skin over at each of the lines and then begins rubbing it with a blunt piece of flint to soften it. Anderson likes her thin fingers — the way the skin doesn't crack and look raw from overwork like the skin on his own hands, but is oiled, shiny and creased with fine, fine lines. For a moment he imagines her hands splayed across him, her dark fingers pulling gently at the small knots in the curls of his chest hair. But it is never that tender. She has no desire for him. Anderson winces at the slow throb spreading deep within him. He is lying down, head-achey from a night on the rum, and crosses his legs, squeezing his thighs together.

Emue, Anderson says propping himself up on his elbow.

Emue stops what she is doing, the animal skin spread across her lap, her belly round as the full moon curved above it. She keeps her eyes on her hands.

Emue, look at me, Anderson mutters.

She lifts her head slightly. He tries to remember the night before, sifting through images and sounds that splinter as soon as he tries to concentrate on them. He remembers waking Emue . . . and the girl . . . the girl was sleeping with her arm across her mother's shoulders. He had pushed the arm away and the girl's eyes snapped open. Velvet brown eyes. Wide and accusing. He couldn't bear those eyes watching him. He had slunk away, back to the hut. He remembers Munro swilling the rum and he had grabbed the bottle from him. He remembers Everitt, laughing, toothless, as he gulped down more rum. After that, nothing.

Emue hangs her head forward, springy curls falling down in front of her eyes. Anderson looks at her smooth shoulders, like wet stones. He sees the black and purple circlet of bruises around her upper arm.

Emue, come here. Lie aside me, Anderson pleads, the words sticking in his throat.

She doesn't move. He can hear her soft, quiet breathing.

Emue. If yer would just lie wid me then I wouldn't . . . then I wouldn't, but he falters mid-sentence because Emue looks up and meets his gaze. She stares right into him and then stands up letting the skin drop to the sand. Turning she walks away and he watches her feet flicking up with each step, the underside pale like shells.

Murray Lagoon

Once inside Caroline's place, Pearl stands with her back to the radiator until the creases of her knees burn against her jeans. The kettle is on, steaming up the window above the kitchen sink, and Uncle Jim shakes rain from his Akubra and places it on the table.

I'm sorry to arrive like this. I don't really know. What I'm doing. I guess.

Cuppa, love? says Caroline.

Pearl nods, Yes please, and moves away from the heater. Jim rattles the Arnott's biscuit tin. Take a seat, Pearl. You've had a big day all right.

She shrugs. I don't know. Too many people back at the house. I can't think.

Do you wanna think right now? Family's what you need. Just being together. No thinking.

Caroline carries the cups of tea over and places them straight on the table. Pearl notices whitened rings all over the wood grain from so many hot cups. Do you take sugar?

No thanks.

Jim lumps several spoonfuls of sugar into his thick black tea and leans back on his chair. He stirs the sugar for a long time and the cup rings out against the spoon. So I'm glad you're here, Pearl. I've got some stuff for you. And look, I'm real sorry. Culture way, you'd be in sorry camp.

Culture way, she's your mother.

Pearl takes a sip of the tea. It is strong and bitter.

In the morning, we'll go walking, all right. Sunrise okay? Tonight, I'll leave you two ladies to yarn. He takes three Monte Carlos and dips them into his tea one after the other, shoving them into his mouth before they collapse. Jim stands and scrabbles through a drawer in the sideboard. He drops an envelope on the table and then makes for the screen door. As he steps outside the cold rushes in and Pearl shivers.

Caroline slides the envelope over towards Pearl. These are for you. Just some photos and things Uncle's been collecting.

The room darkens momentarily as the power surges and the lights go off, and then back on again. Caroline is looking for candles. Everyone's worried about you back at King George, she says, lining up some tea lights on the counter. She places matches beside her. I love a blackout. Always prepared. Outside, the trees toss in the gale. The rain is so loud that Pearl raises her voice.

I know. I'm awful. Nico just got here. I only just picked him up from the ferry. I can't face him. Jim's burning cigarette tip pricks the darkness beyond the screen door. Beyond him, the lagoon is blacker even than the night.

I lost my nephew last week — that's why Uncle's here. And for Nell. He'll stay for Saturday, of course. Caroline bunches her thick dark hair, blonde at the tips, and twists it up into a headband. She wears a black T-shirt and bright

106

clay beads. She is lined but youthful-looking. He was in prison. My nephew he was in prison. Uncle's taking it hard. The young men, they're not learning the law, our law. Uncle feels he's failing. She shakes her head. Why can't you face Nico, huh?

Ah Caro, I feel terrible. Stupid. I'm so sorry about your nephew.

Caroline covers Pearl's hand with her own. She wears silver rings and bangles and her knuckles are dry. Hey, it's all right. Listen to Uncle, though, you need family. That don't mean sometimes it ain't hard work, right sister? She laughs and swigs down the last of her tea.

The screen door bangs open and Jim comes inside, bringing the rain. He's left his boots at the door and walks towards them in his socks. He warms his hands, fanning them over the oil heater, and Pearl notices that his jeans are wet through. Well I'm off to bed, girls. I'll wake you first thing.

Night, Uncle.

Night, Caro. Night, Pearl. Hey Pearl, I reckon you're gonna be okay. He winks at her. If you're anything like that Nell of ours. She's got fire in the blood that one. Or something like that. He laughs and rubs his jaw. Driving out in that storm. Jeez, Pearl.

Pearl smiles. Uncle and Caro have a way of slowing her right down — their gentle attention is without agenda. Open-hearted. Fire in the blood? No, she doesn't want that. She's working on unfurling the tight folds of her heart instead. Or something like that. Becoming more like water. She tips up the envelope and a photo flicks out. A young man, impossibly handsome, impossibly young, wearing an army slouch — bunched smiling cheeks, straight teeth, dark eyes, shiny skin. She turns the photo over. *Solomon, 1944.*

★ ★ ★

The next morning is damp and gentle. Uncle Jim walks slightly ahead — shoulders loose, body forward on the front of his toes, his steps almost skimming the surface. Treading lightly. Pearl and Caroline follow along the dry creek bed.

Keep together, he says. We're a mob. Small one.

Pearl realises her instinct is to hang back. Walk alone. She thinks about this tendency. And then lets herself be carried along in the wake. There is a memory of water here, the way the sand is gouged and clumps of leaf and stick debris wrap themselves around tree trunks and boulders, as if in mid-flight. As if the creek had only right then disappeared. The sun is newly risen, so everything is silver and cold. Everything is washed clean from the storm and the trees shimmy with water. New branches have fallen. Each gum leaf on the floor of the creek bed holds one drop of moisture. Mercury balls. Caroline stoops to pick up a leaf and tips the water in her mouth. Pearl does the same. Later, all the water will disappear, as if it had never rained.

What we are looking for, says Uncle, is the

glint of wings. He stops at a sugar gum, leans the small tomahawk against the trunk, and looks up. He places his ear to the tree and then knocks it. We're listening for a hollow and a buzzing. He smiles. Pearl, come.

Jim moves away and Pearl steps up to listen. She holds the sides of the trunk and presses her ear to the bark. At first, nothing. And then it's like placing a cheek to a person's stomach — a gurgling of water and peristalsis. She's not sure if what she's hearing is the sound of the wind amplified, or water being drawn up by the tree's own vascular system, or her own blood coursing. She closes her eyes.

It's a talking tree, but no bees there, says Jim, starting to walk again. Caroline clasps her hands behind her back and steps in beside Jim with his little backpack banging on his hips. Pearl bends to peel off her shoes and socks and follows them. The sand is cold and lumpy with mallee roots. Jim tells quietly of the black moss growing on the rocks and Pearl knows the moss story holds many more layers of meaning than Jim shares, or even knows himself. He tells of the grass tree being the spurt of the whale — of the connection between whale law and echidna law. Law of the land and law of the sea. Pearl takes one step after another and tries to keep her shoulders loose. Her feet burn with cold. They enter an opening as if crossing a threshold, going down a series of stepped boulders, and the grass trees grow thickly for a while, and they look like little humps of families in all their odd shapes and sizes. Pearl feels a honey warmth spreading through her belly and she can't explain it. She thinks of Nico, and her body softens. Sorry, darling. You could have been here for this too. If I wasn't shutting you out. Caroline stops to crouch and gestures towards a large stone with a flat surface. It is patterned with a series of rings like the rings of trees, or watermarks from the tide on a beach. Pearl squats beside her.

Good place here, says Jim, and slips off his backpack.

Caroline takes a photo of the rock with its undulating pattern. I'll use this, she says. For an artwork. Pearl nods. She is noticing that there are repeating patterns in the bark, in the rocks, in the clouds, in her own fingerprints. Unseen currents running between the leaves and the stones and the wind and the light and the sky. Between the three of them. Connective tissue. She yearns for Nell. And for her sister. She is almost ready to go home. Her hand closes around the scraper in her pocket.

They find no bees and no honey on their walk but Jim leads them to a fire circle and he neatens up the stones and he rakes it clean and he builds a fire. We keep the fire clean, he says. Our cooking place. Jim lays a wire rack on the flames and turns it over. Have to clean the wire too, he says.

Caroline mixes flour and seeds and water in a plastic dish she's brought with her, kneading the mixture into dough, before breaking it up into small pieces.

Pearl, flatten each one slightly, like this. For johnnycakes.

So Pearl moulds the johnnycakes on a flat rock, stacking them into a little pile, and they wait for the fire to be ready.

Uncle Jim, that photo? Solomon? Pearl ventures.

For a long time, Jim says nothing. When the fire's ready, we'll rake back the coals and make an opening for the damper. Here. Jim points with his fire stick.

Caroline nods. Pearl, make the cakes a bit flatter. Too thick like that. They'll puff up.

Pearl presses her fingers into the damper and pulls out the edges.

Sol. Born here on the island. He was kin. Handsome, eh? There's a lotta stuff for you to look through among that lot.

Jim stands and rolls back some of the bigger logs with his long stick. Caroline stands and arches her back then brushes the flour from her T-shirt. An eagle drifts. The smoke wends towards Pearl and then whips back to Jim. The slight tang of salt tells of the nearby ocean. An eagle marks the sky and the ocean rings out. Clouds striate the sky holding nothing. Ants sieve dirt like flour. Beneath ant mounds, feldspar, quartz, gold, kyanite, lepidolite, tourmaline. Fault lines. Water table. All the folds of the world. All the songs. All the scars.

Who was he? Pearl asks.

His aunty came to Raukkan, the mission at Point McLeay, from the island when she was older. Kicked off the island. I grew up on that mission. We could be related — she was Ngarrindjeri. But with our people so scattered,

111

we have to build a picture from fragments. I don't know, love.

Your Nell was gathering information, and Uncle was helping because she was writing a history or something of the island, Caroline adds. Did you know that?

Yeah, so I've been finding everything I can for Nell. Photos, articles, scraps. Anything at all related to this place. Jim spreads the coals flat and repositions the wire rack carefully.

I think she did mention something. Her love letter to the island. It wouldn't surprise me at all, Pearl says, smiling.

She gave me things, I gave her things. Mutual exchange. Jim drops a johnnycake onto the rack. It hurts here, he holds his stomach, that there are gaps in our history starting from them sealing times. For blackfella. And whitefella.

Uncle was so chuffed when Nell found that scraping tool. At Waubs Wall.

Oh my god, Pearl laughs.

What is it?

Oh, I have that here. I've been gripping on to the bloody thing all night. Here, you should have it, Uncle.

He shakes his head. Nah, I reckon that one's yours. Nell tried to give it to me, too.

No please. I want others to see it. Take it back to the cultural museum.

Jim nods and then is wracked with coughing. He leans into his long fire stick. Thumps his chest. For a moment, despite his long-legged height, he seems frail.

Jeez, Uncle.

Flip those johnnies over now, Caro. I reckon it's time.

Caroline uses long metal tongs to pick up the flats of damper and turn them over. They are puffy and striped and perfectly burnt and Pearl's mouth waters. Jim wriggles the wire rack over to new coals.

Pearl lies back in the sand and the sky is clear and thin, a membrane. She closes her eyes, and she can see something like a bright shining tree but wonders if what she is seeing is just her own branching capillaries. Her own membrane. She could sleep now and not go home. She could see Nell's face and try to hold on to the shifting picture. She could will the deep of her womb into perfect balance. She could rest until she was renewed.

The johnnycakes are light and fluffy and steaming inside. Caroline breaks them open and slathers them with butter. She passes one to Pearl. The butter drips over Pearl's knuckles and she licks it up, and then butter drips down her wrist. She can't remember when she last ate so well.

Nell

For more than two weeks I could not get out of bed. I lay knotted in my sheets, burning up, and the white of the walls shimmied and threw off such a glare that I could barely open my eyes. Mother appeared often with fresh glasses of water and lemon, and fussed with the curtains or the bedclothes, until her bustling made me dizzy and I groaned and turned away from her. Oh how I hated her — that deep frown line and those heavy deliberate steps. Fat ankles. In those murky days of illness it was as if she pinned me down with her solidity, her constant attention, and all I wanted to do was fly up through the heights of fever and out of my body. I could feel Sol just over at the next farm. How I wished for him. If he'd walked into that bedroom then, I would have flown right back into myself as if each cell of my body was spreading out, widening in diameter, instead of this tightly wound thing I'd become. I remember the high watermarked ceiling. The gauze curtains lifting up dancer-like and falling suddenly as the breeze dropped. I remember the knobs of the dresser like big open mouths gaping at me. And I remember the floorboards and how the dust turned to gold in the sunlight. I remember the terrible emptiness I felt in that room that once had been mine, but was now the bedroom of a girl who had been scoured down to powder.

When Father met us at the jetty the sky was thick and pewter. He was absurdly tall, and from a distance he seemed frailer, thinner, his suit crumpled and hanging off his sharp shoulder bones, and his hat pressed to his chest. I almost wept when he lifted me out of the boat and tucked me under his arm. He didn't say anything to me at all, but stroked the back of my hand as we walked to the bullock cart. Mother struggled behind with the suitcases. Peter what about the luggage? she called after him. Father just kept walking, not looking at anybody else, as if nothing mattered except he and I.

Just leave them. I'll come back for them.

But she ignored him and I could hear her breathing heavily, straining with the luggage, and following just behind. Father plumped the cushions around me on the back seat, and I looked back at the people scurrying at the wharf like ants when they know it's going to rain. I searched for him, Sol, in everything — along the tracks, in the paddocks, on verandahs — as we made the slow journey home.

1823
Chapman River

William rushes into the hut to find Anderson hacking at his hair with a sharp but dirty knife.

The baby, the baby.

Boy or gerl? Anderson asks as he razors through another hunk of grey and copper coarse hair, throwing it into the fire.

Girl. She's tiny, answers William, his voice quivering with pride.

Anderson finally turns around. Tiny? What's wrong with it?

Nothing, Father. She's just. Small, William says, thinking how tiny the baby's head was against Emue's heavy breast. He thinks the baby is like the sky and the earth all at once with her blue eyes and brown skin.

Do you want to come see her? asks William touching his father's elbow.

Anderson shrugs William's hand away. No. And you are not to be lurkin' down there now. Do yer hear?

Why can't I?

Because you ain't a half-caste, and I don't want you gettin' influenced. Another handful of hair in the flames, sizzling and acrid.

But Father —

No son of yer mother is going to 'sociate with a half-caste, do yer hear me? Anderson grips William by the shoulders as he spits the words inches away from his face. William can smell the rum on his breath.

He meets his father's eyes and whispers, I ain't got no mother.

William hears something break inside Anderson. There's a terrible tearing sound as he throws William to the floor.

★   ★   ★

Anderson holds the boy's hand to the coals and his ears ring and the angry scar on his chest rages livid. The smell makes him gag yet the boy does not scream. He is limp in Anderson's arms. You ain't got your mother's hands now either. He wraps him in a skin and lays him down. Dotes on him. Ferries water back and forth. Strokes his forehead. Wraps his hand. Puts out the fire. Sings to him. Weeps. Clutches at him. William looks up at him with helpless seal pup eyes. It is nice to be needed, Anderson realises.

★   ★   ★

Maringani knows that Poll has been waiting for this. She's seen Poll gazing out across the passage. Gazing home. Making peace with the water. Singing to it. And now all the women are busy attending to Emue and the new wriggling one. William disappeared inside the hut long ago with Anderson — Maringani waited for him, but he never emerged. The other men have started drinking already and follow their own strange loud rhythms. Poll and her own almost walking baby are alone. Maringani watches from the low scrub. Poll is kneeling at the water's edge, her baby sitting up straight-backed on the sedge cloak spread out on the sand. Poll scoops the water over her shoulders and wets herself all over and then gathers the child into her arms and cradles it. Its round legs kick into Poll's ribs. Maringani whispers and hopes the boy is sleeping. She hopes Poll can swim like a seal.

Poll lays the child down onto the sedge cloak,

kneels up, gathers the cloak and swings it round onto her back. She ties the cloak up deftly and Maringani can just make out the little boy's scrubby head at the top of the carrier. Poll begins walking into the water. She turns to look back and Maringani stands up out of the spinifex and rushes to Poll. Maringani strokes her hands up and down Poll's arms and over the baby's head and embraces Poll and licks salt from her neck. Poll shakes her head, rubs her mouth all over Maringani's face and then turns back to the sea. Their two little crowns, mother's and child's, bob in the water like seals. Maringani sees the waves washing over the sedge cloak and Poll's strong arms rising and plunging. Then there are rough hands on Maringani's shoulders. A gruff voice. Everitt's. What's she up ter?

★ ★ ★

Maringani thinks it is punishment enough, the sodden empty sedge cloak. But for Poll's sake she will hide in the knots of the mallee and she will watch. Poll's nakedness is bright against the tree. The ropes cut into her brightness. The tree is weeping for it knows what it is to be cut. Poll does not cry out because her heart is in the sea. Rolling over and under and over. Everitt seems both to be sagging — drooped ugly spine — and sprung tight — jittery dangerous legs. Poll is no more than a seal to him, thinks Maringani. He is swift, slicing the lobe of Poll's ear cleanly. Sealers' knives are always sharp. He sinks to his knees and sobs at Poll's feet. He smokes and it steadies him. Poll is so still she seems to sink back into the tree, oozing sap. Maringani waits and she waits. When Everitt has lunged away down the track muttering, Maringani loosens Poll's ropes. Maringani sponges the blood. Wraps the wound. Brings more water. She sings and she weeps. Later, in the wurlie, she places Emue's baby in Poll's arms, and finally, Poll sleeps, her ear crusting dramatically. Maringani wonders why William has not appeared all evening. She yields into the sealskins and closes her eyes and nestles up to Emue, who is burning hot, and Maringani tries not to see any more blood. We are trapped by all that water, she thinks. And she imagines a luminous canoe, built from Poll's doorway tree, taking them all home on the stars.

King George Beach (Sandy)

Pearl hovers outside the shed door for a moment. Through the smeary window, Diana is half turned away, her dark hair swept behind her ear. The light behind her is yellow and smudged. Diana is reading something and flicking ash straight onto the floor. Pearl almost walks in, but a familiar feeling returns — of not wanting to pull Diana out of one of her subterranean reveries — and so turns for the house instead. I'll face her later.

She enters softly, not sure what she will find, whom she will find. She knows Nico will want a sufficient explanation for her sudden disappearance, and so she is practising a polite, ordered response. Evenly toned. Something adequate like, I didn't mean to be gone for so long. I'm sorry that I worried you. And not — I wanted to drive myself into oblivion. She couldn't say that.

Even now, she doesn't want to be back here. Even now she is irritated with Nico, though he's done nothing wrong. But the expectation that she might owe him an explanation at all is suffocating. She knows she is being awful. An awful person, I am. So she is relieved to find the living room empty. A bare, clean living room. The kids' things packed neatly in the corner, the rugs straight, the cushions fat, and through the window, the sea heaving, the leaves of the scrub nodding and twinkling after so much rain. All morning after their walk she'd helped Uncle Jim clear fallen branches and pile them up in a neat heap — the ground spongy and briny as they trampled a path through the samphire. The wood smoke clinging in the damp air a presage of winter, even though it is almost April. The easy work of it had been soothing — finding a grip on the wet branches, pulling them from each other as if untangling knotted hair, dragging them along the path, heaving them satisfyingly onto the pile — all of this had taken her attention and dulled it. The gentle conversation with Jim, punctuated only by his coughing, by his thumping his chest to clear phlegm. And the shallow lagoon, glittering, a giant handprint in the sand, was more striking than she remembered it. Cratered like a clay pan. She stood on its crusted edge and made no wishes. For once her thoughts were as flat and as quiet as the lagoon.

Ah, so you're back! Lucy slings a cloth over her shoulder, looks at Pearl inquiringly, hugs her tightly. For a long time they don't pull away, and Pearl is relieved. There's no telling off. There are no lectures. Lucy smells good like shampoo.

So are you okay?

I'm fine. I feel a lot better. Where's Nico?

Walking with Joe and the kids. Don't worry, he's good. I did as you requested. She smiles.

Pearl flops into the armchair and swings her legs over the arm rest. Digs her thumbs into her temples.

No, get up. Come with me out to the shed. See Mum.

Pearl groans.

C'mon, while everyone else is out.

Diana has been sorting Nell's trestle of beach flotsam — the shells grouped together, the driftwood piled up, sea-eagle feathers all in a woven basket, the stones, glass, bits of netting, shark eggs, fossils, urchins, beaks, claws, skeletons, carapaces, tiny skulls arranged systematically in little boxes. And then a stack of papers on the cleared end. Nell's green shoebox. Some sketches. Pearl takes it all in — wonders how Diana can already be tidying, rummaging through everything like picking through bones. She bites the inside of her cheek. Says nothing.

Jesus, Pearl. What were you thinking? Diana regards her sceptically. Nico only just got here!

Pearl purses her lips. I can't explain, she thinks.

Well, I guess grief is selfish, Diana says matter-of-factly.

Pearl ignores her, and thinks, I could say something to wound you, too, but I won't. She points to the sketches. What are these?

The top one is clearly of Nell — peering into the distance, resolute mouth, haughty eyes. A charcoal. The intricate detail, in the hair, the earrings, the lines of the forehead, is not something Pearl has seen in Nell's work before. It is more Nell than Nell.

Diana comes to stand next to Pearl. They're mine, she says quietly. I did them.

Pearl begins laying the sketches beside each

other. They are luminous and shadowy both. Restless. Nell always looking away. And all of them side by side, a kaleidoscope of Nell. The shed heaves and groans in the buffeting wind.

She was the only model I had.

When did you do them?

They're beautiful, Mum, says Lucy.

I thought if I could paint her perfectly it would mean . . . I threw them out in a rage. Found them yesterday. I'm surprised, actually. She kept them. Though she was vain!

Diana wanders over to the stool by the easel. Shakes the cigarette packet. Casts it aside. Perches on the stool daintily. Pearl knows what she's thinking. Needs to make this pack last — the shop's a good hour's drive away.

It was when Dad died. I hated Nell. Being left with her.

To Pearl, the pictures are full of regard for the subject. They shine. Behind Diana is just a haze of graceful rain through the little square of window. Everything still again. The clouds over the bay striated with rose and gold. Soft light.

Lucy hefts a cardboard box onto the trestle. I found these, too. She pulls out tissue paper like stuffing. I thought we could use them for the wake. Lucy unwraps the little packages — tea cups and saucers. She wipes them out with a cloth and begins lining them up delicately. They are an assortment of gold rims, bright colours, geometric patterns, floral designs, fine handles.

Nell and her bloody cups, says Diana. If you unwrap them, we'll only have to pack them all up again. Another thing to add to the list. Lucy drops a cup and it rattles loudly in its saucer.

Pearl tries to control her breathing. Digs her fingers into the skin of her stomach and twists it up. Why's that?

God. Because everything has to be packed up. This whole complete mess. Diana waves her arm to indicate the whole of the shed. She shakes a cigarette from the packet and lights it. And before you say anything, Pearl, you know it has to be this way. Diana blows the smoke out long and slow.

Does it? She faces Diana squarely.

Well are you going to move in? Take care of the place?

I live in Melbourne. Pearl brushes sand from the trestle.

Exactly!

Lewis's mum is there.

Could it be a holiday place for us all? Could it not? Lucy ventures.

Diana rolls up her sleeves and shakes her bangles to sit low on her wrists. Pearl knows this gesture well — a kind of taking the floor as if she's about to deliver a monologue. Luce, I'm fifty-two years old. I still rent. I drive a bomb. I work in an art supply shop. We'll go thirds in everything. I promise. I need this. Or buy me out. Go on, Pearl. Buy me out.

Pearl opens the green shoebox and unfolds the tissue paper. The red woollen caps are slightly sticky to the touch, sweating lanolin. We grew up here, Di, she says quietly.

You grew up here, Lucy says quickly. Only you. Not me. Lucy drops the empty cup and saucer box to the ground with a kind of annoyed flourish.

Anyone seen the glass scraper out of there? Diana nods at the shoebox and looks sharply at Pearl. I'm trying to gather everything precious together. In one special place.

Why would you say that anyway, about buying you out? You know I can't afford it. And the bloody scraper. I gave it to Jim. Pearl winds her hair up into a spiral over her shoulder.

What?

I said, I gave it to Jim.

Why? Lucy and Diana ask at the same time.

I don't know why. I just wanted to. Except now she misses the gravitas of the scraper in the palm of her hand. I never properly lived here either, Lucy. And we *both* spent a lot of time here.

Well, you more so.

Pearl cannot believe Lucy is being so petulant. How quickly the mood between them changes.

It was not only that last night Pearl had wanted to drive herself into oblivion, but also she wanted to keep away this inevitable drowning. There is so much water between them all. When she was little, she liked it best when she was here with Nell, and Lucy and Diana were back on the mainland, the shoals and seaways of Backstairs Passage between them. Now they are so near, but still, she cannot get to them. She swims underwater and her lungs burst with holding her breath. Only the light tells her which way to resurface. Suddenly, she misses Nico.

Ah god! Let's just get through the next few

days. We don't need to be packing up yet, Mum. Let's slow things down, Lucy offers. So much to think about, actually. Lucy sighs.

Typical of you to assume everything belongs to you, Pearl. That scraper was the one thing of my mother's I wanted to have for myself. And Lucy we do need to be packing now — I've only got two weeks off.

Oh and then what? Pack up and sell in two weeks? Pearl picks fluff out of one of the little woollen hats. They are so fragile now they could disintegrate. She tries to remember their story. Orange-red in colour, they were worn by the Tasmanian women in place of their customary ochre caps, in the sealing days, Nell explained. But why did Nell have them? Pearl closes the lid to the shoebox.

I just mean, we should do some packing while we are all here together. Diana is quiet now. She seems suddenly small and hunched.

I'm having no part of the packing up. Of any of it. It's that I actually can't. Pearl turns away. She plucks a pelican feather from the trestle and caresses it along the inside of her neck. When she opens the door, it's like all the water gushes out of the shed, carries her along in its wake. She could ride the wave right down to the ocean until she has no breath left. Dive in like a seal. This is Diana's decision to make. She knows that.

Well there is something for you, Diana calls out. She strides over and thrusts an envelope against Pearl's chest.

What is it, asks Lucy.

A story or something. I started reading it last night.

But it has my name on the front?

Diana shrugs. I just wanted to make sure it wasn't getting wet inside — shed's leaking. The black scraper's in it.

What?

It's in the story. Diana raises her sharp eyebrows into a little triangulated point. Lucy has these eyebrows too.

Once outside, Pearl realises all Nell's things have been packed up from the verandah. Her skirt taken from the line. The deckchairs stacked neatly against the side wall. She can hear Lucy and Diana talking in low voices. Today she is ovulating — she can feel it in her breasts even without the reminder that she knows is waiting on her dead phone. If Nico wasn't here now they wouldn't have to try. Pearl rips open the envelope. Inside is a little red notebook, the size of her outspread hands. She shoves it under her jumper. Walking towards the dune she remembers something Uncle Jim said that morning. This is sorry place. We are closer to our dead here.

Pearl is scared that if she leaves the island, she will never come back. Especially if Nell's house is gone. Jim wasn't just here for Nell, he had said. He was here on other sorry business. I come here to be close to my nephew. You feel it in your body, Pearl. In your miwi. Tell me about miwi again, she said. You feel it behind the navel. It's a knowing. About place. It's everything — your life force. Listen to your miwi. She

127

crouches in the sand and prays not to the water this time but to the dirt. Its firmness. Its heady crushed-grass wet eucalypt smell.

Nell, she whispers.

⋆   ⋆   ⋆

It always takes a day or two, Nico remembers, to leave the city behind. To not want to compulsively check his emails, to not keep thinking about his patients. Leaving his phone in the bedroom just now had taken actual willpower. It takes a while to relax, he reminds himself, and rolls his shoulders. It feels good to walk. It feels good to inhale deeply the after rain smell. Not the rain on bitumen smell of the city, but the rain on sand and scrub smell. Damp beach. He is last in the procession, with Joe leading and the kids in between. The creek will probably be too shallow for catching marron, but they had all needed to get out of the house for a while. Joe's idea. Pearl's sudden departure last night has everyone on edge. Lewis walks in front of Nico, helping Ariel keep up — holding her hand to guide her over stumps and moving branches out of the way for her. Nico can't believe how long Lewis's legs have grown — how slim and tall and blond and lanky he has become. So different from Nico's own olive skin, his dark curled hair. How sweet Lewis is being now, and he wonders how much longer he'll be able to think of him as 'sweet'. Lewis turns twelve next year and already his boyishness is chiselling into something new.

Nico had been nervous travelling over. The morning before Pearl left they'd argued. Not argued exactly but acknowledged between them some kind of unnavigable distance. She'd sat on the edge of the bed and said, When I look at you sometimes, it feels like I don't know you. It was probably the worst thing she'd ever said to him. He wonders how it has got to this. She is so angry with him, is that it? He wanted to say, But it's you, it's you who's different. Instead, he just got up and hopped in the shower. Later, he wrote her a note: *Let's get to know each other?* He actually meant the gesture, but wondered if she'd read the tone as facetious. And really he felt she was the one that needed to try harder — she needed to accept that they weren't going to have a child together. For some unfathomable reason, it was not going to work. This was a problem he did not know how to fix. And he liked to always be able to fix things — his patients' sore backs, their headaches. Or broken door knobs, or Lewis's shoes, or Pearl's lamp — all manageable. It was a challenge for him to be so unable to intervene on this. He'd given up long ago, he realises.

Joe halts up ahead and Alfie, who's been riding on his back, slides down to the ground. This is the spot, I reckon. Joe uncaps his water bottle and takes a swig. His shoulders glisten with sunscreen. He is a man who is never cold. Always in shorts, always bare-armed.

Yup okay, Nico calls out, catching up with them all.

Alfie is already shoes off and in the creek. Hey

mate, don't get your clothes wet, Joe says. But it's too late; Alfie has plonked right in. Ariel helps Joe separate out the nets, laying them side by side. Lewis jumps across a series of rocks to get to the other side of the creek and then scrambles up the steep bank, slipping. Ariel laughs at him. Nico kicks off his shoes and rolls up his pants. The water is warm on top and icy below and tannin-coloured. His feet look particularly white under water. Dead fish, he thinks.

Where are the yabbies? Alfie says, poking at the water with a discarded branch he's found floating.

I think you might be scaring them away, Joe says. Come out of there and help us with the nets.

Nico lifts Alfie up from underneath the armpits and hoists him out.

Dad, do you want me to find you a hiking stick? A really strong one? Lewis says, already fossicking on the other side of the creek.

That'd be great. Nico wades a little deeper. The sun on his neck begins loosening tension.

I want a special stick. I want a stick, Ariel says, abandoning the nets and making her way over to Lewis.

Hey careful there, it gets a bit deep in the middle, Nico says.

It isn't deep, Nico, see? And Ariel almost flits across, nymph-like. She can't make it up the steep bank, though, and slides down to the water's edge. Lewis, help.

Righto, who wants to lay a net? Joe says.

130

I do, I do. Alfie jumps up and down.

Ariel? Do you want to? Joe says, holding up two nets. She is crossed arms and frowning. I want a stick and Lewis won't help me get up this crazy side. Her voice wobbles.

Joe sighs. Ary, we'll find sticks in a minute. Let Lewis alone. He'll be done soon.

I actually think it's a bit stagnant, Joe says quietly, coming to stand beside Nico.

Best continue with the plan though, right? They both laugh.

Yes, hopefully we don't catch any, Joe says. Not sure I want to eat something outta here.

Nico agrees. So still it's like soup.

Alfie struggles with the bucket-shaped net. It's almost half his size. Joe huddles over him and they wade a little further along, fussing with the net together. Midges fly up, disturbed. Nico carries a net over to Ariel, and she smiles up at him gap-toothed. Lewis, did you find me a stick? And she stands up enthusiastically.

Yep, Ariel. And got this one for you too, Dad. Lewis leans over and extends the branch out to Nico. It is mostly straight and sturdy — just a little bent knob in the middle.

Hey, nice one. I love it. Come on you two, this net's yours.

Ariel and Lewis inspect the creek together finding a good spot. They carry the net between them, the hiking sticks having now been carefully lined up on the bank of the creek, ready for the walk home.

Do you think Pearl will be back by now? Lewis calls out.

Nico shrugs. Yeah soon, I think. But he doesn't know. As soon as he'd seen her waiting for them at the ferry terminal yesterday, pacing, he knew she was . . . something. He'd embraced her and she was all jumpy and eyes flashing. On the drive home, he'd told her that he could take more leave. Stay longer. She dismissed him and said Lewis couldn't miss so much school. Did she even want him here? He was starting to feel so out of place with her. This whole thing is an effing mess, he thinks. At breakfast Joe had told him that Lucy was pregnant. Thirteen weeks. Luce is worried about telling Pearl, he had said. Thinks she might be too upset at the moment. He asked whether Nico agreed. Nico suggested it would be better to just tell her. She'll be pleased for you. No, Joe said, Lucy doesn't want to yet. I'm just giving you the heads up.

Nico is sitting now on a sandy patch, elbows resting on knees, and drops his head in his hands. It's ridiculous actually, he thinks. Why tell me and not Pearl? He considers now that perhaps Pearl is in worse shape than even he realised. Theirs was a private grief, he'd thought. Even Lewis is worried about her. Every hour since waking he's asked when Pearl will be back. Nico stands suddenly, wishing he'd brought his phone.

I reckon we should head back soon.

Lewis glances up, surprised. Straightening, he pushes his wet jeans up to his knees, jamming them into place. Dad, you should just go back. We're okay here. Bring us the burley first, though.

132

Nico splashes into the creek. He crouches and helps Lewis tie the stocking of burley securely to the drop net.

Poor things, Ariel says. They won't be able to get out. Joe stands behind her now and puts his hands on her shoulders. Alfie is still digging around with the branch, looking worried.

That's the point, Ary, Lewis says, positioning the net carefully against a slimy rock, pinning it down.

And for a moment Nico remembers the cracking sound as he'd cut through the head and thorax, of marron, a few summers ago when Joe had first shown him how to split them open. It had been like dissecting a kind of alien. He'd worried at his knifing skills, but quickly learnt the swift flicking action of the wrist. It was messy work, yet he much preferred it to fishing, which he did not enjoy at all. The interminable waiting, the dealing with the hooks and the blood and the scales. The sad fish eyes. But this he loves. That a brown creek like this holds such delicate crustaceous secrets is a kind of impossible wonder. He wraps his arms around Lewis and kisses the top of his head.

I'm heading back now. That okay?

Joe nods. Yeah course, we'll just pack up here and see you back there. Joe gives Nico a look that says something like, Everything will work out okay.

Don't forget your stick, Nico, Ariel calls out. Yours is the biggest one.

★ ★ ★

The stick is actually useful. He walks in a kind of swinging rhythm, leaning into the staff and punctuating his steps. Punctuating his thoughts with the crunch of shell grit underfoot. He is hungry again. He never eats as much at home as he does here. It's like the body wakes up. Nico focuses on dropping his shoulders, opening his chest, keeping his pelvis even. So many hours he's spent adjusting other people's spines and hips and necks that his own body is all cramped up. He'd like to feel better; he'd like to rest. He'd like Pearl to let him in, let him stay. For such a long while he'd loved her before they were together. And it's like that time all over again. He keeps waiting for a sign that she wants him.

The last part of the walk is steep and he slows, his lungs working hard. As the back paddock, the shed, the house, the washing line, the muscular sea come into view, he sees Pearl sitting on the dune, knees drawn in close. Her shoulders are fine and straight. Her hair is brassy. She's strong, he remembers. But he makes a promise to be gentle with her. He catches his breath. The island will work its way on us as it always does, he reassures himself. I'll wait.

★   ★   ★

When Pearl and Nico visited Nico's relatives in Crete, Pearl had missed Nell terribly. Achingly — and she couldn't articulate to Nico her strange mood that wasn't quite homesickness, but was a restless longing nonetheless. She wanted Nell to trample alongside her in the

134

aromatic wildflowers that grew on the mountains; she wanted Nell to cradle in her palm the white round stones Pearl collected along the coast. And she wanted Nell to lie in the sweet tickling grass that smelt so much of home and look up to cypress trees (not like home) growing haphazardly from rock faces. She wanted to share with Nell the feel of the island's ancientness. She wanted Nell to know this island as she knew her own. All its ragged edges. And its nostalgic light. She wanted Nell to know it so that she herself could understand it too.

It was Nell who had shown Pearl the quiet private things of her childhood island. Not the 'grand swathes', as Diana mockingly called Nell's constant imparting of local history, but the small gleaming things. Bright salt-encrusted rock pools, rubbery shark eggs, lichen-covered boulders lying prone like seals, hard sandy roads that shone in the night from the quartzite, soak holes, she-oaks, abrasive cliff tops, bush tracks, Waubs Wall, ruins, lagoons, sea glass, fleshy leaves of pigface, salt pans, Lubra Creek, dank wind shelters and blonde grassy paddocks. In Kissamos, Pearl tore out handfuls of dittany of Crete to make into a therapeutic tea and wondered how she would describe the mountainy taste of it to Nell. She also couldn't wait to tell Nell about its most enigmatic quality — it was used to expel arrows from the body. This quality was first noticed by shepherds whose goats went straight for the herb when they'd been accidentally struck by an arrow. It was a wound-healer, used to heal Aeneas in Virgil's

135

Trojan Wars. It was barely palatable, said Nico, but Pearl loved that such an unassuming flower, woolly and velvety and pungently carpeting the mountains, could bear such history. At the palace of Knossos she had leant against a portico and, weary and heavy with menstrual pain, had cried and the tears as they dried made her cheeks tight and hot. It was a combination of physical exhaustion — sunstroke even, as she found the ruins of Knossos to be dusty and glaring and overwhelmingly desolate — and a sense of displacement.

Later in the hotel room, she'd tried to explain it to Nico. It's that I can't fully connect to the idea of this being both a mythological site, birthplace of Zeus even, and a living, functioning, twenty-first-century island with traffic and cities and pollution and so many layers of ruins. I can't fathom it. It makes me feel very small somehow.

I know what you mean. The first time I came here, I was completely spooked. Nico stood framed by the alcove doorway. She thought of Adonis, the way his hair curled at his neck and his shoulders so shapely and young. Was this a ridiculous impression of him to carry around with her from that time, she wonders now. It had been their first time away together without Lewis. For a brief moment she had Nico all to herself.

But you're from here. Well it's in your blood anyway.

I guess. It is in a way. But mostly because the climate, the colours, the smells are so familiar. So much like home — Australia, I mean. Nico

136

came to sit beside her on the bed. He picked up one of the blue and white woven cushions and held it at his stomach.

It is and it isn't. The mountains feel different. It's like wandering in a biblical landscape. Pearl drew up her knees and leant against Nico.

Earlier than that even. And it's not because you studied Ancient History, right? It's something you feel?

Yeah.

It's like, we can know something because it is a grand narrative, documented, archived, critiqued, passed along through popular culture — and we can *know* something. He took off his belt and the buckle clunked on the terracotta floor. He unbuttoned his jeans.

Pearl smiled to herself and thought about the philosophy lectures she'd struggled through as an undergraduate. Episteme and gnosis. The different kinds of knowing. She hadn't really understood them. Perhaps only intellectually.

Gnosis, she said.

What?

Doesn't matter.

Nico rolled onto his side and ran his thumb along her cheekbone. Pearl's hair was still wet from the shower and she shifted closer to Nico, out of the wet patch on the pillow. The blue shutters were open, and the breeze coming through prickled along her skin. He put his hand flat to her breast and she felt her womb tighten, against the dull thud of cramps.

Our little funny island, Nico. I miss it when I'm here. Moreso than in Melbourne.

I know. It's . . . enigmatic.

Not just that. Compared to here, its story is so quiet.

Untold maybe?

Pearl turned her back to Nico, and he wrapped tight around her, pressing his hand between her legs. The wetness was more than just blood and he slipped easily in. Pearl's thoughts emptied like her skull was a bowl of light, and when Nico stopped moving for a moment, holding her firm against him, his arm hooked under her breasts, she clutched at him deep inside and she came high and juddering and loudly, and he moaned. Lying spooned against her, the wetness between them pooling, he whispered, Don't worry, Pearl. It's early days. We can keep trying. We will keep trying.

But it's like everywhere we go, I lose something.

You haven't lost anything. You just got your period again.

He turned her towards him and cupped her face with both hands. Pearl, it'll be okay. Look how perfect you are. He ran his hand over her hips and grinned, his teeth shining.

And lying there on those dense white sheets, the boats clanging in their moorings outside the window, she'd already lost hope. But she said, I promise not to worry. Then closed her eyes and saw a little girl on the mountain, picking wild-flowers, and she was running away from Pearl like Crete was her place and she could never leave. Nell would know what to do. *Gnosis*. Tell her a story and make things all right.

Nell

So it was by accident that I finally did see Sol again. I had only been back from the mainland about eight weeks and was still light-headed and weakened by that terrible flu or breakdown or whatever it was that came over me on my return. But I'd managed to convince Father that I needed an outing, that I needed to get some sunshine and do something normal, and so he'd taken me with him into Penneshaw to collect the post and buy some flour and a few other things for Mother. As we entered the general store, everyone turned to look at me. May Walker the post-mistress, and Aunty Hettie, and Aunty Hettie's grand-niece Charlotte with her new baby boy, Elijah — and even he gawped at me with his brown eyes. I could not take my gaze from that baby. He was older than mine would be, and his nose ran with clear snot and Charlotte looked tired. How was it that Charlotte, that whiny girl not much older than me, got to hold on to her child? And mine cried for me somewhere else. Father laid his hand on the back of my shoulder. Well good day to you all, ladies, how are we all keeping?

Good afternoon, Peter. Nell. Dear girl you look terrible. So thin. I heard you took ill. Very sorry to hear. Are you feeling any better now?

May said, taking off her glasses and squinting at us, a stack of post dangling in her hands.

I, um, yes I'm —

She's just grand now thank you, May. Having an outing. Getting some air. Father leant into me and whispered, Go take a little walk, darling. Stretch your legs. I'll get what we need and meet you back in half an hour or so, yes?

I nodded and kissed him quickly on the cheek. Okay.

But as I turned to leave, Hettie called out, Nell.

Aunty? I said quietly.

I felt Father stiffen. No more questions, Hettie. She's not herself yet. Still recovering.

Aunty looked so much older, and as she spoke her eyes were milky or glassy or something. Tears? And I wondered what she wanted to say.

It's okay, Father. I'm okay.

Aunty Hettie came towards me and took hold of my hands. She was short and compact, and her high cheekbones were shiny like a burnished apple. Come see me for a tonic. You need something. Day after next. You'll bring her to me won't you, Peter?

I hadn't seen Hettie since I'd been sent away. I wanted to ask her about Sol. I wanted to ask her about everything, but Father and May and Charlotte were all staring at us too warily. I couldn't speak.

Mrs Walcott. Thank you for your concern, but Nell is just fine now. She'll be right as rain soon. Just needs some more rest, Father said, a little too roughly.

Right as rain. Right as rain, I thought. What does that even mean? I am not right. Not right. Not rain. There's never any rain.

I would like that very much thank you, Hettie. Father will bring me, won't you Daddy?

Father shook his head so imperceptibly that I pretended not to notice. Aunty smiled and let go of my hands suddenly and nudged me towards the door with a nod. Good girl.

Before Father could protest any further, I stumbled out into the glare and silver ribbons danced in my line of vision. My head throbbed and I dug my palms into my temples a little too viciously. I stood very still and let myself adjust to the brightness, the scooped deep sky, and the platinum mirror of ocean. When it was this hot, I felt exposed. My eyes watered and my scalp itched with sweat. There was just the slightest wind coming off the sea, but all it did was dry my lips. I steadied myself on the railing outside the post office and looked over towards the mainland. I could just make it out, fawning provocatively in the far distance. My baby was over there. And here I was imprisoned by sea walls on this island that a year ago had been all I needed. Sol and me, our honey, and this little piece of island flung out to sea — that was all we both ever needed. Now I was exiled and my entire being from deep in my chest poured out towards Adelaide and to that little boy I never held. I understand now what Emue might have felt then, the pull of the other side, like an enchantment. A fierce and endless and over-whelming pour of energy, white and hot, but useless and pointless and completely unmanageable. I gripped my chest with both hands and twisted my fingernails deep into my skin. It was satisfying to feel my nails draw blood. It stung pleasurably. I looked down the road that led to the sea and there he was. Sol.

I knew that lanky body anywhere — the deep runnel between his shoulder blades. Blue shirt clinging. Narrow hips. Impossibly long legs. Bare feet. His dark hair had grown longer, I noted. Sol was striding purposely (I assumed) up the road that led to 'The Aboriginal' — the pocket of land on the eastern side of Penneshaw.

I didn't call out to Sol, didn't chase after him. Just watched. Mute. He hadn't seen me, so very cautiously I began to follow him. I had imagined this moment many times, but never like this. He was supposed to turn up at the girls' hostel and rescue me, and if not there, once I was home, he was supposed to tap on my bedroom window or just walk brazenly in against Mother's wishes and hold me hard against his ribcage. It was not meant to be like this. I didn't call out because I wanted to observe him. I wanted to know how he was in the world without me. Foolish, foolish girl, I was. It was then that I lost him. Not when I fell pregnant, not when I was exiled in shame on the mainland, and not upon my coming home and during those weeks of breakdown, but in that half an hour after I first spotted him walking along the coast road. It was right then that I lost him.

I wondered where he could possibly be going, and because he was walking so briskly I, too, sped up to not lose sight of him. My body was not used to exercising. It was strange feeling so unlike me. Before, I was strong. You'll get your strength back, darling, Mother had said. I hoped to somehow defy her. My thigh muscles burnt and my hips ached.

But Sol. Where was he going? I was crazed with all sorts of reckless thoughts. And as he rounded the shoulder of the bay thick with vegetation, I lost sight of him. I hiked up my skirt, scrunching the material in tight fists, and half ran half walked after him, my boots scuffing in the dirt. The hair in my bun fell loose. Everything was so very still. Poised. No wind. Even the sea was compliant and gentle. Flat as glass. No sensible person was out in this heat. What was Father thinking, sending me out for a walk? I wondered angrily. I was drawing too much attention, so he got rid of me. And Sol, wouldn't he have seen our cart in the main street? Why hadn't he tried to find me? As I approached the edge of the beach, I could just make out Sol, that blue shirt again, between the tangled trees. I stopped for a moment and caught my breath, my heartbeat thudding loudly in my ears. At that moment he turned and looked over his shoulder, as if he knew he was being watched, and then he stopped completely and turned back to face the ocean. He faced the sea for a good couple of minutes like some kind of sentinel, his hands shoved deep in his pockets. I held my breath; the trees held their breath. The sky waited. Then he began walking again, away from the beach and up the hill that faced the shoreline and that was dotted with just a handful of houses. Sol Sol Sol, I whispered desperately. Turn around.

When he stopped outside the Simpsons' little white hump of cottage and swung open their gate, I flushed with inexplicable rage. Eliza Simpson. He was quickly swallowed up inside the house and I picked my way along the road slipping into the scrub that fringed the dunes. I sank to my knees in the sandy dirt and waited by Frenchmans Rock. I knew the words inscribed without even looking. I'd recited them that many times, they were like a song to me — *Expédition de découverte par le commandant Baudin sur le Géographe 1803*. I looked up to Tigers Hill, the little patch of land where dear Tiger Simpson often set up camp. Father would be wondering where I was now, but I didn't care. I realised that my worst fears were true: Sol hadn't given me a second thought when I left. It was obvious. He had a spring in his step; he was light. If I'd been close enough to hear, he would have surely been whistling. He was the same open-chested, 'clicking my heels' Sol as always. Nothing had changed for him. He was not a broken thing.

We had walked along this road more than a year ago now, delivering honey to old Mrs Seymour when she broke her hip. Chatting to Tiger Simpson along the way as he tried to catch a lift into Kingscote. We couldn't hold hands then because people would look at us funny, but we walked so close together I could feel the heat coming from him, the hairs of our arms just brushing. Sol carried the box of honey jars, and I

144

nursed a cake that Mother had baked for Mrs Seymour. As we got to the beach we heard crying, and four boys, perhaps twelve years old, came running towards us.

She's fallen over, the children said as they ran past us. And I thought I heard them snickering.

Down on the beach we saw a little girl, stranded, weeping. I tried to keep up with Sol as he bounded down to her. He got to her first, and I saw him pass her a hankie and kneel at her level. It was then I noticed a white wicker doll's pram upturned, and dolls scattered. Broken dolls — heads and legs strewn. The girl was dark-skinned and wore a thin red dress. I didn't know her.

What's happened, little one, Sol asked her ever so gently. He placed her plaits carefully over her shoulders, and wiped her tears away with his thumb.

I turned the pram the right way up, and began gathering the dolls and brushing the sand from them.

They broke my dolls.

Those boys?

She nodded and hung her head. I was taking them for a walk. They teased me. Said I was too old for dolls.

Little buggers, Sol said, and stood to see if he could still see them. He would've clobbered them.

We put the dolls back together as best we could and I walked the pram and the dolls and the honey and the cake up the beach, the wheels jagging in the sand infuriatingly. Sol carried the girl, and I can still see those little arms of hers wrapped around his neck. When we got to the road, she said she was okay to walk home, and she kissed Sol's hand. He gave her a jar of honey, and she grinned so big and toothy. Sol and I watched her disappear into the distance, pushing her pram, and he snuck a hand around my waist. For the briefest of moments I nuzzled my face into his shoulder. He was hot and I licked the sweat on his neck.

On the way home, we stopped off at the grass tree. I took off my dress and hung it in the fronds. We didn't make love, not yet, but it was good to kiss with our skins touching. His hair was dark against my bright thighs; I gasped. When he put his mouth between my legs, even through my knickers, I felt myself swell to meet him, and I pushed his head hard against me.

Squatting there spying on Sol, I pushed that memory away and undid my top buttons. I must have been a pitiful sight. The sweat made my armpits itch. After some time, enough time for my headache to take a deep hold like my brain was banging loose in my skull, the front door of the cottage opened again and out came Sol. He turned and spoke to someone in the doorway, but it was too far away for me to make out who it was. Eliza, probably. I rose steadily and twisted my hair back into a knot. My cheeks burnt. I would confront Sol, I decided, so I waited in the shade of the trees, jealousy flaring through me, setting my mouth grim and my fingers twitchy. I was fire. I could set the trees on fire. I had wanted to be beautiful when we met again, to pick up where we'd left off, but now that I was actually seeing him I realised just how angry I was. We could never pick up again. I was broken now, and he hadn't had to go through anything. Hadn't even written me a word. Not a single word. Had he even asked after me? I brushed the twigs from my skirt and stepped out into the middle of the road. When he saw me, he began running, and shouting my name. Nell, Nell, Jesus, Nell.

He threw his arms around me and picked me up. Oh my god, Nell. It's you.

I wanted to collapse into him, bury my face in his hot neck, but my body wouldn't let me. For a while now it had been doing its own thing. I was stiff as a board. He set me back down and cupped my face in his hands.

Nell. Darling. What is it? What's happened?

He looked tired. Great brown circles around his eyes. He was unshaven, giving his face a kind of rough look. Older, he looked older.

I shoved him hard in the chest. No letters. Not even a single word.

Sol tried to respond but I wouldn't let him speak. How could you? You didn't even think of me, did you —

Nell please, I —

And now Eliza Simpson. Like I was nothing —

What? Nell —

Shut up. I hate you.

Sol tried to embrace me — Please, Nell — but I pummelled him. It felt good to make hard physical contact. I punched him vigorously in the upper arm, until he grabbed me forcefully and pinned me in a hard embrace. For a moment, out of exhaustion and relief, I dropped my forehead into his chest. We said nothing, but he was breathing hard and fast and I was trembling all over. But then I remembered with a sort of panic those little scrunched red and waxy faces peeping out of blankets at the home — all those other babies with their mothers and mine gone. Did I see for a moment a thatch of dark wet hair? I just don't know. Say goodbye, the nurse said, and then she took him away. Just like that.

I burst free of Sol, whose own body was starting to relax into mine. Say goodbye. I hate you. Just like that.

I'd wounded him. Sol's jaw tensed and he backed away, but I couldn't bear to look at him. I just turned and bolted.

Father remembers it differently. When he couldn't find me, he set out himself along the road. He says he saw me arguing with Sol. He saw Sol getting rough with me, and then I'd broken free and run away.

Don't you go anywhere near her ever again, Father shouted, his voice sprung tight, even though Sol had, by then, stopped speechless in his tracks.

Father says Sol just stood there running his hands through his hair maniacally, and was still standing there when later we passed him in the bullock cart. I looked for him everywhere, scanning the bay and the road and out the front of the pub, but couldn't see him. My heart sank. Even on the road home, I looked for him between the trees that bowed towards each other in wooden tunnels over the road. He was gone. Gone. And Gem-Gem. I realised with sudden dread that Sol's little dog, his shadow, his familiar, had not been with him. Oh, Sol. It was then I cried out, choked with tears. Oh god, what have I done?

You've got to forget him now, Nell. He's caused you nothing but pain. He's driven you almost crazy. Father's hands on the reins were sunburnt, and he held the reins from underneath to keep them out of the sun. I worried that the bullocks would veer, that he wasn't in control. We bumped jarringly along the pot-holed track.

Your mother and I are just so worried about you, Nell. She was a mess while you were gone. An absolute mess. We need to get back to how we were. I just can't bear it any longer, Nell. You've got to forget him.

I was incredulous. *You* can't bear it any longer, I thought. Forget whom, I wondered. Did he mean Sol or the baby Samuel?

Then why did you make me do it? I knew as I said the words, I was gutting him. It was Mother that made me do it. I knew that. But I wanted him to suffer. Why had he let it happen? Why hadn't he protected me, as a father should?

He brought the bullocks to a skidding halt and we slid in the shale along the side of the track. The smell coming off the bullocks was pungent — like off milk. He turned to me and took off his hat, tears in his eyes. Behind him a sliver of water beside the track shone like the scales of whiting. I imagined a great big fish flopping by the road.

I want to show you something.

149

I still have that letter from his solicitor, tatty and overly folded, that he took from his pocket. And the words still sting — but they shut me up for such a long time. I was that great silver fish flopping out of water, each word scraping away a scale, until I was denuded, pink raw, burning in that interminable sun.

1828
American River

William can hardly remember what it was like before Minnie arrived. Minnie, the little sister he and Maringani both now share. And certainly before Maringani and the women came that first night, shivering and whimpering with their hands tied behind their backs. If he remembers back to those times it is just a blur of seal blood and rough voices and always feeling a little bit hungry and wishing his father would carry him sometimes.

He thinks of the days when Minnie was just a walking baby, following Maringani and him around like a babbling, curious shadow. It seems so long ago now that his father worried about him 'sociatin' with Minnie he can hardly remember the night Anderson held his hand to the coals. The scar is more white than pink now. Clumped and smooth like melted wax. Maringani had wrapped his burnt hand with leaves for days afterwards, and William has not looked his father in the eye ever since. He had managed to keep visiting his sister in secret until eventually,

150

because Maringani was able to keep Minnie out of the way of Anderson, his father seemed to forget about her. William carried her on his back before she was walking, while he and Maringani went digging for kuti, or laying snares for wallabies, or hunting for mutton bird eggs. Minnie's plump arms around his neck were worth his disfigured palm, William remembers thinking.

Now everything has changed again. William feels himself more serious, the long uncluttered days stretching narrowly into a tight feeling. Something uncompromising. He can no longer slip between shadows unnoticed because everything he does and says has a weight to it now, even in his imagination; he looks like a man, so he is suddenly expected to behave like one. But what is it to be a man? Does it mean everything is yours for the taking, even the light of hope from the eyes of another? He shudders at the thought of ever hurting Maringani. Anderson needs him more than ever now. The men are building a ship near the salt lagoon and William must cut down trees, gather salt for ballast, and hold battens in place till his arms judder and twitch with strain.

Maringani is more distant and William doesn't think it is because they are spending less time together. He notices that she won't look him in the eyes like she used to and sometimes she doesn't really want to talk with him. Emue, Poll and Maringani take off on what he assumes are hunting trips for days at a time, sometimes taking Minnie or sometimes leaving her with Mooney and Puss. The men occupied with building the ship don't seem to mind the long absences of the women. When Maringani returns from the trips she is increasingly quieter and more serious. To William, she still moves like a bird, but she is rounding out in secret places.

And the last time she came back, she was scarred across her upper arms and back like the older women. The small cicatrices form a deliberate pattern, which he can't make out and which he doesn't stare at for overly long because he knows she doesn't want him to.

Now she collects salt from the lagoon for curing skins, along with Emue and Poll, and Anderson watches her. William works on the other side of the lagoon because the men need more salt back at the ship. He stands up to flex his back and have a swig of water from his pannikin, when he sees Anderson standing on the edge of the lagoon. It is unusual for Anderson to be so still and so quiet. William can on most occasions detect his looming presence. Anderson is looking straight at Maringani as he blows smoke from the corner of his mouth. William doesn't appreciate it. He has come to know a certain expression of his father's, his mouth drawn into a hard line and his eyes filmy with exhaustion, that William finds disturbing. He knows not to speak to him when he looks like that but he can bear his father's gawping at Maringani no longer.

Needin' somethin'? I'm just 'bout done here, William calls out to Anderson.

Get back to the cove, Anderson says, stalking away.

William pours the rest of his water over his hands and down his neck and tries to dismiss the white heat of panic. He rubs his eyes with his wet hands and manages a quick glance at Maringani, who watches him. She bows her head and her hair falls in front of her face — clouds obscuring the sun. He turns and abandons the lagoon, following the staccato strides of Anderson down to where the half-built schooner lies, the ribcage of a giant fallen animal; and the men, like industrious ants picking clean the bones. Except they're not picking clean, they're putting flesh on bones, thinks William. Always wanting more.

★   ★   ★

Anderson decides that after the shipbuilding is complete, he and the men will go on another Sabine expedition. He is tired of Emue and Poll and Mooney and Puss coming and going as they please as if they belong to no one.

Yes. I will cotch meself a wife. A young 'un, Anderson mutters to himself, taking a swill of rum.

What's that? William asks, dumping more wood on the fire.

I was just fancyin' meself a new gin, son.

Anderson moves back from the fire — the mallee roots catch and the hut brightens.

You s'pose you can just take 'em as you please, do yer? William says slow and quiet.

I do. And besides, next time you'll be coming wid us.

I won't.

Anderson puts down the pannikin of rum and wipes his mouth with the back of his hand.

So you think yer too good for a gin do yer? Yer think yerself better'n me? I seen yer makin' eyes at the gerl. Yer not foolin' me. It's allers bin the way to steal gins and maybe when all this land hereaway is full wid settlers, they'll yarn 'bout the 'old times' and us islanders grabbin' black women for wives. Anderson laughs but is stopped short by the look on William's face. Beatrice used to sometimes look at him like that. Disappointed. Ashamed. He waits for William to speak, but his son remains far away.

Yer think yer can get by wid no woman do yer. No purty lady is goin' to have yer. And there ain't none hereabouts. Not long afore now yer'll be wantin' some game, son. And black game it'll be.

Shaking his head, William spits into the fire. Emue's more 'an just game to yer. Don't yer see. Yer nothin'. Yer think yer'd be sellin' skins wid out Emue? Yer need 'er.

I agrees wid yer, son, but I can still 'ave that *and* fresh game.

William makes to leave and Anderson rises shakily to his feet. Call the gerl. Go on. 'Ave yerself a treat. Why yer holdin' back? Or is she *more* 'an just game to yer?

Anderson shoves William towards the opening of the hut, Go on, son.

William tries to shake him off. Leave me be.

154

I won't until yer agree to come gal-huntin',
Anderson says, his hand tight around William's
upper arm. And when William purses his mouth
into a hard line, Anderson staggers outside into
the cold air and calls for Maringani.

★ ★ ★

Maringani sits with Emue, Poll and the other
women around the fire, talking softly while
dinner cooks: a shoulder cut off from the young
seals put directly on the coals. Every now and
again Poll turns the spitting meat with a stick
until it is almost done. Minnie lolls in
Maringani's lap, the weight of her affection
soothing, but uncomfortable, as her pointy
elbows push against soft stomach or breast. The
men's voices are getting loud and brash across
the river, jarring the quiet of the purple dusk.
Yesterday they bartered a hundred skins for a
store of rum from a merchant ship. Maringani
clicks her tongue disapprovingly, lowers her
head, and talks in a hushed voice to Emue, as if
by making herself quieter the men might forget
she is there. She pulls William's thick woollen
coat around her and Minnie more tightly, shivers
and stares into the curling smoke. The coat
smells of campfire and dried fish. She hopes
Anderson will not call for her. Emue looks over
and Maringani knows she is hoping the same
thing. She begins to sing in a low, lilting voice.
Poll joins her and the song distracts Maringani
momentarily from the rising volume of shouts at
the men's camp. Minnie becomes still in her lap,

but throws dry leaves into the fire one at a time. Together they watch the crackle and release of wisping eucalyptus smoke.

When the meat is ready, the women and the two girls share it out between them, and eat listening to the swagger in the laughter and the crashing about that is coming from the men's camp. Afterwards, they rub the oil from their hands up their arms and along their legs to keep out the cold.

Hey Polecat, shouts Anderson from up the track, send Mari down wid yer.

Maringani stiffens and Emue leans in to her and whispers, Nginbulun, nginbulun. Take Minnie.

Minnie's hand grips her own as she flings the rest of her meat into the fire, runs to the wurlie, grabs some skins and flees with the night and the stars on her back. She glances back, and Emue is walking slowly down the track to the main hut. Minnie yanks at Maringani's wrist.

★   ★   ★

William is almost relieved when he sees Emue appear out of the scrub, rather than Maringani. But as soon as his father speaks, he realises that it is not relief he feels, but an overwhelming guilt. He knows that he can do nothing to protect Emue against his father.

Where's Mari? I called fer Mari, not you . . . yer black bitch, Anderson hisses, steadying himself against the outside flank of the hut. His face is blotchy and his eyes are pale and glassy.

156

William takes small, silent steps in a wide arc to try and move behind his father without him noticing. He hedges sideways. The other men are in the hut, chortling over one another in loud, gruff tones. William can smell burnt fat and tobacco.

Gone, Emue says, looking away.

Where she gone? slurs Anderson, wiping spittle from the corners of his mouth and then raising his arm at Emue. Yer bitch. Yer lyin', and he lurches towards Emue, his hand coming down hard across her face before William has time to intervene. He rams his boots into Emue's stomach over and over. William notices the glint of sharp rock in Anderson's hand. Sees him fall.

Leave it, Father. Leave 'er, William cries, before everything goes quiet, but for the blood pounding in his ears. The rage in William is hot and sharp in his chest. He has never moved so fast, skimming lightly past the flayed skins hanging and the mess of bottles and kindling.

William pulls his father off Emue by grabbing him under the arms and rolling him sideways. Anderson is too drunk to resist properly, although he spits at William's feet and tries to get up, but cannot support himself and keeps falling down, a puppet with cut strings.

I'm yerr farrther . . . hisses Anderson trying to swipe at William, who kicks his hand away sharply, getting him in the ribs as he does so. Anderson moans and rolls in the dirt. Wheezing.

William smooths Emue's long sailor's shirt back down over her body and pulls up her trousers. He bundles sealskins under her head

157

and spreads one over the top of her.

You a gin lover, are yer? calls out Everitt, flicking his roll-up at William. Everitt leans against the hut, his mouth contorting in a smug grin.

Yeah he just can't help himself, can he? Leave 'er be so we can all 'ave a go at the hag.

William could break their skulls. He scrabbles for rocks and hurls them at the men. He can hardly breathe.

Get away. He slides in the dirt and scoops up more stones. Everitt and Munro laugh nervously, sensing the force of him — perhaps his father's son after all — and retreat into the hut. Gin lover, one of them calls out, disappearing inside.

Poll, Mooney and Puss emerge from the bushes and crouch down beside Emue's head, whispering to each other. Poll smooths Emue's hair away from her temple. A bruise is purpling, thickening.

Fire, she murmurs to William.

The four of them manage to lift her enough from the ground so that William can find his feet beneath the weight of Emue and grip his left arm firmly under her knees and his right arm beneath her shoulders, swinging himself upright. He staggers along the track to the women's camp, his eyes fixed on Poll, who walks ahead. It is dark by now, but the white sand of the track and the flecks of quartz glimmer in the moonlight. The shallow river water is cold. Anderson and his men don't follow — too drunk now. Once William and Poll have her safe inside the wurlie, William stokes up the fire while Poll sits with

Emue singing gently. With a heavy stone, Poll is bruising yalkari leaves against another flat piece of rock. Mooney and Puss are on lookout, listening.

Where's Mari and Minnie? William asks.

Poll doesn't answer him, just keeps on preparing the leaves and points with her lips towards the scrub.

Will they be right do yer think? William responds, straightening up and looking out into the shadowy bushes.

Again Poll doesn't answer, but she looks up at him with watery eyes and makes a slight nod. She then bows her head towards Emue. William walks over to the entrance of the wurlie.

What can I do, he asks as he kneels down and has a closer look at Emue's injury. It is then that he notices the blood trickling out from the corner of her eye.

I hear minka bird today, Poll says softly.

Minka bird? What's a minka bird?

Small bird. Got eyelashes. Long 'uns. Always hidin'. Crying like a woman. That mean a woman is going ter die, Poll continues as she applies the leaves to where Emue has been hit.

William feels as though someone is kneeling on his chest.

She gonna be right? he whispers.

Poll answers by jutting her chin and pointing her lips towards the inky sea.

William swallows as he considers the near impossibility of her request. It's a wild stretch of shoals and crosscurrents and William's not sure they'll make it in a rowboat, the only vessel he could feasibly steal without attracting attention. He replies, The mainland?

Poll holds his gaze, and he knows by the firm set of her eyes that she means for Emue to be returned, to be taken home.

near *Hog Bay*

Maringani lays the skins down on the sandy patch she has cleared and puts William's coat over her and Minnie as a cover. For now, they will camp by the lagoon. She dares not light a fire in case Anderson has decided to go looking for them. Minnie tucks her bare feet between Maringani's legs for warmth, her hard knees jutting into Maringani's ribs. Maringani strokes the hair away from Minnie's face until her whimpering gives over to a deep and exhausted sleep. Maringani isn't sure exactly how long they have walked for, or quite where they have ended up, but her calves feel tight and there is an ache deep inside each hip joint from stumbling through the dark with her sister on her back. In the light of morning she will be able to work out where they are and find some food. She knows there will be trouble back at the camp. She knows that she and Minnie will have to stay away for some time. Maringani shudders, remembering the damp, sweaty smell of Anderson. The weight of him and the raspy breath of him hot in her ear, just one moon ago. She whispers to the moon. *Weellum*.

King George Beach (Sandy)

Pearl wakes with something like panic. She'd been dreaming of fire. Flames wrapped around a grass tree like a banner coiling and swinging in the wind. An upward stream of embers and eddying flicks of light. Spiky leaves like a flare of fireworks, then black nothing. And the spear that runs right through the middle of the tree smouldering orange like a lamp, a beacon. But it was the sound that woke her. A crackling rushing whip and roar as if she were underneath a plane. The terrifying suddenness of fire, lingering now as dream residue. And an acrid burning in her nose, like the fine hairs had been singed. Face, stinging hot.

Nico's arm is draped heavy across her hip. She moves slightly to shift him and he gathers her in. They're sleeping in a swag on the floor of the lean-to. The mattress feels hard and compact beneath her.

You okay?

Um, yeah. But he has gone back to sleep. Lewis makes little sighing noises in the bed beside them.

She can't shake the feel of the dream. An alertness, as if she's shot through with something foreign like metal. A quickening. A burning tree seared in her mind. And the feeling that she's somehow implicated. The red wine that last night softened the edges of everything leaves her raw and sharp now. Bloody shocking headache. There are no hints of white at the gaps in the curtains. Not even dawn yet. The house creaks and shifts like a boat — its old joints accommodating the slack and pull of the elements. Pearl always dreams brightly here.

But she remembers being scared here, too. As a child, Pearl would often still be awake when Nell came to check on her, the sound of the sea so loud that Pearl imagined it to be giants looming up the dune, crinkling paper in their oversized hands. The outside so vast, she felt lonely. Stooping to fit underneath the top bunk, Nell would peel back her covers, laugh at her granddaughter's wide eyes, and take Pearl to bed with her. Lying beside Nell writing and sketching in her journal, Pearl would fall asleep instantly, her irrational fears dissolving as she pressed against the solid form of Nell.

She scratches at her scalp and sand rolls under her fingers. Nell always shook the sheets out before the girls went to sleep. Lucy was like the princess and the pea and couldn't sleep if there was a speck of sand in the bed. Pearl just wanted company. But she's frightened now too. She squashes her hands to her breastbone to stop the flurry of wings that beat in her chest. Great pelican wings. Nico runs his hand along her thigh and then rests it on her stomach, as if he reads her, and in his sleep his penis swells against her hip. But she feels like a trapped animal. Today is Saturday. Day of the wake. Wakefulness. She is too awake.

* ★ *

Nico wraps himself around Pearl from behind, props her up. Her hair is damp — he'd washed it for her in the bath earlier — and as she leans back into him, he rests his chin on the top of her head and breathes her in. Orange blossom. He knows she is heightened today, too open; he can feel her heart hammering through her ribcage. There is a particular energy at funerals, he thinks, a kind of charge that runs through the air making everyone tense and electric and Pearl is taking it all on. Nico can't wait for this part to be over and then he can down a Scotch. Pearl will have red wine and her body will get softer. He has decided that today his job is to be with her and to hold her up. Really, she's lost a mother. And lately, he is just so worried about her falling into an even bigger gap of sorrow. Three years they've been trying to have a child, and she is strung out. Even this morning, he knew it was still on her mind. Always on her mind. And always in her body — like she carries a heavy twisted root of absence, and is growing taut and stooped around it.

Nico calls Lewis over to stand beside them, and they all three look up to watch a flock of birds arc one way then turn back on themselves and curve the other way, retracing retracing retracing like the tide. Fine black lines against a white sky. How do they know what to do, Nico wonders. How do any of us know what to do?

He feels sorry for Diana, who seems adrift. Joe stands with his arm around her, at least. Alfie wants to be picked up, put down, picked up by Lucy. Ariel fidgets. Jim and David talk to each other in low murmurs. People float past and squeeze Pearl's hand and kiss her forehead and whisper comfort. Wind-whipped faces. Sun-scorched. Hard, kind faces. And they all begin to move inside. How do you feel anything in such a concocted place, he thinks. Neat chairs, trickling water, tulips everywhere with their fragile bending necks. Nell lying over there. When they'd arrived, Pearl had said, I want to stay outside — I need natural light, trees, dirt, insects, wind. I want to carry Nell home, and put her in the earth, she'd said. So weightless, Nell would be now. And he imagined himself carrying Nell's body through the scrub, past the grass trees, and running like a fugitive. Earlier, when they'd looked at her, it was like she was carved from some other material. Not flesh. Finer than paper, sunken, chiselled, lightweight. Nell, but not Nell at all.

Nico remembers when he'd first met Nell. Lewis was only five then and he and Pearl were just at the beginning. He'd never been to the island before and he couldn't believe how pristine it was. Even though there were paddocks and farmland, there was still so much scrub, still so much untouched. He loved how the gums grew in canopies over the dirt roads, softening everything into winding, wooded tunnels, and how the greens and yellows of the foliage seemed somehow more concentrated. He loved the uncluttered skyline, the clean and fierce ocean. The sweet dry air. He had never wanted to leave.

It was bright and spacious where his dear Melbourne was muted, moody.

They'd come off the ferry and, after first greeting Pearl, Nell hugged him and Lewis like she'd always known them. Nell's hair was completely white and surrounded her face in a soft dense halo, her cheekbones were high and fine and she had a kind of haughty look that might have been more to do with her very straight posture rather than something in her attitude. Pearl was like Nell moreso than like Diana — grandmother and granddaughter both had that sort of shining quality that he loved, and when the two of them were together he thought of two flowers bending in exactly the same way towards the sun.

The service is about to begin and Pearl turns to him. He takes her hand and jams it on his thigh. Every now and again her hand jolts with a tremor and he stills it. Sometimes when she is tired, she looks even more beautiful, her eyelids damp and shiny like tulips, he thinks. And before long he cannot stop noiselessly weeping. The tears slide in runnels down the lines of his face. He knows somehow it is disturbing, even annoying Pearl, who sits still and rigid, but he does not know how to stop. It is almost ridiculous. Is it because he is worried that Pearl will move even further away from him, go deeper into herself, now that Nell has gone? Will she leave him? Or is it simply because he is sad about Nell? He cannot think straight, but it is clearer and clearer that nothing in his life seems to fit together. Mostly he spends his time in the car driving between the practice and home and Lewis's school and Annie's house, and Lewis's soccer training, so that by the time he sees Pearl he feels scoured out on the inside. And being with Pearl does renew him, but she looks at him these days as if he is some strange animal that she doesn't quite know what to do with. He feels as if he is not quite in his own skin.

He thinks about something Nell said to him on his first visit to the island. Nell had taken them to the Contemplation Steps just before dropping them to the ferry for home. Pearl and Nico sat beside each other on the polished wood sculpture — the natural curves and hollows of the wood forming a canoe-like seat perched high on the hill. Lewis sat at their feet and traced over the names set in concrete — Tuery, Suke, Mooney — while Nell stood looking out to the mainland, explaining to Lewis that the steps were built to remember the Aboriginal women who were stolen and brought here from the mainland, and Tasmania. Little Bird, Long 'Un, Sally Cooper. Lewis had wanted to touch every single name and even though they were running late for the ferry, Nell said curtly, Don't rush him — the names are disappearing. She stood at the top of the hill, with her hair flying out in all directions, and Nico had felt a little bit terrified of her then. Later, as he'd stepped away from Nell to board the ferry she'd grabbed his arm and hissed loudly towards him, head inclined, I like you, Nico, and please please, love that girl. Love that girl.

I do.

Yes, but Nico, is it enough?

He thinks about those words now. What did Nell possibly mean? He'd dismissed them at the time. But was everything already mapped out? Did she already know something? And with a slow spreading feeling of desolation, he realises now that perhaps his love is not enough. He cannot give Pearl the thing she most wants.

Lewis places his hand on the back of Nico's shoulder. It brings Nico back to himself with a jolt. He wipes his face with his sleeve and kisses Lewis on the cheek, and then turns to Pearl and puts his mouth to her ear. Let's move back to Adelaide. Let's make things better, honey. Do you want to?

She looks at him puzzled and then laughs shaking her head. Ssshh, Nico.

Yet he thinks he sees something in her that he hasn't seen in a long time — something clear and solid like relief, and he could burst with crazy joy. I'm a mess, he realises.

★　★　★

It is about halfway through Uncle Jim's eulogy when Diana decides she will not read out the words she has scribbled down. Diana hasn't accounted for feeling so strange. The blood drums in her ears and everyone around her is moving too fast or too slow. And her thoughts keep wandering as if they are leaking right out to the edges of the room. She hopes she's turned the hose off properly at her flat in Adelaide, imagines a lake in the pit of her front garden,

167

ducks dipping their wing tips in as they skim past. I'm drowning. She thinks resentfully about all Nell's stuff. It will take months to sort through. Old bat, hoarding things. And she wonders how much more time off work she can realistically wrangle out of her manager, even given what's going on. Another week or two? But can she afford it?

She can hear the wheel and screech of corellas outside, even above Uncle Jim's voice and everyone coughing and shifting in their chairs. Too heightened, she thinks, and wishes she'd taken something to dull the brightness, the alertness. When she was pregnant with Pearl everything sharpened, especially her hearing. High-pitched hums reverberated in the height of her skull and kept her from sleeping. Everything tasted awful, too. Strong and metallic. Bitter. She imagined the pregnancy was some kind of honing of the senses that could help with her creativity. Instead, she became too jittery to even hold a pencil, and the lines on the page didn't come out how they were meant to. She found it devastating, like she'd been taken over. And Nell could hardly deal with her. Sit still, she would snap. Or, You look peaky. Are you not sleeping properly? Sometimes she felt like that seventeen-year-old Diana was hiding some-where, crouching in a dry hollow of rock, protecting herself, waiting until it was safe to come out again.

Uncle's voice is deep and round and it's something to hold on to. Such a calm man, she thinks. But she's missed most of what he's saying. All she can focus on is Ariel's knees like scrubbed little mushrooms blooming on the seat beside her. Ariel swings her feet and the mushrooms bob up and down. She imagines how she would draw them: velvet white caps pushing up through the black earth. When Uncle introduces her to speak she shakes her head and feels a roomful of eyes at the back of her neck, and the air still and thin like she's at high altitude.

Lucy leans and takes her elbow. I can read it out for you, Mum?

Diana shakes her head again. Not now. Sorry love.

Lucy shoots a dark look across at Pearl. It's not because of the argument earlier, Diana wishes she could explain. It's because there is simply nothing more to say. Nell is gone. There's just the earth taking everything back in as it will, even those silken mushrooms.

Nell

I want to set fire to our tree. I want to set fire to our tree so that it can keep watching over where we've been. If our tree remains, then we too remain. I want to hear it roaring with flame and with life. I want to smell the spitting oil of it, follow the volumes of smoke wrapping thickly upwards and not be afraid. But I am afraid. I don't want to set the island on fire — I nearly did that once, emptying coals I thought had burnt out into the scrub at my back door. It took only a couple of minutes for flames to lick menacingly through the low-lying grasses. Marian and Red and I stamped them out, panic-stricken. Perhaps it is enough to just imagine our tree burning. Write it. Perhaps this is something words can do — make sense of grief. Give shape to the unknowing. Give form to that which cannot be enacted. Resurrect memory. Set down the future.

But I've known the power of words and I've been hurt by them. Grown into cruel shapes by them. When Mother found my notes from Sol, the notes we hid so carefully, she stole from me. Those words were mine and they were as private as our kisses, but when she read them, our tryst became an awful exposed ugly thing — well that's how it felt. I would not write again, I decided then, because pieces of me were in my writing and I had to protect them. Keep myself cloistered. But I did write to Sol from that shameful place in Brighton. It was a final desperate attempt, and it was the only way I thought to handle my longing for him, my confusion, my loneliness. I prayed for those words to transform us. Carry us out of this. It soothed me to tell him things, to imagine we were having a conversation, like before. I might as well have been writing in the sand. Mother intercepted those words too.

The grass tree when it burns begins in the heart and burns outwards. The grass tree when it burns sheds its blackened skin and releases its seeds like an offering. The grass tree when it burns sounds like the she-oak moaning in the wind. To sleep under a she-oak is to hear the wailing that kept Ngurunderi awake after his wives drowned. Uncle Jim told me this. When the leaves of the she-oak chafe together it is to hear the secret language of the tree — the speaking tree whose sacred messages are not mine to know. But this I know. Ngurunderi's wives in their effort to escape their husband after breaking taboo built a raft from grass trees and reeds and crossed Lake Albert on the mainland. At the spot where they landed, their raft turned back into rushes and grass trees. The women transmuted with their landscape. The grass trees that lead crookedly down to our creek — Sol's and mine — preside like elders over a slowly unfurling landscape. Steadfast and ancient, they know deep time. Bearing witness. It comforts me to think that when Sol and I were falling in love, they watched over us. The trunk of a grass tree grows just one centimetre a year, morphed into odd bent shapes by drought and fire and the position of the sun. To move a grass tree is to risk losing it. It must be replanted with the exact same side facing north or it will die. Sun and fire and a little water — these are the things it needs, shivering into flower only after wildfire. The heart of the grass tree tastes sweet, Aunty Hettie says.

Instead, I want to set fire to our tree. I will set fire to all of these words — these jottings, excavations, resurrections. Beautiful tinder. Belonging only to me. And this time, it will be my choice to extinguish them. To make these words ash.

Only my heart story in my little red book shall remain. This is the vow. Sol, it is our precious thing.

1828
Antechamber Bay

Anderson wakes and finds Emue gone. He scrapes crust from his lips with his teeth. It is early and the other men are still sleeping, but Anderson's shivering has woken him. He is wearing nothing from the waist down. Outside the hut, the ground is cold and hard in the early dawn, and he sits up carefully. If he moves his head too fast the ache between his eyes makes him nauseous. He staggers to his feet and urinates beside the hut. Taking one of the skins pegged out for curing, he wraps it around his waist, coughs, dislodges some phlegm and then stumbles into the hut.

Where's Polecat? Need water, he spits under his breath.

Piebald is asleep in Anderson's spot. He kicks him in his side and Piebald grumbles but doesn't move. Anderson, noticing that William's sleeping place is empty, groans at the spinning room as he lies down in the pile of skins. His stomach is growling and burning with the acid of the rum. He wants to go and lash Emue for not being there with some food and drink for him, but he is too weak to move.

By mid-morning the heat bearing down on the hut is stifling and finding himself alone he makes to call out to the boy but he can't summon his voice. There is a dull thudding like he can hear the blood thumping along the vessels in his brain, and his voice is thin and fragile against such a din. He stumbles out into the daylight. Leaning against the hut he shields his eyes with the crook of his elbow. The day is a bowl of fire.

Where's me boy?

Munro and Everitt look up from where they are trying to resurrect the evening fire.

We 'aven't seen 'im, replies Munro as he stirs up the coals.

Anderson tightens the sealskin around his waist with one hand and makes his way over to the campfire, tripping and cursing a few times as he does so.

Get the boy and the gins would yer, Everitt,

Anderson mutters as he settles himself down next to Munro.

Everitt glares at him. I'm presently occupied makin' tea.

Well, presently occupy yerself findin' me boy, Anderson says, singsong.

Everitt mumbles something under his breath, spitting into the coals, but makes no move to stand up.

I think Piebald was headin' down there. William'll be there, Munro offers tentatively.

Anderson shoots a look at Everitt, fingering the scar on his chest as if to smooth it.

I want Everitt to go look for the boy. I ain't interested in what Piebald is up to.

Piebald emerges from the scrub coming off the path that leads to the women's camp.

Gone. Emue, Poll, Mooney, Puss, the rowboat. All gone, Piebald announces, his bare shoulder glistening whiter than the rest of him, as does the skin of his elbows, too.

Hunting? Anderson asks, still staring at Everitt.

Piebald shakes his head. Boat's gone. And baskets.

Anderson shrugs. You saw the boy?

Nup. 'Aven't seen him all morning. 'Aven't laid eyes on him since last night, responds Piebald.

Anderson gets up and strides towards the track, knocking into Piebald as he passes. Munro follows, while Everitt scowls and remains seated by the fire.

Praps we should look along the inlet. Mebbee

they took the boat there, Piebald says as he follows Anderson down the track.

Anderson kicks sand into the remnants of a fire and then scans the inside of the wurlie. Some of the women's pouches and nearly all of the skins are gone.

Find the boy, Piebald. Find 'im now. Emue'll get a hidin'.

She already got 'un.

Whadda yer mean? Whadda yer saying? Anderson leers, his face inches away from Piebald's.

I mean to say that yer gave Emue more 'an a thrashing last night. Piebald glances at Munro for backup, but Munro is mute.

Yer don't know what yer saying. Anderson gives Piebald a quick shove in the chest.

Piebald stumbles a few steps backwards, narrows his eyes at Anderson and whispers, You ought to start 'preciatin' the gins. Look at us, dressed head to toe in skins. We look like 'em, don't you see. And they look like us. We is all in this together now.

He turns away, heading off towards the inlet. I'll find the boy, Piebald calls gruffly over his shoulder.

Anderson crawls into the wurlie and covers himself up with the one remaining skin. He is overcome with sickness, but when the gins return he wants to be there. He likes the smell of it in here.

Yer right? Munro asks, crouching at the entrance to the wurlie.

Jus' leave me. Leave me. Find Will. He'll know

175

where they is, Anderson responds, unsettled by Piebald's words.

★ ★ ★

By evening, Anderson is more than agitated. Mooney and Puss have returned from a day out gathering wiltjeri, munthari and nganangi, but there is no sign of William, Emue, Poll, or even Maringani or Minnie. Piebald and Munro have conducted a thorough search of the nearby inlet, which has proven unsuccessful, and the other women, harangued by Anderson, seem unsure of the whereabouts of Emue and Poll.

Where are they? You know where they is? Stop lyin', yer bitches, Anderson says, grabbing Puss around the arm and leering at her bowed head.

Leave her be, Piebald warns, shoving Anderson's hand away and putting his arm around Puss's shoulders, drawing her to him protectively.

They'll be back in the morning. They do this aller time. Jus' steady yerself, Munro says, holding a dram of rum out for Anderson.

Anderson whisks the rum from Munro, swills it and wipes his mouth clean with the back of his hand.

I told that boy not ter hang about the gins. Now they've taken 'im as their own. He thinks he's a bloody black.

Anderson looks across to the other side of the fire and sees Mooney with her smooth, round face watching him. She is dressed in Munro's shirt and baggy trousers. Munro is wrapped in wallaby skin. The firelight is reflected in Mooney's shining black eyes. He doesn't like the way she is staring at him and is about to say something when Munro passes her some meat. She doesn't eat the meat straight away. It is the best bit, the tail of the wallaby, which she had kept aside for Munro, but he nods to reassure her and tentatively she eats it, turning away slightly from him, smiling.

Anderson can barely contain his disgust. The sight of the other men with their gins is sickening; he heaves himself up and disappears inside the hut. Once inside he paces back and forth, cursing under his breath, slamming his fist into the palm of the other hand. Why has everyone turned against him, when it is he who holds it all together? Crashing his way out of the hut, Anderson strides past the men and the women and heads off into the scrub. He can hear Piebald calling after him and Everitt possibly taunting him, but if no one else is going to find the boy and the gins then he will have to take matters into his own hands. For a moment, he reels, remembering the last time he did that, and the smell of William's flesh burning.

near Hog Bay

Anderson crashes heavy-footed through the undergrowth, his arms held above his head knocking away branches and spider webs and saplings. There is a feeling in his limbs like he is weighted down — like his blood is thick and bubbling. He's felt like this once before: he thought William had drowned. The lurching panic had overwhelmed him, and then William had popped his head up out of the black still water, grinning at Anderson, and choking. Oh to find solace in that ruddy face now. That face that makes him boil with fury. There is something of himself — better than himself — in William. Where is he, though? Something's awfully wrong, he thinks to himself. He shudders, hearing again the scream of that gin when Everitt tied her up to the tree. And afterwards, the silence so deafening Anderson had been sick. It was here. Lubra Creek. It was here, he realises with a quickening dread. All he knows now is that he needs to walk — get out of here — needs to feel like he is in charge of the situation. His brain seems to pound inside his skull. The sea is to his right, to the north-east, he is sure of that, and as long as he doesn't wander too far inland then he can avoid getting lost. Once, he had navigated himself from one end of the island to the other with one of the dogs and a knife. But now Anderson's thoughts are far from concentrating on tracking where he is. He is thinking about William's disobedience of late and what he will do with him when he finds him. If he finds him? After giving his son a hiding he will have to put a stop to the over-friendliness between William and the gins. How? How? A son should show more respect to his father, he thinks to himself. *William, William.*

But there is something else troubling him. It is Emue. Some nights ago he'd had a dream, the residual feeling of which he has not been able to shake for days. In the dream Emue had turned to him and smiled. Her face was open to him, her wide smile revealing her large straight teeth, and in her eyes, a softness that told him there was no discord between them. When he'd woken, Emue wouldn't look at him, and when he finally cupped her chin in his hand and made her look at him, he saw that he repelled her. But he was seeing her in a whole new way. He needed her. Not just because, together, they doubled their output in skins, and not because she knew the body of the land — its private, secret places that offered up honey, and fruit, and roots, and flesh to sustain him — but because the smell of her made him calm. And sometimes frenzied. Reassuring like the taste of milk when you're hungry. Would she ever just rest her head on his chest like Beatrice used to? Then he could breathe deep the crown of her head, and she could sleep, and he could let all the tight places in his body go. But it's too late, she hates me, he realises sinking to his knees. And it's also the thought that those other bastards are just sniggering at him behind his back, getting around with their gins like they're kings and queens, that's made him unsettled. A heavy axe swinging and breaking things. They were all nothing without him. This bad feeling is all because the scrimshaw went missing. He'd scoured every gap and hollow in the sugar gum where he usually kept it, but it was gone. It was an omen. He had made it as an invocation to Beatrice, and now she had abandoned him, too.

179

He needed Emue more than ever. He needed to be held. But his dream had been a cruel trick to make him suffer. Emue, you are nothing without me, he shouts to the frowning sky. Beatrice.

He collapses to his knees and begins to crawl, reaching out his hands to feel what's ahead. Anderson searches the stars for reference but they give little comfort. They aren't as they should be. In fact nothing is as it should be. The sound of the ocean has disappeared and he can no longer make out the curls of smoke from the sealing camp he has left behind. He sinks back onto his knees, cups his hands around his mouth and yells out his son's name. The wind stirs as if to mock him and a bird lets out a shrill cry as if it has been disturbed, although Anderson thinks it is also calling out Weellum. The drooping she-oaks loom at him menacingly and there are no soft landings for his hands and knees. Everything pricks and pierces and stings. He has forgotten which direction he is heading in. That daft boy, look what he's done to me, he thinks, wondering if he has actually mouthed the words or just imagined them. Then he remembers he's seen Emue smile at William like she'd smiled at him in the dream. I'll knock 'im down, he imagines, fuelled by helpless jealousy. I should have left him where he came from. Mauritius. But William was strong and a good boy and so helpful. I need him, I need him, Anderson repeats. Standing up to stretch out the cramping in his knees, Anderson strains to make out the distant purr of the sea. He can hear a noise but he isn't sure if it is waves or just a ringing in his ears. And then he feels something roar past him and he yelps like a frightened dog. The force and speed of the passing sensation almost knocks him from his feet and suddenly he is shivering all over. Anderson stands frozen and listens; there's nothing to hear but his own ragged breathing. What are the trees saying? Why do they taunt me? What a fool I am, he thinks. Even Emue knows not to wander about in the dark. Too many spirits in this place. He shouts again for Emue, who knows him better than any.

★　★　★

Maringani is the one who comes. She'd followed the sound of moaning, not imagining for a second the cries would belong to Anderson. For a long while she just sits and considers him. His sturdy frame is sprawled awkwardly like a thick, fallen branch. The skin of his lips is cracked and blistered and he breathes in shallow jerks. Maringani has never seen him so reduced. He needs water, she thinks to herself, but there is none to be found here. These strange pale men are too loud in their thinking, in their talking, in their walking, to really hear anything, to really see anything at all. Skulls too thin for this bright sun. She wonders what they know. How they've learnt it. They can build ships, all right, and that magic drink that makes them wild and as awkward as seals out of water, they can make that. And those beautiful bottles of glass. Oh yes, they are clever in their own way. They know how to grow things that don't belong, so you don't have to always go looking for tucker. But what will they do when all the seals are gone? It seems to Maringani that these pale men just want lots and lots and lots of one thing. Won't everything start to fall apart? She knows they won't last long, unless, like Weellum, they start listening.

Maringani stands and reaches into the rough, thick leaves of the grass tree that spreads beside her. She separates the fronds as gently as if she is finding the place where the hair parts on Weellum's head, moving slowly so as not to cut herself on the sharp edges of the leaves. Once she has made space enough for her body, she wriggles in close to the stem of the grass tree. This one reaches high above her. Old one, she thinks to herself. From her sedge basket she takes a chiselled stone and begins cutting away the leaves at the base of the stem. The sun is hot on her hair and the stem of the grass tree is scratchy, rough. Anderson whimpers, and there is a quickening in her belly. A little fish flipping over and over. She strips away the leaves in quick deft slices and the sharp edges cut her hands. She raps the base of the stem quickly and the tender white root falls into her hands, the skirt of the grass tree rustling against her shoulders. Kinyeri, the heart of the grass tree, water when there is none. It fits perfectly in her hands, white and vulnerable, and she is sorry to take the heart from the tree. Now, it will die.

Kneeling beside Anderson, she slides her arm under his head and props him up. He smells sour, and she turns her face away. Almost runs away. But it is Weellum's kin, and because of that, she cannot leave him to die.

Emue? he mutters as he tries to focus on Maringani.

She bites a piece from the heart; it is woody and sweet in her mouth and she spits it into her hand before placing it on Anderson's lips. He makes to choke on it, but she lifts his head up a little, and orders him to chew. And at first it's as though he's never had anything in his mouth before, but soon enough he is sucking on the pulp obediently.

He stares up at her. A seal pup, she thinks. When a flicker of recognition passes in the light of his eyes she knows it is time to leave. The kinyeri will revive him. But he is a too-loud man. He did wrong. The rest is up to him. She places his head back down, and holds the heart against his lips a moment. He nuzzles towards it. Then Maringani places the heart on his chest, white against the dark of his hair, heart upon heart, and cradles his flailing hands around it. He grips it and sobs, turning onto his side, folding himself up. As she slices his upper arm with the hard edge of a leaf torn from the heart, he barely cries out. He is a fallen grass tree, kildjeri, and marked now, she thinks, before disappearing into the waiting scrub, taking the flowering stem of the tree with her. She hears him calling to Emue. His voice is gentle. Changed. Maringani calls for Emue too. And sucks the nectar from the little yellowy flowers. Wings in her mouth.

King George Beach (Sandy)

Joe steps back and admires the basket-like mound of twigs and kindling that he and David have gathered. It's almost sculptural, Joe says.

David is collecting up the logs scattered around the place and is sorting them into piles by size. Yeah, mate.

But I reckon we need some more medium and big logs for once it's going.

Yep. David straightens his felt hat, scans the beach, and flips open a packet of cigarettes. Might have to chop some more.

Joe is glad for this time away from the house. The service had been quite beautiful, but he'd spent most of the time torn between worry for Lucy and worry for Diana. By the time it was all over he felt like he needed to run, or swim, or chop wood, or wank, or just stand on Nell's verandah and let himself be blasted clean through by the wind. But Joe and David had decided it might be a special thing to have a bonfire on the beach that night. They'd bring down cushions and blankets and beers and wine and sun their faces by the fire. Nell would have approved, they'd reasoned, even if they'd had to convince Pearl and Lucy it was a good idea. I just can't be bothered, Lucy protested. But you won't have to do a thing. She'd rolled her eyes at him.

David cups his hand round the end of the cigarette and lights it, turning his back away from the wind. He throws the packet at Joe. Here. Have one. You've earnt it.

Ah thanks.

Joe appreciates that David doesn't say much, but that he's a man that pays attention. His father-in-law is a tall man with a barrel chest, and strong planes to his face. When he smiles his face crumples. Always, he wears a dark leather jacket with the collar up, and Joe thinks of him as some kind of Indiana Jones-like figure. Even his daughters think of him as sort of heroic.

It had taken them nearly an hour to get the wood down from the side of the house. They'd stood at the top of the dune and hurled it down in stages, sniggering like schoolboys. And then they'd scoured the scrub for kindling. At one point they'd converged and they sort of fell back into the sand together like weary camels. It was late in the afternoon and already a white smudge of moon was showing. David had told him that the evening before he'd dreamt about this exact moment, with the moon just there, and the air getting cold and the smoke of his cigarette curling up in perfect spirals. Joe had told him about Lucy being pregnant again. David had squeezed his arm in congratulations, and then asked about Pearl. Now they smoke and gaze at their handiwork.

Gonna be a shame to set it alight. It's bloody

beautiful, David says.

But Joe can't wait to see the blaze of it. He's proud of what they've made. He can't wait, in fact, for this day to be over.

It hadn't started well. Diana and Pearl had argued in the kitchen. Pearl read Diana's words for the funeral — Diana having left them on the table — and she'd told her mother that this was not the day to publicly vent her grievances with Nell. Joe had walked in at that point, and Diana turned to him.

But Joe I should be honest, shouldn't I? I'm not going to say too much, but I'm also not going to paint the relationship as something it wasn't.

Why would you be painting anything? This is just a chance for you to say goodbye to Nell, Pearl countered.

Joe offered to read the notes, and he saw in those words a woman in desperate shock. He suggested that Diana take out the bit about Nell kicking her out of home at seventeen and keep it more focused in the present. Lucy had chimed in then, and said that this was all beside the point. There wasn't time to worry about what everyone was going to be saying, and Diana could mention whatever she bloody wanted to. Joe wondered if Lucy was on the verge of getting hysterical. He folded up the papers and handed them back to Diana.

Lucy's right. It's up to you Diana.

Pearl glowered at them all, and turned brusquely from the room. Joe sank his head into his hands and did a rare thing. He prayed.

186

Please, please, let us all get through the day unscathed. Ariel slid her thin little arms around his neck and lifted his face up with her forehead. Are you all right, Daddy?

Joe looked into Ariel's eyes and was galvanised. I am *much* better now. And he slung her over his shoulder and spun her around. She gripped his shirt and squealed. Alfie tottered into Joe's legs and wanted a turn too, but they all fell into a heap on the mat. Then Joe noticed Lewis standing shyly in the doorway, his hair washed and combed, and wearing a suit, so that he looked like a sort of shrunken old man with a shining face.

Alfie's turn next and then it's Lewis's.

Joe saw something like sunlight break across Lewis's face. Being eleven, he had started holding himself back where once he would have rushed in. Is this how childhood disappears, Joe thought, in the slow holding back of yourself?

Please stop razzing them up, Joe, you're messing up everyone's hair, Lucy said, just as he'd hoisted Lewis over his shoulder.

So it would be a wonderful thing to finally set the pyre ablaze, thinks Joe, and this day could burn away into something softer and kinder and more tolerable.

The others start snaking down the dune, Diana with Alfie on her hip, Ariel slipping and skidding, Lewis running in great leaping strides, Nico and Uncle Jim carrying the esky between them, and Pearl, Lucy, Marian, Red and Caroline balancing their way carefully down, loaded up with cushions and blankets.

187

David is standing in the shallows with his jeans rolled up. He looks beyond the ragged line of them all coming down the hill to Nell's house squatting behind the sandhills. From the shoreline you can hardly see the house; only the sloped green galvanised iron roof, which blends in with the scrub, and in the late afternoon the glint of the sun reflecting off the top of the windows. Now it's lit up from the inside like a lantern, and he wonders whether the sound would carry down the hill if he put the stereo on up there. David watches Joe instruct the children to screw up pieces of newspaper and stuff it into the construction of branches. They squat around its perimeter like lost bees nudging the outside of the hive.

When David and Joe kneel down and hold a flame to the tinder, there is a network of snaking orange before it catches, fierce and bright, and everyone steps back, sloshing their champagne over the tops of their glasses.

To Nell, says Jim. You old bugger. He raises up not a glass of champagne like the others, but a dented metal water bottle and pours water over his face.

To Nell, the others respond in unison. And Ariel spontaneously claps.

Later, with the ring of faces softened by fire glow, the children drowsy in laps, and Van Morrison's 'Beside You' crooning down the hill, David wonders whether, essentially, he's made an irrevocable mistake. The feeling has been gnawing at him for years really but tonight it grows into something sinewy and rangy and pins him down. It sits on his chest and taunts him. He wishes he could take it all back. Perhaps then he and Diana might have made it. But when they found out Diana was pregnant with Lucy, he insisted they get Pearl back from Nell. Let's be a family, he pleaded with Diana. Pearl belongs here with us. Her biological father was a sandy-haired country boy, as David liked to imagine then, who'd fallen in over his head with Diana, and been left like roadkill in her wake. He'd moved to Darwin before Pearl was born and was not going to have much of a role, if any, in Pearl's life, and so David wanted to be there not only for his beautiful huntress Diana, but also for the little dimpled daughter.

Diana was in the bath, with him perched on the edge, when he announced his idea, and his heart was melting for her. She was so delicate-boned and tragic. She almost shone in the water, her breasts dewy and milky with pregnancy. And those big sad eyes — he just wanted to wrap his coat around her, like in the Rolling Stones song, and protect her. Diana wasn't like anyone else he'd been with. They merged together like white light and her face when they made love was clearer than quartz. But she lowered her eyes and shook her head. I'm not sure, David. I'm just not sure about it at all. When they arrived at Nell's to collect Pearl, Nell slammed the door in their faces. Yet Pearl eventually came to live with them — David found a lawyer — and things between him and Diana were never the same again. Or Diana and Nell for that matter. Or between anyone.

David glances over at Diana now. They are all sitting in a ring around the fire. The sun has slipped into the sea and the sky bleeds red. Already, the night is coming on cold. Diana and Nico are talking. David knows Nico tries hard with her, perhaps hoping to be some kind of bridge. Diana is deftly rolling a joint. Her face has a deepening beauty, he thinks, like antique fabric. She hasn't spoken a word to him yet, but when 'Sweet Thing' came on she'd winked at him, or so he imagined.

So I found Nell's stash, she says, giggling.

Lucy and Pearl break into laughter at this and lean in, clutching on to one another, Lucy eventually wrapping her arms around Pearl and holding her close. David's heart lurches, and for a moment it's like he's thrown the clinging animal from his chest. He's been watching Pearl swig from a bottle of red all evening and he thinks, God, she's worse than me.

You're such a teenager, Mum, says Lucy. And David knows it to be true.

Be warned, it's very strong, Marian says, the sheen of her teeth catching in the firelight.

Red giggles. Yes, remember the last time we smoked it with Nell? We ended up down at Pelican Lagoon at midnight fossicking for animal bones to go in her sculpture.

Oh yes, I remember!

I can't believe Nell was seventy-seven and still smoked that stuff, says Lucy.

Ah, but she took it for her back pain, didn't you know? Diana says teasingly.

⋆ ⋆ ⋆

David lies back on the sand and above him the stars are crushed glass. When they arrived home with Pearl that first day, Diana just stared at her daughter from underneath a crochet blanket his mother had made and simply did not know what to do with her. David was gentle with both of them and tried to find ways to bring them together — he bought a baby swing and showed Diana how to strap Pearl into it, or he put a doll and a pile of doll's clothes between them on the floor. Sometimes he would just place Pearl directly in Diana's lap, and Diana would look at him sharply, and Pearl would wriggle around and reach her arms out for him. It was a little better when Lucy came along because Diana seemed gentle again like when they'd first met. Pearl was interested in everything to do with Lucy and followed Diana around like a flitting shadow. But by the end of Lucy's first year, Diana's face hardened and where once she'd slithered on top of him in the middle of the night, placing him gently inside her, now she turned away from him, and the dark smudges beneath her eyes became even more pronounced.

The joint gets passed around the circle and when it reaches David, he takes a long deliberate puff and stands unsteadily on his feet. He makes his way over to Diana, hands the joint to Red and reaches out to Diana, bowing slightly. Dance with me?

Everyone is silent, and Diana stiffens. In a gentlemanly effort to break the tension, Joe turns to Lucy and asks her to dance with him. And then Marian and Red help each other up and embrace. When Diana rests her head on his shoulder and he places his hand at the small of her back, he closes his eyes and wishes he'd understood her better. He knows now he'd put her on a pedestal — his ideal woman. But she was just an ordinary girl, probably with postnatal depression. He'd hoped Diana would return to herself one day and to him. Her body hasn't changed a bit, he thinks, but she burns hot and he can't find her rhythm. Through the thin silk of her shirt he can feel her shivering ever so slightly with tears. Stepping lightly like a ballerina.

★ ★ ★

When Diana places her cheek on the cool leather of David's jacket she loses all sense of orientation. She's falling but he holds her up around the waist and she is weightless. She is expanding out towards the stars and then she is shrinking to a point of light, and David is the fulcrum. I am Alice in Wonderland, she thinks. The smoky sandalwood smell of David is so familiar she can finally rest. It's like there's more space inside her skull, her shoulders are wider, her hips more spreading. Her womb aches and she presses against him. She hadn't been ready for his love all those years ago — the intensity of it, his neediness. This is the last time they'll be this close, she knows. When the tears come they seep like water from the face of a mountain. A slow and necessary leaking out, like she's become too full.

★   ★   ★

Uncle dances with his black Akubra on, head bowed towards Pearl, and she concentrates hard on her little footsteps in the uneven sand so as not to topple over, and trying not to lean too hard on Jim's arm. There's a wheeze in his chest — a whistle on the in-breath. He is springy, wiry, ageless even. The same age as Nell, Pearl wonders. As a child, she remembers him coming to visit the house whenever he came to the island, and she'd always thought of him as older than Nell, but now she's not so sure.

Jeez you remind me of Nell, Jim laughs, and the corners of his eyes crinkle.

Why?

Jim takes a deep, slow breath and exhales a long thoughtful hum. Hard to pin down. Lightning eyes. Smart eyes. Pearl winces.

Not to offend, Pearl. You're both sort of mysterious. I bet you keep that poor Nico on his toes. Jim laughs again and coughs turning his head away from Pearl.

Uncle?

I'm fine. He stands still for a moment and thumps his chest. Pearl stands back, her hand resting on his elbow, and Jim's cough is deep and gravelly. Caroline glances up at him with concern. He winks at her.

The wind picks up and Pearl shivers. She is tired suddenly. The fire creaks and pops and the sea whispers. Everything seems to pulse and quiver around her — like there are unseen currents running between the spinifex and the stones and the wind and the firelight and the blue-black sky and the murmur of voices. A humming. Connective tissue.

Sorry, Pearl. I've had a bit of a cold. Jim puts his arm tightly around Pearl's shoulders.

It's okay, Jim. And it's getting late — chilly. Perhaps we should head up.

Jim nods and reaches into his pocket. I want you to have this, Pearl. He places something small and tapered into her hand. She peers at it and it looks like a piece of polished yellowing wood — tooth-shaped. It is carved, and in the firelight she can't make out the pattern.

It's a scrimshaw. Old one.

Oh. Wow, Jim. Where's it from?

Aunty Hettie passed it along to the cultural centre. At the Coorong. She said it was made by a sealer. Islander. I was going to give it to Nell — she always admired it. But, well, it's yours. For you. It's bone.

He shakes his head and takes the cigarette packet from his breast pocket. His hands tremble slightly as he places a cigarette at his lips and his face is illuminated at the flare of the match. Jim exhales and the smoke clings in the cold air.

Pearl holds the bone to her forehead and it is so smooth, so worn. She shivers.

194

Caroline stands and takes Jim's elbow. It's getting cold, Uncle. We should be getting going.

He sighs, Yep it's about that time, Caro.

Pearl takes Nico's hand and pulls him up to standing. I'm tired. Let's head up too.

★   ★   ★

Getting back up to the house is difficult. The sand dunes are steep and in the dark it's hard to stay on the path rutted with roots. Pearl, carrying an esky and a blanket, keeps slipping forward onto all fours. Nico, following behind, squares his palms to the back of her thighs for support but then he's falling down too and Pearl is laughing so much she loses all the strength in her arms.

I can't do this, Nico. I'm just gonna dump everything and come back for it in the morning.

He puts his arms around her and rolls her off the path. His hand is hot and dry as it snakes up the inside of her T-shirt. When they kiss, they mash their lips together hard, teeth clashing.

Nico, you're not helping. I need to get up this damn hill. In. To. Bed.

But when he takes her breast firm in his hand, pressing down on the nipple, she moves closer to him and the sand is cool and yielding against her shoulders.

Oh my god, you two. Lucy gives Pearl a friendly kick in the side, and then dumps a pile of cushions on the esky. Fuck! I can't carry another thing! So steep.

Leave those, Lucy, I'll get them. Nico sits up

195

and rearranges Pearl's T-shirt gently, pulling it down.

Lucy frowns and moves aside for Joe, who is staggering up the dune, occasionally falling to his knees with Alfie draped over his shoulder, and Pearl thinks to herself how absurdly loud the crickets are. Whirring through her brain with mad song.

Later, when they're in the bedroom, Pearl confronts Nico in a hushed voice because Lewis is sleeping. What did you mean?

About what? Nico pulls the covers up around the hump of Lewis.

About Lucy not carrying anything?

I didn't mean anything. Just that it was too hard. We're all drunk and tired. What a fucking day!

Lucy hardly drank a thing. I'm her sister. I notice these things. She's pregnant, isn't she?

Nico moves behind Pearl and brushes his lips on the back of her neck, hand to the inner edge of her hipbone. Come to bed. It's so late.

But she spins away from him, crashing into the dresser. There is a crunch as her hand lands in the tray of jewellery. She pulls her earrings out and chucks them down, and fumbles with the clasp of her necklace.

Fuck's sake! Why's it a big secret. What must you all think of me?

She could start a spot fire. Little rings of flame all around the bedroom. She could make an inferno.

Nico lies down on the swag and sighs. We just thought about getting through today. That you

196

had enough to deal with.

Oh my god, Nico.

And she thinks of Lucy, fertile as a river. Putting out spot fires. Beautiful sister. She could cry but the wine makes her agitated. Sexual. But she won't make love to Nico. Not now. He is barely awake. Just cajoling her. And her body is a fine-feathered thing. Downy and silken but armoured with feathers. Like a high priestess in a jacket of wings. No one can reach me now, she thinks. And she sinks beside Nico and lays her palm in his, all the heat gone out of her sadness and rage because what is there to rail against? Lucy's joy? You don't need to manage me. Don't keep things from me, Nico. I love my sister.

Sorry, Pearl. I just don't know. I can hardly bear it sometimes, he says, eyes closed. She watches him drift away from her, as he falls asleep. A drowning man — she wishes she could pull him back out of the deep to be with her.

And when he sleeps she cannot. There is the son and the father breathing heavily and her own self, separate from them, taut with wakefulness. There is the moon like a great lamp mooning naughtily at the window. And there is Nell, like an uncharted map. All those tracks she left behind, thinks Pearl. Will I never rest? Will we ever know what to do? She disentangles from Nico, he's plummeted into black sleep now; she regards him resentfully for a moment, and then crawls along the floorboards to her satchel slung by the door. Stuffed deep inside is the little red book.

Nell

When Aunty Hettie and Sol came to petition their case — to petition for me — I'd already been sent away. I was at the place with white wooden cots all in a row and shining linoleum floors. I was at the place with swaddled-up babies in white wooden cots. I was at the place that smelt of disinfectant and talcum and something rank like the smell of sweat when you're afraid. I was at the place where they give you a different name — a pseudonym — so as not to sully your own name. I was at a place where some girls — the older ones — got to keep their babies, and some handed them over like they were a pat of butter, and others, like me, had them wrenched away, like breaking off a branch from a tree.

I visited Aunty Hettie after our meeting at the post office. Her kitchen was sparse and cool. Flagstone floor, heavy wooden table and an assortment of dining chairs, sideboard, meat safe and a shelf much like a bookshelf, with rows of herbal tinctures in large amber bottles neatly set out. Woven baskets, flattish and long-handled, hung from hooks at various heights on the walls. Sister baskets. A vase of sedge sat in the middle of the sideboard, the grass sweeping gracefully over the lip of the vase. Beside the vase there were sedge rushes wrapped in damp hessian sugar bags. A bitter smell hung in the room and then I realised something was simmering on the gas top, making the lid of the pot rattle. As if to read my thoughts — Dandelion leaves, she said. For cleansing the liver.

I hadn't really thought about how dark-skinned she was until then. It made her seem younger than her eighty-odd years — her skin tone even and smooth, whereas my own mother's face, forty years younger, was blooming with sun-spots and already sagging around the edges. I felt mean for the thought but Aunty was more like kin to me than my own mother. I'd always loved watching her small hands and narrow wrists as she wove the sedge grass into mats and baskets, or adjusted her shell necklaces that hung opalescent at her lined throat; she had a girlish way of moving, and she and Sol both had the same mouth — distinct and expressive. She kissed me on both cheeks and then stroked her hand from my forehead all the way over my head and down to the base of the neck, when she greeted me. She left her hand there for a while like I belonged with her. I didn't want to ever leave.

Aunty ushered me to the kitchen table and began taking some of the amber bottles down from the shelf and placing them on the sideboard. I read their labels. Parsley. Sage. Yarrow. Rosehips. Skullcap. She took the pot from the stove, placed it on a slab of marbled stone beside the sink, and then turned to me, wiping her hands on her apron.

You've been through too much.

How did she know? I shifted uncomfortably in the chair.

Don't look so surprised. You left a girl and came back a mother. Without child.

I liked that she said I was a mother. Even with no child to look after. Even with my breasts wrapped tight in bandages to stop them from leaking.

I watched mesmerised, and reeling slightly, as she poured small amounts of the tincture from each bottle into a glass measuring cylinder.

What's in those bottles?

Herbs. Tinctures. I'm a herbalist. But I know other things too. From my dark mothers and sisters. More than I can say. I know about yalkari, nganangi, kalari and kinyeri, too. I take things from both worlds and make something new.

Both worlds?

Don't look so serious, girl. You're in both worlds too. She laughed, and I noticed some of her teeth were missing. I'll make us a cuppa.

The dandelion tea had an earthy taste, not what I was used to, but I sipped it slowly, hoping it would calm the shake in my hands. I didn't know what was wrong with me lately. But my body would quiver and shudder as if I were in a panic, even when I was doing something as simple as folding the sheets, or checking the fences along the boundary. She watched my hands. We'll add some oats or chamomile to your tonic, she said.

While I sipped the brew from the bitter leaves,

Aunty sat across from me, an unfinished weaving before her on the table. She slid it over.

I've started it off, she said, it begins in the centre and spirals outwards. Now you do it. Do you remember how?

I looked at her blankly. She picked up another weaving and demonstrated how to stitch the main thread over the bundle of rushes, adding more rounds of the circle. Not too tight, not too loose. You have to keep adding in the rushes — not all at once, she said — like adding to a family. Keep it growing. When you finish you can't see where it ends because there is no end, like an umbilicus.

A year ago, I'd been adept at it. Now, my fingers felt clumsy, too big for the sinewy reeds, but the more I paid attention, the more soothing, steadying, it became. The rhythm of it seemed to focus my whole self, instead of being this scattered thing. Pieces of me everywhere. Hanging on fences. Hettie's fingers were articulate with the rushes, over and through, and after a long stretch of quiet she told me this story, for stories and weaving go together, she said.

When Sol and I came to the farm to speak for you — to try to make your folks understand — you'd already been sent away. We didn't know where.

Sent away — yes, I thought. Sent away like dirty washing to be laundered. I said nothing and waited for Aunty Hettie to continue. She spoke slowly and in perfect time with her careful deft weaving.

Your mother said that you had a job for the autumn with some cousins in Adelaide. We had to believe her. We were patient people, and Sol said that he would hang on for as long as it took, that his wish to marry you was not something that he could make go away.

I swallowed some tea and wondered whether she'd heard how loud my gulp was.

We were prepared for resistance, so we put our offer on the table. It was all we had. Sol was old enough to take on the farm, and I brought the papers to show that it had been transferred in his name. As you know, this was my great-grandfather's land — he was granted it by the government because his wife was Aboriginal. That's what they did back then. They hoped to encourage European-style farming among the 'natives'. But anyway, in this case, that granny of mine was a curse. We was offering you a home and income, but it wasn't enough. We pleaded: you would still live next door to your own family and Sol could be of help to them too.

I watched the spiral of her weaving slowly grow. But none of that mattered. We were a black mark on your name, your mother said. We had too much dark blood in us and it would keep showing up in your babies and in your babies' babies.

I swallowed. And all of those scattered parts of me came flying back in like great angry wings. So what, I said. So what!

Aunty smiled. You're a generation on. You understand things they cannot. Understanding takes many lifetimes. Let me tell you a story? She looked at me, her eyebrows raised into a question. I recognised Sol in her eyes.

Please, Aunty. Yes.

⋆ ⋆ ⋆

Back in the sealing days, before we were settled and when all that was needed to survive was all that was traded — salt, skins and Aboriginal wives — there was a woman brought here from the mainland called Emue. She had many children with her Ngarrindjeri family, and one of her daughters was caught too and taken to the island. We don't know much about the children Emue had with her sealer man — the records are scant. You see, before 1836, it's like islanders didn't exist, or were too 'uncivilised' to go on the colonial records.

One day Emue was brought home in a dinghy by a young sealer and another woman, a relative. Emue was dead by the time the boat washed up on the shore and the young man was half drowned. Emue's people revived the boy by placing his frozen body in a scooped-out hole of warm sand, heated by fire. They buried him up to his neck until he woke up. He became an initiated man, you see, Nell? Do you see what I'm saying? After Emue had been properly buried, and the boy had recovered, he returned in the dinghy to the island. Before he left, he promised that he would take care of Emue's daughter and bring her back home too. But he and the girl never did return to the mainland. Perhaps they tried but the passage of water separating the island is so very treacherous. We just don't know. When the sealers took our women, they left gaps in our history that we won't ever fill. But the story of that young boy and that young girl, and the stories of many other such unions between blackfella and whitefella, they belong to us. I am a descendant of this heritage. We must acknowledge our sisters and the blood they shed — the children they carried. This is a two-way exchange.

And because of your child, because of Sol, you must know this. We are all in this together now. Dear Nell, we are all stitched in together.

★ ★ ★

I smoothed the reeds in my lap and saw my baby boy floating towards me on a raft made of rushes. I saw not water, but waves of blood.

Make a place in your heart, Aunty said. Oh but that place, Sol, it hurt so much. Diana, Pearl, it hurts so much.

Charlotte came sweeping into the kitchen then, plonking the baby Elijah on the floor. I watched him — the film of spit on his lip, the bony bumps on his skull, the tight curls, the way his knees fell outwards like butterfly wings — and then Charlotte scooped him up, glaring at me.

What?

I held the weaving tight in my hands, knuckles whitening. Aunty stood and took the baby from Charlotte.

Mind your tongue. Nell's our guest.

Charlotte leant against the sink and scowled at me. Just been over at the Simpsons'. Tom's enlisted. And Sol, too. Leaving tomorrow. She looked right into me, her eyes glistening with a kind of greedy pleasure.

So there I was, burnt to the ground. And not even seventeen yet. Aunty Het my witness, like a guardian angel. He was leaving. And on his own accord. Either way, I lost him.

No one wants to marry our boys, Aunty said, and my cheeks flared. And so we are losing our land, our farms. Again and again. On the mainland, we're herded into missions. Here, we're frozen out. We are removed over and over.

I took a swallow, and kept weaving, my fingers less clumsy now. In fact, I'd never felt so alert. Aunty Hettie had an autonomy that I admired then and have now grown to deeply appreciate. And it was only during that conversation that I became conscious for the first time of her heritage and all it meant and all it was. All she'd strived to hold on to. I'd not seen Sol and me as any different from each other. But we were. It wasn't just my parents' disapproval, disgust even, that we faced; this was a bedrock of prejudice, denial and theft that we may never break open.

If no one marries us, then we have no children to pass the land on to. You have to understand, Nell, Sol doesn't have a choice. He must enlist. Take that tonic three times a day with food. A big spoonful. You'll start to get your spirit back soon enough. And about Sol, you have to let him go. Let him find his own peace. There were tears in her eyes.

When I climbed back into the cart for home, Father didn't say a word, but kissed me on the forehead, and he was so gentle in his big coat and his scratchy stubble was so familiar that I wanted to cry on his shoulder. But I pushed him away. I wanted to hate him but I was too spent. Broken. Anyway I knew Mother was the one who had put her foot down, so I didn't berate him. Great wracking tears made me feel like weeing, I was that full of water and dandelion tea. My hand closed around the black glass scraper Aunty had given me from Sol. He had found it when he was out yaccaring. After my parents bought Aunty's land, I never saw her again. Before she left for the mainland, Aunty gave me other things, too — I keep them in this pale green shoebox like talismans. What can they tell me what can they tell me what can they tell me of you? Old dusty things. And Hettie, I am sorry. Dear Aunty, give me words. At least just those. Sol. Sun. Song of songs.

> *Bind me as a seal upon your heart,*
> *a sign upon your arm*
>
> *for love is as fierce as death,*
> *its jealousy bitter as the grave.*
> *Even its sparks are a raging fire,*
> *a devouring flame.*
>
> *Great seas cannot extinguish love,*
> *no river can sweep it away.*

1828
Backstairs Passage

William wonders whether the cold of Emue, her skin like wet stones now, is seeping into his own body. His shoulders ache and it's because his arms are so numb. He could break bits of himself off, like cleaving ice, but he keeps rowing, his gaze set on the steady outline of Poll. They are just a little slit in the ocean — a little fissure seaming through — the water black and heavy and surging around them as if they're in the clutches of an animal. He shifts his feet away from Emue. Poll sings. William remembers sleeping in a channel of rock wrapped in seaweed. Oh what he'd give for that seaweed now. Its embrace. It seems they are suspended in the mid-point, the crumpled hills in the distance never any closer. William dares to glance down at Emue and, all wrapped up like that, she is like a seal.

The night keeps coming on. The sky getting higher and higher — blankets of cloud peeling away, so the bones of his skull burn cold. The stars burn holes, too. But Poll does not stop rowing — her arms are strong — and her song weaves around him, stitching him all in. Keeping him going on. He wonders how long it will take for them to become more sea than boat. How long to dissolve into her seductions? Would it be an embrace? He holds on to Poll's song like a thread. She scoops water from the boat and it gleams like fat thrown onto a fire. Last time she'd tried to cross this passage she hadn't made it. Everitt carried her from the shore and then chopped off her ear. William thinks of Poll's baby rolling somewhere beneath them. Wrapped in her sedge cloak. And he imagines himself wrapped in a sedge cloak and closes his eyes. He imagines he is a seal wrapped in blubber. He rubs the scar on his hand. The sea, his kin.

near Encounter Bay

The light when it lands is like his mother standing over him — the face he once knew. Her hands blaze like a furnace. The sand is a lance. He is naked, but it is still too hot. There are voices and they overlap and overlap like waves getting closer. He makes out words from Maringani's language. He understands the way they curl and ring. Maringani. If only for her cool fingers on his swollen lips. They will burst like waikeries. There are many hands and he is lifted, floating on songs and whisperings. William opens his eyes and the sky shudders white and is scored with black lines. Crows, dawuldi, he thinks, and then a hand smooths his brow and palms his eyes shut. He is rubbed all over, a sea of hands, and his skin might be falling off. They could just be rubbing at his bones. Scouring him down to ash. But then he's lifted gently again and placed into a recess. He feels the hands putting his flesh back on. Patting it firmly in. Building him up again with hot sand. Enclosing him. There is smoke and it curls and rings around him. It rings out with the clean smell of ti-tree. And there are men with old faces, and younger faces too, watching him, talking in low voices. Their chests are bare and painted. He dreams he is growing fur like a seal. Or perhaps he is a wallaby roasting in a hole.

★   ★   ★

Days later and he is painted in ochre. He can't remember getting here but thinks they might have sailed on the stars in a bark canoe. Poll is different. She's hacked her hair and she is caked in mud and she keens. All the women scratch and cut at themselves; the men keep the fire going in a circle of ti-trees. William is swept up with the men, falling in with their rhythms, of hunting and singing, tending the fires, and keeping watch, and he is buoyed by them. Their strength, their ordered world, their acceptance of him. He observes carefully. Emue sits on a raised platform — her head bent forward. Shoulders slumped. She is wrapped in branches. The fire is a long way beneath her, and the smoke wreaths and conceals and then clears again. The body drips down, the men say. And William is sometimes frightened by the acrid smell lurking beneath the aroma of burning ti-tree. He remembers his own hand burning. The spirit travels up, they say, and point to the Milky Way. Ngurunderi's canoe. The bones will remain. To be buried, they say. This goes on for many days and William sleeps more than he ever has before. He dreams every time of pelicans — their feathers sweeping over Emue and sweeping out her wurlie, like Poll had done before they left. Sweeping and sweeping until his dreams are brushed clean and he wakes again to the high-pitched wailing. The women's voices are carried up with the smoke and stretched out along the clouds. He wonders if Maringani can hear them. He looks across to the island — the water is a sleeping wild animal between them.

★ ★ ★

William wipes the red paint from his body in long deliberate strokes. This covering has protected him for weeks now and he's afraid of what scraping it away will bring. But the men have instructed him — he is ready. Narambi. His skin underneath is startlingly white after the earthy dry red he's become used to. Yet his body feels unusually energised — like it could never be cold again. His blood is singing. And as he rubs at the ochre his penis is impossibly taut. Ignoring it, he concentrates on wiping away the red from all the hidden places — behind the knees, at the back of his skull, in his hairline. When he emerges blinking and new and so brightly naked, he is given a plonggi, fighting club, a wakaldi, shield, and a taralyi, throwing stick. He is given other things, too, and foods to break taboo.

He sits face to face with the old feller who grasps William's left hand with his own lined left hand, and William's navel with his right hand. Navel cord exchange — belonging now among the men. Flicking and clicking his fingers away, the old feller releases William, and William notices that he can no longer smell burning ti-tree. How many moons has it been, he wonders. He asks about Emue. She is buried now, old feller says. Her bones face west. She travels over the waters on the symbolic raft of her burial platform. She returns to the island, place of crossing over. William knows he must return now too. This time he will be given safe passage. Maringani — he can't even say her name but utters it over and over again mutely in the pit of his throat. The smoke has changed his voice.

near King George Beach (Sandy)

Maringani kneels at the shoreline and the waves break on her knees. Today the sun is quiet, gentle. The rushing foam swirls at her thighs and she leans forward to stop from tipping. But she should allow the water to carry her, she thinks, and the tide paws reassuringly as if to take her in. It has been three moons since she and Minnie fled from the camp. Every day she scans the ocean for a sign. Does Weellum think of her? All she knows is that without Emue and without Weellum she is cold in her bones. She is worried she'll be caught by rough hands. Is Anderson even alive, she wonders. It will take more than kinyeri to save him.

Maringani is becoming lighter than a pelican feather even as her belly grows. The other side of the water is a moving shadow that she tries to set down with her gaze. But it keeps drifting.

She crawls into the waves and they slam at her shoulders and she rolls over and over in the bubbles. There are clouds massing over the distant mainland and she wonders if this is the sign. With long slow strokes she swims past where the waves break and she feels a kind of fizzing inside, like she's no more than foam. She is so buoyant she cannot make headway, but she holds Weellum's face in her mind and it propels her forward. Maringani rolls onto her back and points her feet towards the shore and works her arms like rudders to keep afloat. She'll have to pace herself. Become like a pelican. Swim, fly, dive.

On the beach is Minnie, working a stick into the sand for kuti. Minnie glances up and waves at Maringani furiously. Maringani gestures back and her throat is suddenly swollen with salt. She chokes and she is no longer light but a heavy stone sinking. She slips under and Minnie is running. Under the water there are all kinds of singing. And the sound of wings beating. Her lungs tighten and her blood screams and she pops back up to the surface. Circling low between Maringani and Minnie is a nori, pelican, her ngatji, protector. It sails on the wind and she follows it. Her arms become great white feathers, the black tips rustling. Maringani glides into the shore and Minnie tumbles through the shallows towards her. They embrace and the pelican looks on before standing to its magnificent height, plumping its wings and gulping as it takes flight. Maringani grips on to Minnie's soft warm body and sobs into Minnie's thin chest. Minnie leads Maringani out of the water to the dry sand, sits her down carefully, and then squeezes the water from her hair and drapes herself over Maringani's cold red shoulders. It takes some time to stop shuddering, but now when she looks towards the mainland she can see nothing at all. Just the clouds bleeding thickly into the sea. Minnie hands her a pelican feather and sits firmly in Maringani's lap.

King George Beach (Sandy)

The ground is cold underfoot from the night. All
the heat of the previous day sucked away like
Pearl is walking on a grave. But it will be hot
later. This is just a dawn respite. Time of the
birds. Drops of light fall through the leaves,
spreading gold. The she-oaks are whispering
loudly, sounding the new day. She read the
whole thing last night — Nell's little book — and
now everything takes on a new tenor of meaning.
Pearl had looked in on Diana sleeping and
thought of waking her, pulling her out into this
precarious morning. How much had she read of
Nell's story? But there was a kind of perfection
in being the only one awake in a house heavy
with sleep and sorrow, so she'd left her mother
like she was abandoning ship. Almost ran from
the house before she could be noticed. Nico will
sleep for hours yet, she thinks with annoyance.
Her eyes are raw and her shoulders ache with
insomnia. Everything she held to be true is
blurring; her whole self is leaking out at the
seams. She is amorphous and only the trees hold
her up. When she finds the old beehive she kicks
it to pieces. It is satisfying to break it heartily,
even as shudders of pain jolt into her hips and
knees and lower back. It crumbles easily, like it
was held together with the finest of stitching. But

it is rot that makes everything, in the end, break down. Her feet throb and they're cold. She thought Nell had always told her everything. So why did the story of Maringani and William leave her feeling as if some great part of herself had cleaved away — rocks tumbling into the ocean. Why is it we can never know anyone, not mothers, not sisters, not lovers, she thinks. We just fumble along. Her thoughts are dramatic with tiredness, she knows, but she indulges them. She is like the beehive. No longer held together.

Nico's footfalls are soft. He is soft, she thinks, when she sees him coming along the track, the sun just catching the ends of his hair like wires of copper.

Honey! Are you okay? What are you doing? He kneels in front of her, his face crumpled with weariness and worry.

It's so early. I didn't want to wake you. I just —

Come here.

For a long time she rests with her head on his chest, trying to fall in with his breathing, trying not to tremble. She's twitchy. There's just the rise and fall of him and the fullness of sky and the light burning away at the morning. When they kiss it is only a whisper. Soft lips to soft lips. Slow-moving honey. Heating. Pooling. And when she moves him inside her, she knows that in the inmost part of her she is molten. They are the sun burning away the dross of cloud. Oh that face of his — like a face from ancient times, smooth and clear now, and warrior-like — she cradles it and anchors her fingers in his hair. He smiles and it makes him young. They are seamless. This is not the desperate clinging it has been of late, but a singing inside; this is a coming together. Skin to skin. She wears nothing now but the fine periwinkle necklace that was wrapped up inside the envelope from last night. Nico lets the string of shells fall gently into his mouth, as she leans over him. And the she-oaks cry out, and the sun ignites, and she never wants to be anywhere else, but here with the smell of them everywhere.

★　★　★

As a young child, Diana had often wondered what it would be like to live inside a shell. She would squint inside their spiralled chambers and try to fathom what was in the middle. Breaking them apart didn't help because then they were no longer themselves. She used to ask her father over and over what it would be like, and he'd always say: It would be, dear girl, to know what it is to be carried along. Diana liked that idea — to just let the swell of the ocean take you — to follow the pull of the moon, to fit exactly inside your covering. But lately, the thought of such surrender has terrified her. She's been too passive and she's being crushed.

Now she no longer desires a maisonette backing onto a train line but a round house, a humpy with no right angles, or a burrow, even a lighthouse — something curved and graceful yet grounded. It has to be comfortable though, and clean. And not subject to currents or riptides. And so she begins, the drawing flowing easily out of her, and the pencil just sharp enough to satisfyingly ignite the page. The house is curved, so that the wind from any direction could never lash against it, and it is bone white like a weathered shell. It is enough just to draw it. In fact, it is drawing that always frees her in the end.

She'd woken early, before dawn, to Pearl opening the door and peering in, but Diana pretended she was asleep. David was in her dream and she wanted to hang on to the fragment, walk through the dream again in her mind before she forgot it. But it was too late. By the time Pearl had creaked the floorboards and unlocked the back door — she imagined her daughter mounting a white horse behind the house and simply galloping away — she'd lost David again. Dancing with him last night at the bonfire she realised she had no outer covering, and that what she needed was a shell house, even if just metaphorically. Protection.

After everyone else had gone up to the house for the night, the two of them walked along the shoreline, shell fragments crunching beneath their bare feet. There was a gap between them, at least an arm's length, as if their closeness earlier had only been possible when they were part of the larger group. Diana thought perhaps this had always been the case. She enjoyed David most when they were in the company of others. He was lighter. Less focused on her. Charming, funny even. And then when they were alone he became serious, critical, brooding. Suffocating. Something in him was softer now, though, and she felt uselessly sad for how things had gone between them.

You never really belonged here, did you, Di?

What do you mean? Her voice was tight. Astute — that's what Nell had always said about him. Dangerously astute. Yes!

Well, I just mean that you've always had to get away from here as fast as you can. Always itching to leave. Not really a country girl at heart. But this time . . . is different, I imagine? And in the way his voice kind of faltered she knew that he loved her. Not like before. But without agenda and with sorrow.

She thought about what he said. It was just that everything happened so slowly here on the island. And everyone knew you. It was either too windy or too sunny or too deathly quiet. Exposed. Sandy. Diana had never been out-doorsy — not like the other island children — with their bleached by the sun hair and long brown limbs, surfboards attached to their hips, their freckled shoulders and their ability to swim like they had gills. Diana was afraid of waves, of being dunked by waves, and hated how sand got into everything. Ears, fingernails, scalp. Nell, too, had been different from the mothers of her friends. She wasn't a tea and scones kind of a woman; she wasn't in the crochet club (though she loved to crochet); and she wasn't a member of the Pioneer Association, although she knew everything there was to know about the history of the island. She was more of a fierce loner, especially after Reg died. The married women saw her as a threat to the wandering eyes of their husbands, or so Nell thought, and so she befriended the rabble as she called it, the flotsam and jetsam that turned up on the island. There was at least one thing Diana did have in common with her mother. With those they loved, they were uncompromising.

When Diana fled to Adelaide as a young woman after Pearl was born, the suburbs with their plush gardens and flat neat tree-lined streets were well kept, well mannered. Adelaide was the stately elder. Composed. Whenever she stayed on the island too long, she started to feel like her mind was losing its sharpness. Like she was pickling and she might never have the wherewithal to get up and leave. She could petrify.

The girls are finding it hard. There's a lot to do. And —

You want to be here?

I don't. Well. Yes, I do, she said quietly.

David fumbled in his jacket pocket and found his cigarettes. He stopped to light one and then loped up to the dry sand and eased himself down. Diana hovered uncertain until he took off his jacket and spread it out for her, patting it encouragingly. She sat beside him, hugging her knees to her chest, tiredness chilling in the small of her back and making her yawn in great gulps.

So she's left the house to you. What will you do?

Diana had given this a lot of thought, but last

219

night hadn't been able to answer David. He hadn't pushed her, he'd just said, Do something for yourself, Diana, but don't rush. Mull it over. She hated mulling, so her first instinct had been to sell — a clean slate. She needed the money, really needed the money, and sitting at Nell's trestle table delicately shading the side of the round house with cross hatching, the pencil making a soothing sighing sound, she considers the two things her mother has given her: art, and now shelter where she thought there'd be none. But the shelter doesn't have to be here, in this wily place. She could build anywhere. With the money, she could start over.

There is the beginning of a plan, but it is too early to take root. She will try to talk to Joe about it later, hopefully, without interference from the daughters.

When she finishes the drawing of the round house and is satisfied with how she's managed to turn a vague sensation of being unmoored into something material, something she can visualise — a thought projected — she takes another piece of paper and places it on top of the sketch, securing it with a couple of stones. Diana moves carefully and deliberately, building up to another urge, which had come to her in a flash during yesterday's funeral service.

The cap of the ultramarine blue tube of paint is stuck fast. Diana rummages in the drawer for pliers and then remembers they'll be hanging on the far wall, a black outline traced around their shape — like they're in a crime scene. She supposes this *is* a trespass, of sorts.

Nanny Di, what are you doing?

Diana turns with a start, pliers in hand, to Ariel framed in the doorway, the sky behind her still milky it's so early.

How come everyone's up already? Ariel says rubbing her eyes. I heard Pearl go and then Nico. And you're up. And Mummy's being sick in the toilet. And Daddy's cross because I woke up Alfie. I didn't mean to.

Diana hears the edge of hysteria in Ariel's voice. She's so over-tired, poor little thing.

Come here, sweetheart. You can help Nanny.

Ariel makes her way around the trestle and folds into Diana, her fairy floss hair so light it tickles Diana's clavicle as she bends over her granddaughter. Ariel's thin little matchstick arms are cold and Diana rubs them and then drapes her own cardigan around Ariel.

But what are you doing, Nanny? You're always in here these days. Mummy said so.

Taking Ariel's hand, Diana leads her to the easel, lifting her up on the stool. I guess I just like it out here. It's very peaceful.

Is it because you're sad about old Nell?

Diana takes a swallow, her back to Ariel as she struggles with the stuck cap and the pliers. Of course they've all been talking about her. Probably even with David, too.

Nanny?

Yes, I am sad. A little bit. About old Nell. She smiles.

But what she doesn't say is that mostly it's because she likes the smell of sheds, especially the painty, dry, comforting smell of this one. And

221

Nell's private coveted space is somehow now slowly becoming hers. She's never been this close to Nell before.

Diana can feel Ariel watching her sceptically as she sets out the palette, the linseed oil and the brushes she cleaned earlier. When she squeezes the blue from the tube, having freed the cap, it is glossy and thick, and Ariel makes a small gasp of pleasure.

Nanny. Are we painting?

Diana doesn't answer but begins adding a little of the linseed oil to the blob of paint and mixing it through. This is not her medium, and she knows it will be impossible to get exactly the same hue and thickness that Nell has used. Her eyes flit between the dried layer of blue on the canvas and the swell of wet paint she's working up with the brush. It takes days, weeks, sometimes, for oils to dry, so the painting is still a changing thing, and Diana begins working in the new layer with a kind of restrained ferocity, painting over Nell's last strokes. It's a feeling of being underwater as she becomes lost in the blue, eddying in the swirls and currents made by her own hand. She doesn't notice Ariel slipping down from the stool and coming to stand at her side, even as Ariel places her hand on Diana's free elbow, steadying her. Filling in the background, working the paint right to the edges and then back in to the outline of the grass tree, she is happy with the way this final layer of blue, Madonna blue, deep and glistening, thrusts the central image forward.

It's a baby made of bones, Ariel says with finality, as though she's been trying to work it out all this time, and breaking Diana's one-pointed focus.

You think?

Ariel sneaks a hand up to finger the pointy tip of the shells.

No, Ariel, don't touch. It's wet.

The little girl withdraws her hand as if she's been slapped. And then Diana is sorry she's snapped at her. She puts the brush down and stands back from the painting, sweeping her arm around Ariel's shoulders.

What do you think, Ariel? Happy with the blue? Diana would like to keep going, but she'll let this layer dry as it is now, shocked at how like Nell she sounded when she scolded her granddaughter.

Yes, Nanny, Ariel whispers, barely audible.

Do you know what those shells are, sweetie?

Diana can feel the quick breathing of her granddaughter through the slip of cardigan, her shoulders shuddering slightly, the back of her neck a little damp. She's always run at a higher temperature, this one. A higher speed, higher metabolism, as if she's burning on some other fast-acting fuel. She was born early, her little body whittled to just the essentials, all bone and muscle and sparkling wide eyes. Gappy teeth. Diana sits on the stool and lifts Ariel into her lap, stroking her damp hair away from her high, glossy forehead.

Let me tell you a story.

Ariel nods and leans back into Diana, her

frame softening now she's been forgiven.

Great-granny Nell had a special shoebox with some very precious things in it. Did she ever show it to you?

No.

Okay. Well some of the things in that box were two necklaces made out of those little shells like the ones in the painting. They're called periwinkles. From a tiny seasnail.

Like teeth. Did Nell wear them — were they hers?

Diana has often wondered that herself. Had tried many times to suggest Nell donate all the objects in the box to the South Australian Museum, or even the Penneshaw Folk Museum. It seemed selfish her holding on to them for so long. Diana didn't get it.

Did Nell cut them up for the painting?

The thought hadn't occurred to Diana, but of course, she probably did do that. She lifts Ariel from her lap, the edge of the stool digging hard into the back of her thighs, and stands.

Maybe. Go on. You can touch the shells now. Just be very gentle.

But Ariel shakes her head. I don't want to now, Nanny, they're too old.

A tendril of memory floats and settles, and Diana stares at a fixed point on the far wall in order to prevent the memory from vanishing. To let it take hold. She strokes Ariel's hair, bundling it into a ponytail, and is careful with her memory while her hands are busy.

★   ★   ★

The day was overcast and rangy and Nell was determined that the two of them were to go on an expedition. Diana, just thirteen, was reluctant, not wanting to spend that long in the car with Nell, and probably hoping to take advantage of the rare opportunity to be left alone for a while, to listen to singles in the living room at full volume. Well one single, the only one she owned — The Hollies's 'Just One Look' — bought from a funny new little section in the Kingscote store, with only just a handful of records to choose from. Not many made their way across the waters to the island. Slim pickings. She'd pleaded with Reg to buy it for her, and he had. But Nell wouldn't be deterred on this day — Diana was coming with her. Nell packed lunch: honey sandwiches, apples, and a thermos of water with lemon slices poked in.

The only thing Diana remembers about the car ride, apart from it being long and hot, is that she got her period on the way and Nell hadn't been very sympathetic, just gave her an old hand towel to shove in her undies, and kept on going.

You're not going to let a bit of blood hold you back are you, Miss Diana? Don't be that kind of girl.

Sometimes Diana wondered if Nell wished she were a boy. And she couldn't stand it when she called her Miss Diana, mockingly, as if she were that kind of girl. So, with her belly cramping and the blood drying sticky between her thighs, they bumped along, Diana holding back tears of frustration. When they took the turn-off into the Gill property, just past the Chapman River, Nell

225

slowed the car as they followed the line of dense pines that edged the dusty road. Nell stuck her arm out the window and waved at Alan Gill mowing in the distance as they passed him, having a kind of arrangement with him that she could visit the property any time. On his land was Lubra Creek, a gathering place for Aboriginal women in the sealing time, and a place Nell liked to visit often, usually alone.

Nell steered the car carefully past the shearing sheds and the back of the old farmhouse 'Freshfields', built by Nat Thomas, a sealer, and his Tasmanian Aboriginal wife, Betty, in 1827, and now owned by the Gill family. Sheets flapped on the hills hoist and a sandy-coloured dog, shaky with age, barked at them half-heartedly as they drove past. Following the edge of another paddock opening out into hills that undulated to the sea and to Lubra Creek on the left, Nell brought the car to a gentle halt on the side of a grassy slope. Nell sat for a moment with the windows down, hushed by the sweeping views of the ocean. Diana couldn't wait to get out of the car, needing to stand and stretch out her cramping belly, but as soon as she stepped into the thick grass, the blood rushed and she had to hold the towel firm. Nell pretended not to notice and Diana could have thrown a rock at her mother except she was too sad.

Nell set off briskly down the slope to Lubra Creek, and Diana could do nothing but follow. She remembers it being beautiful despite her bad mood, thick canopies of mallee, gold-green light, a goanna, watchful — like a gatekeeper. Diana settled against a horizontal branch and splashed her face with water from the thermos, watching Nell squat in the dry creek bed running her fingers through the powdery sand. No water here anymore, just sheep skulls and cattle bones, scattered, like petrified wood. Diana already knew the story of Lubra Creek. This was a women's place, a gathering place for the 'wives' of sealers. But there'd been violence here, too — Nell made sure Diana knew about that — the women punished and tied to trees. Flogged. That word made Diana want to throw up, and it was one of the reasons that she didn't like to go there, thinking of that word. Too many ghosts. Not Nell, though; she thought it a place of power.

Why are you always sulking, Diana? Nell had said, the air hanging fragile between them. It's a beautiful day; we could picnic here. Read a book. Did you bring a book? I bet you didn't even bring a book.

Diana was incredulous. Why would she have thought to bring a book? She didn't even know really what they were doing. She kicked at the sand and stalked back towards the car without replying, thinking she would lie on the back seat. Curl up in the fetal position and wait for the surges of menstrual pain to pass. She'd never been able to talk to Nell about those kinds of things, girl things. She just had to struggle along as if it wasn't happening — like she was in total command and not a bloody disaster, the stuffed-in towel doing absolutely nothing. Diana doesn't remember, now, how long she waited for

227

Nell in the back of the car, welded with sweat to the vinyl seats, but when Nell returned she was gentler — found a box of tissues in the glove box and got rid of the damned towel. Gave her a sandwich, the crusts drying at the edges, but the honey was sugary and revived her.

Come on, I want to show you something else. Something you haven't seen before. Waubs Wall.

They drove to the opposite side of the property back past the homestead and the pine trees and the low stone wall with the plaque that told of Nat and Betty Thomas, and parked the car at the edge of a gully, before scrabbling their way down to the base of a hill.

Wait here, while I go and find the opening, Nell said, squeezing Diana's shoulder.

Diana watched Nell as she almost crawled through little gaps in the bush trying to find a path inwards, and then back out again shaking her head in consternation. The wind was picking up and Diana clamped her hat down firmly, and danced to keep the ants from crawling into her sandals. Why were they here? She remembers thinking that perhaps it was something to do with Reg being away — perhaps Nell felt they should do something, just girls. Diana hoped it was that, but you never knew with Nell. Something else entirely could have been going on.

A little spyhole in the hill, Nell announced, once they'd climbed up. It was steep and sheer behind Waubs Wall. No flat ground to rest upon, just panoramic views of Antechamber Bay, and barely a trace of wind behind the dense screen of scrub. The flattish sandstones were placed on top of one another, creating a kind of rudimentary wall, more than ten metres long, though it was collapsing in places, and at least a metre high. But this wasn't the work of a stonemason, Nell explained, leaning slightly on the wall to catch her breath. Diana wondered how on earth she'd managed to get up here, bashing through bush in Nell's wake, sliding on the narrow animal tracks and scratching her legs and palms.

You could have told me to wear proper shoes, Diana said, emptying the dirt from her sandals.

And she remembers Nell looking hurt then. I've never taken anyone here, not even Reg. I'm surprised I remembered how to even find it.

Well, who was she anyway? Waub?

Nell eased herself down, finding a scrap of stone to perch on, knees hugged in. No one really knows exactly. She was an Aboriginal woman and she lived here, alone, for many years behind this wall. Built it herself.

Why alone?

Well that's the question. For protection? Ostracised perhaps? Uncle Jim thinks there was tension at times between the mainland women and the Tasmanians. But then those caps, you know the red caps I've got, they were a gift from the Van Diemen's Land women to Uncle's people. And the necklaces. A show of friendship? I don't know.

They ate their apples in silence and, finally being out of the wind, Diana began to feel more settled. The pain in her lower belly was just a dull ache now, and they perched there for at least an hour, watching the ocean shimmer and ripple, Nell writing things in her little notebook and chewing the end of her pencil. Diana thinking, with some shame, that it would be a good place to kiss a boy, and wondering when it would be she would have her first kiss. She liked a boy called Rube, and when she listened to The Hollies, she imagined it was Rube singing those words just for her. How foolish she'd been, though, pinning her hopes and dreams on boys too young to know what to do with love. Lust, even. She had always given too much away. There was Pearl's father, too — Paul. She had latched on to him as a way of extricating herself from Nell, she realises now. The first boy to pay her any attention. He was sweet — picked her wilty flowers and wrote her little funny notes. Pearl got her bright blonde hair from him. Every now and again Pearl meets up with him and his wife for lunch. He's so shy with me, Pearl always says afterwards.

When Diana and Nell left the hideaway, Diana grabbed a small stone from the wall and put it in her pocket, wanting a souvenir of not just the day, but of Nell's earlier meanness. Diana was keeping tally. As they stumbled out at the bottom of the gully, she felt guilty and chucked the stone back into the scrub when Nell wasn't looking, struck suddenly by the superstitious thought of being punished — in an other-worldly sense. As she looked back at the sheer face of the hill, she saw that the opening in the bushes where they'd just emerged, the little gap, was no longer visible; it had simply healed over and disappeared.

Places could swallow you up. She didn't think she'd ever be able to find this spot again.

On the way home Nell pulled over when she saw a flowering grass tree. Diana watched from the window as Nell stood for what seemed an eternity in front of the tree, finally picking off some of the little cream flowers growing along its spike. By the time they got home the flowers had shrivelled on the dashboard and Nell brushed them unceremoniously out the car door into the dirt, and popped one in her mouth. She thought Nell quite mad then. But after Nell had gone inside, Diana too ate one of the flowers. Sweet and dissolving.

Diana is surprised at herself for remembering this detail. But this day's imprinted deep in her body.

Nanny, finished painting?

Ariel is crouching on the concrete now, sweeping the sandy floor with the edge of a feather, whispering to herself — acting out the central character in her imaginary game.

It's finished now, she says, wringing her hands. The sudden ache in the guts, chest, womb, bowels, jaw, ears: grief.

I'm hungry.

Why don't you go back to the house, then, and I'll just finish off here?

No, Nanny, I want to stay with you. And don't worry, I won't tell anyone you finished Nell's painting.

Let's get you some breakfast, little nymph; I'll clean up later. All Diana can think is that she needs to flee the shed. Spooked all of a sudden.

As if Nell was watching her on high. Disapprovingly.

Nanny, you're hugging me too tight.

And as they stumble out into the glare of morning — the salty clean bracing wind of it — Diana knows her decision has been made.

Nell

It could be that I'm going crazy, of course. It would not surprise me at all. Just me and my ghosts and my silly desperate thoughts knocking around here now. Sometimes I have the urge to flee from this undoing because the house seems so full, so bristling, so listening. So lonely. I put down my pen and stand quickly so the chair crashes backwards satisfyingly. Briefly, I am naked in the middle of the lounge room floor while I think where my bathers have got to. Reg is there, reminding me to take a hat and cover my shoulders. I laugh at how shocking I must look to Reg now. He saw me neither very young nor very old. I only had a few strands of silver in my hair then and I was proud of them like I'd earnt them. I plucked them out and lined them up on the dresser. Between my breasts was a vertical line like a faint fold and Reg loved rippling his fingers across it. My thighs were strong then and my belly was curved and pliant. My buttocks more of a handful than Reg could manage. I rummage through the pile of clean washing on the couch and Reg wraps his arms around me and he carries me across the threshold and down the winding path of the dune. My hair whips up in his face and he stumbles, but I am light in his arms, so he finds his feet. My nipples prick in the damp air; Reg's rough thumbs are joists in my back. And then I'm kneeling on the sand and he is gone. Vanished. My kneecaps shrink from the jolt of the fall. A pool of water glints in the sun and calls me over and I hear Reg singing 'You Are My Sunshine' in the distance. This was our driving in the car together song. When I stand the sun is a beautiful sealskin around my shoulders. Its colours are mottled, speckled almost, and run from chocolate to grey to something luminous and pewter. Sealskins can forecast the weather, or so I've been told — when the hair rises up, a storm is coming; when the hair lies silky smooth and soft, the day will be fair. A storm is coming. There is blood on my lip and the salt of it the salt of it the salt of it. Is pleasure. I lower myself into the rockpool and the cold of it seems to clamp all the loose muscle of my limbs to the bone. It sharpens me. Underwater, my skin is blanched young and taut and the paint under my nails flakes away. I float on my back but my legs will not stay up. I keep righting myself vertically like those Japanese papier-maché dolls that won't fall over. Diana comes to me, but she is a little girl and she is crying. Has she always been searching for her brother in the rocks and the caves? Seal Brother. Did she always know? Or did I forget to tell her? I couldn't find him either — he didn't want to know me. There was a veto against me making contact. And yet, the memory of Sol is lessening. It's just a wisp and a brightening. I close my eyes and the smell of salt cleans my throat and empties the skull.

My dove in the clefts of the rock,
in the shadow of the cliff,
let me see you, all of you!
Let me hear your voice,
your delicious song.
I love to look at you.

And then Pearl comes to me, her whole body spread across the sky like pregnant rain. She just keeps swelling and swelling, so that I can't tell my size anymore. I could be a pomegranate seed. A spear of samphire. Or I am an entire bedrock. Once I took Pearl to Red Cliffs with Marian and Red. She was ten. We slathered ourselves in the mud that oozed by the water's edge and when it dried our skin pulled tight and we laughed because we were terracotta pots and it would not wash off. If I could make Pearl rain now I would I would. Wash everything clean. Please don't make her wait heavy any longer. She'll grow strange, like me. If I could weep for all lost children I would. So I weep for my own and my tonsils ache. My cheeks ache. I grow a covering like I'm being zippered up — sleek and fine — and suddenly I'm no longer cold. I am perfect. When the next wave sucks back toward the ocean, I glide over the lip of the pool, grazing my belly, juddering at the bladderwrack with my fin, and swim deep down to the bottom, holding my breath. This is where I must go. Beyond words.

Maringani slices the glass scraper along the last of the flesh, cutting the fat and sinew away from the kangaroo skin in quick, jagged motions. Emue's scraper — cool and heavy and smooth. She remembers it in the curve of Emue's hand, and smiles at how neatly it fits her own. Once Maringani has scraped all the flesh from the skin, she turns the tool on its side to use the sharp edge; she cuts two long pieces from the pelts and places them side by side in the sand with the fur facing up. Weellum, kneeling opposite Maringani, holds out a whale ear bone filled with water. She glances up at him and he is looking straight at her, and she notices for the first time that he has a tiny scar by his right eye. She lowers her eyes and flicks sand from the edges of the damp fur. She has missed him. So many moons he has been away. And she won't ask him about Emue, she already knows. Weellum places the curled-up bone with water, in front of Maringani, his thumb accidentally brushing past her breast. His hands rest on the sides of the vessel, and she thinks the container frilly like coral or flowers. William's hands are brown, with wide palms and strong, thick nails. She remembers the dry warmth of them as they skimmed past her, imagines his calluses running along her belly skin. The air thickens like honey. Weellum takes her right hand in both of his and gently unfurls Maringani's fingers from the scraper. She allows him to take the tool from her and place it in the sand. Weellum lowers her hand into the water. She doesn't look at him. Rubbing his thumbs along the inside of her palms and along the lengths of each finger, he washes the sticky kangaroo fat from her. Delicately, he lifts her right hand from the bowl and places it onto her thigh; Maringani watches him looking at the water that runs in rivulets down behind her knee. He takes her other hand, entwines his around hers, and then begins to wash it carefully. Maringani whisks it away, wiping it dry on her shirt. She looks along the curve of the bay to see Minnie crouching in the shallows.

Come. Stand, she says quietly to Weellum.

Traces of dried salt crust around William's calves and ankles — pearly against the red-brown of his skin. She turns on her knees from him and gathers her tools from her sister basket.

$\star$ $\star$ $\star$

William gets up and places one foot and then the other onto the pelts. They feel soft and smooth against the soles of his feet. Maringani pulls the skin up and moulds it around each foot, pressing the edges together firmly. Taking a thin piece of bone sharpened into a point on one end, Maringani sews the shoes together with finely rolled sinew. William looks down at the crown of her head, at her black hair hanging in waves stiff with salt. He stands very still as she sews, feeling the tug as the bone needle is pulled firmly through the kangaroo skin. He feels the tug in his groin. When Maringani has sewn both shoes she presses her hands deliberately into the skin, moulding it, so that it will dry perfectly in the shape of his feet.

Thank yer, William flexes his toes inside the shoes, feeling the coarseness of the kangaroo fur, but also the warmth and protection it gives his feet, raw with cuts and salt from walking on the pointed rocks at the edges of the bay.

Maringani has already moved away to the water's edge. William watches her and wonders whether there is a swelling of her belly that he hasn't noticed before. His cheeks burn at the thought of this. Women are like trees, he thinks. Growing essential fruit. But how will he know what to do? He never wants to hear her scream, like Emue, when Anderson makes her lie with him. He eases back in the sand and remembers the pressure of her fingers against his feet; imagines the temperature of her skin, tight and smooth across her perfectly round belly.

July, 1829

William is reminded of Minnie. There are smears of dried blood on the baby's head and a white, waxy coating that makes it appear lighter-skinned than it is. When Minnie was born he had watched with curious dread from the bushes, and perhaps it was that experience he had called on now to help Maringani. William kisses Maringani's glistening forehead. The skin of her

238

cheeks is polished crimson. As it sucks noisily, the baby's wet, fuzzy hair gleams against Maringani's full breast in the firelight. Maringani motions for William to sit beside her. Kneeling down gently, he smooths the damp curls clinging at Maringani's neck and then takes hold of the baby's foot. It is softer than anything he has ever felt, the sole criss-crossed with thousands of tiny creases, like a crinkled, unblemished square of silk. Maringani leans her head back on the pile of skins and closes her eyes. She is barely able to hold the baby from exhaustion or something else that William is unable to read in her. William slides his arm underneath hers and moves her carefully so that she is propped against him. He has learnt to be so very gentle with her body, learnt to make it sing with his. He puts his arms under hers and supports the baby against her breast. Maringani's hair tickles his chin, so he rubs his whiskers into the crown of her head and he can feel the perfect weight of her body as she sinks against him.

★   ★   ★

Maringani watches William with the baby. It is wrapped in a sling, secured to his chest. Maringani refuses to look at the child, even as he passes it to her for nursing.

Mari yer should see 'is eyelashes — they long. Like yers. Brown eyes. They is gettin' darker. William sits beside her with the fleshy lump lying on his knees, its feet pawing at William's stomach. Maringani turns her face away.

239

Mari, William whispers. I've brought you some ngalaii, he says, holding out the honey he has collected in a wolokaii from the stem of the grass tree, just how she had taught him.

I knows yer tired. I knows, Maringani, I knows. I'll help yer. I'll take 'im away and yer can rest, he says, as she takes the sponge of honey from him.

Bundling up the little boy and putting his little finger in its mouth to placate it, he pads quietly away.

Maringani catches a glimpse of the baby's dark hair against the curve of William's arm as they disappear behind a line of skins drying in the heat of the afternoon; she takes a deep suck of honey to keep her from falling.

★   ★   ★

William decides that Maringani isn't interested in the baby because she is still missing Emue. After he'd returned from the mainland and when he'd finally found Maringani again living alone with Minnie in the bush, he'd asked her if she wanted to go home. But she had wanted to stay. With him. Maringani never utters Emue's name, but there is a faraway look to her now that he can't penetrate. Perhaps she misses the other women too? Poll, who'd stayed on the mainland, and Mooney and Puss, who were god knows where. He imagined after the camp disbanded that Mooney and Puss had stayed with their men. But there was no telling what those women would do once they put their mind to something.

Unease gripped him across the shoulders. His people, all broken up. And his fault, too. He should have protected Emue. And now here's someone so new and helpless on his watch. William worries how they will get sealskins now — how they will get enough with just the two of them hunting, and how they will get their lays without Anderson and the merchant ships. He realises that, for the time being at least, he is the protector of this baby, and he is reluctant to leave him alone with Maringani. Mari needs time to recover. Then he'll know what to do. Wallen's farm perhaps?

William straps the baby on his back and only unwraps it when he hands it to Maringani for its milk. He can't think of anything more dizzying than the smell of the baby's damp neck. He will protect this baby. And when its small fingers grasp at Maringani's hair William's heart just about shatters because she bats those brown hands away. He ignores the copper sheen when the baby's own hair catches the light because it is unthinkable to see Anderson in him. William wants to name the child but Maringani shakes her head at every name he suggests. For weeks, he is just 'boy', until William decides that a son deserves a proper name. He calls him Samuel. Minnie calls him pangar, seal, and Maringani doesn't call him anything at all.

Melbourne

Pearl uses the story-wire now, too. It sits on the little shelf behind her desk and she hopes it can help her understand. From her window, the small square of lawn holds shadows as the day slips away. A low Melbourne sky. The story-wire belonged to a friend, was all Nell had said — but it's for scratching out stories in the sand. Pearl sweeps crumbs from the desk and then leans back in her chair, pressing her spine into the top strut and cracking her shoulders. Sometimes she is afraid of words and what they will bring — the way they can shape things; but also, how open one must be to receive them. They could burn you down to ash, or give you wings, fins, gills. She has read Nell's little book three times. Almost every scene sets off a recollection: something Nell has told her, the overwhelming physicality of an island location, a conversation, a dream, a memory, a smell. All of these things inside the story. It is like a topography — this book. Everything she knows of Nell can be tracked. And everything she doesn't know. Pearl places the story-wire round her neck and closes her eyes. She wants to recall the salt-collecting day, almost eight months ago now.

She'd half run half slid down the dune to the beach, the canvas bag with all the salt-collecting things banging against her legs rhythmically. Nell followed more carefully behind with the water bottles and her cloth hat scrunched up in her hand. When Nell caught up with Pearl they'd walked to the furthest end of the bay, the sun firm on their necks. Nell paused every now and again to pick up shells, but also to cough. Planting her hand square in the middle of her chest she coughed lightly, more like a clearing of the throat, and then some bright or worn shell or stone would catch her eye in the sand and she'd stoop from the hips to inspect. Pearl wondered whether Nell was trying to take attention away from her breathlessness. It was like walking the length of the beach with a child — they got nowhere.

Will you see Diana on your way home? Nell had asked.

Probably not. I have to be back for the school holidays. We've got Lewis for the whole lot this time. I'll call her tonight maybe.

And how is Lewis?

He's um, quite lovely and a bit . . . quiet.

Oh?

Well, I don't know. We're very close but I can never quite get to him. He worries a lot, I think. About his mum. About us. Something like that.

It must be confusing for him, going back and forth.

Well yes. But he's fine with it.

The conversation went something like that and Pearl remembers now that she'd been annoyed with Nell bringing up the back and forth. As if she was such an expert. But then,

Pearl supposes, she was.

The water nipped gently at Pearl's ankles, her chipped silver nail polish glinting in the colourless water. She remembers that image like a photograph. And the whole uncluttered expanse of the bay lying before them — the dramatic slate cliffs in the distance too sheer, as if they'd been split clean like a log. Something cleaved.

They'd talked about Crete and how beautiful the beaches were there, but how they were strewn with litter. And they talked about how Nico was desperate to take photos without any rubbish in the background. Or even people. We're so lucky to have this, she'd said to Nell, gesturing to take in the whole lot, the water, the dunes, the muddy frothy inlet.

Yes, I remember, Nell said. You sent me your 'rubbish series' of photographs. And a mountain herb pressed between pages.

Oh god. I did. Yes.

It still has a smell to it. Even three years later.

Well getting close to four years now, thinks Pearl, and she sucks in sharply as if she's been struck in the chest. The same reaction she'd had then on the beach.

Nell had grabbed Pearl's wrist and squeezed it, pecked Pearl quickly on the cheek. Pearl leant down and pulled on her sandshoes, and Nell began clambering up the first clump of rocks. Pearl followed, scrunching up her toes inside the damp and gritty shoes. The rocks were nibbed and spiked and pitted and held bowls of shining water in large craters. She is like a mountain goat, thought Pearl, observing Nell's quickening pace once they were on uneven terrain. Her arms and legs were brown angled sticks, her skin buffed to sheeny velvet, as she picked on ahead. Pearl remembers this imprint of summer — how bright the sun was compared to the quiet deep dusk of now. Of winter.

They reached a rockpool, neck-deep, and the water gushed in from the ocean side. She'd swum in the same pool with Nico and Lewis in the days after Nell's wake, and when they'd hopped out and were all wrapped up in their towels, they noticed a black stingray butterflying around the white scaly edges of the rockpool. Pearl and Nico looked at each other in alarm and didn't mention it to Lewis. She gazed into the depression and made a wish. The same one. In Crete, she lit votive candles inside humpy whitewashed churches. On Kangaroo Island, she prayed mostly to water.

It was reading about Maringani scraping salt at the lagoon that took her back here, to the rockpools and the salt and the stingrays, and to Nell squatting down, hitching up her skirt into her knickers. Nell clamped her hat on her head impatiently, as she always did, like she was annoyed by having to worry about such inconveniences. Pearl hurried over, wincing at the pointy rocks digging in even through the rubber sole of her shoes. She crouched beside Nell and slipped the canvas bag from her shoulder. She passed Nell a spoon and set out the containers. The salt was bright, tessellated, and crusted the edge of the dry pool in rough

245

crystals. Pearl stuck her finger into it, the top layer cracking. Nell scraped the spoon through the whitest part and collected the salt, banging the spoon on the container's edge to plop out the contents. Pearl followed with her own spoon, careful to avoid the watery grey parts. The edges of her fingernails stung. This is a memory overlaid and overlaid from every time she's collected salt with Nell. The stinging was because she bit her fingernails.

Nell had asked her about work. The bookshop. And they'd discussed how books made a room beautiful. They'd mentioned the smell of paper. Pearl told Nell that once she'd been asked to recommend a book for a dying child. How do you ever choose such a book? When the customer left, the book all prettily wrapped, she'd cried.

The two of them had then moved wordlessly over to the next pool and started on a new container. There was salt in little dips and curves everywhere like white shadows. Like snow. The scraping rhythmical, Nell first and then Pearl shadowing.

I was always writing little books and poems when I was a girl. I've got drawers full of them. Little books all stapled together with funny names, like *Duck Girl*, Nell explained.

Ha. You do? You should show me.

I'm writing a bit at the moment, Nell had said.

It was the first Pearl had heard about writing. She'd always thought painting was Nell's thing.

I don't have *things*, Nell said, irritated. I'm what you might call a dormant writer. I was always writing as a girl. Making up stories. But I stopped at some point. Just couldn't. My words were drops of rain disappearing on concrete.

Pearl remembers Nell's face then. Brown, strong, lean. A warrior. This image of Nell is forever emblazoned.

She wanted to ask her more about the writing, but Nell was already walking off around the next corner of rocks, one hand wedged into the small of her back, the other steadying herself on rock ledges. And so there it was. The only time they'd ever spoken about writing, a passing conversation, etched now forever, and this story unfolding before her. What was Pearl to do with it?

Afterwards they'd spread the salt out thinly on trays to dry off in the sun. There is still a whole jar of salt left from that day, sitting on her kitchen bench in the next room, a little of it spooned into an earthen dish for crushing straight onto cooking. The salt day was the last day she ever spent with Nell — she has run through every detail of it over and over and over again, combing their conversation. Sitting at her desk now, she looks up the word 'dormant'. *Lying asleep or as if asleep. Torpid. In a state of rest. Quiescent. Inoperative. In abeyance.* Are you still a writer if you don't write? How long had Nell been dormant? What awoke her out of torpor and why? She looks up the word 'write'. Etymologically speaking, its meaning is associated with cutting, rubbing, tearing, scoring, incising, writhing. All of these activities can be done to the body, thinks Pearl, as much or more so, as to sand or bark or clay or paper. Is writing a kind of writhing, she wonders. Did Nell come to accept that to write is to also incise, involve herself bodily? Pearl has a headache. The only thing she knows is this. We each have a body. And we each have a story. In the end, only the story remains. And Nell's is just so full of gaps, so dripping with honey-drenched holes. She rests her palm on Nell's little red book. Her beautiful heart story. She opens to the very last page.

Nell

So, the story went something like this, but of course, it's not the beginning. Sol's ancestors — long before Maringani and William — already knew white danger would come from the sea; the fires of knowledge had warned them so. Their sacred story fires were always burning, before the pale men arrived, and are still burning, so that as I write this, I know my words fall short. That beyond words there are ways of seeing, ways of knowing, that illumine the currents between all things — the connective tissue of the universe.

All I have of Sol now is his story-wire — a lightning rod to bring down words — and the smell of smoke in my clothes from all that burns.

Pearl, I hope you read this story, and I hope you understand that I've held it in me always, but that I had to wait for the words to come. That now I burn with fever. Fire that renews. And dear Pearl, please release this story from the heart place where it grew.

1831
Three Wells River

William has been told the story many times but still doesn't believe it. He imagines his father unbreakable. A tree that will not fall. A fire that will not go out. Hewn of rock and timber, is Anderson. Sturdy stuff. He is of this earth. Taken by water, in the end. William sees it clearly in his mind — the way his father's body must have turned over and over, filled to the gills with water, becoming debris, swollen with dying and rolling in the undertow. There was nothing to be done, Munro said, he drowned. Would Anderson have thought of William in those last moments? Of his mother? Emue? Maringani? He shudders. But William's days are spread out cleanly now without a wrinkle. Here at the settlement there is plenty to be done with the crops and the hogs and the wallaby skinning. And now there's no Anderson to take them by surprise. The girls are safe. And baby Samuel. Yet he aches for his father — the briny, manly smell of him a primal stirring — even if it makes him sick to think of it and that awful night and the faraway look of Maringani sometimes. She is better here, just being with the women, 'Guvner' Wallen's wives, Sal and Suke, and the others from Van Diemen's Land with their close curly hair, and different song in their voice — Palawa — and Mooney, who is here with Munro. William remembers when he'd first clapped eyes on Maringani — the jut of her chin and her wide scared eyes, straight hair like reeds. But especially he remembers how much light she brought. She was like an unexpected flower quivering in the new air. Even then, she made him smile in spite of himself. Even then, he worried for her knowing what men could do.

He turns the soil, black and loamy, spreading it over the first green shoots of the potatoes, covering them up for they grow in darkness. Like me, he thinks, not able to remember much of anything but the cold and the dirt and his father's big hands before Maringani came. Behind him are the rows of cabbages, little nubs still forming in the folds of their leaves, and the fowls strutting and scratching and clacking between them. And further in the distance, on the sloping bank of the river, is Wallen's log hut, leaning crooked to the west — held up it seems — by the stone chimney built at one end. The bark of the exterior is rough, stringy, and all the piccaninnies, as Wallen calls them, like to pull at the fibres until Guvner chases them away with his stick. But he is gentle with them. And this is what William admires most in the guvner — he is a kind of chief hereabouts but doesn't use his lordship to make others small or do his bidding. Not like it was before. And so here they all are, chipping in, the men more like their wives now, draped in skins and digging for water. Talking in language. Smelling like foxes, say the ones who don't stay — say the ones who pass through, tossed in by the sea, taking skins and salt — leaving rum, sugar and heavy-booted footprints. William doesn't envy them at all. No, this is the life.

He checks on the watermelons by knocking on them. They're a way off yet.

Lately, he's been thinking there never was a mother, or house, otherwise wouldn't he have a memory, even just a song of one? His skin, though not like Maringani's, darkens up in the sun and he is always in the sun, and it doesn't blister and peel and welt like Anderson's. If he makes the space in his skull very still and spacious, he thinks his first impressions are of green green light, mosquitoes, saltwater, singing. Somewhere else.

★   ★   ★

Maringani can feel it again. First it was a dream, a knowing, and now it's a quickening inside. It will come when the nights are getting colder, when the Maringani stars appear in the sky, but before the song of the whales, kondoli. In her sleep she sings it into being. As she weaves, she stitches in time to this new heartbeat, winding the rushes over and through, the mat growing in her lap like her family's growing. Different, this time, she knows. Maringani sits with Sal — Maggerlede to the women — at the entrance to the wurlie. Sal with her grubs and kalathami, native currants, stored in her frizzy hair, and the dogs lying around her, muzzling in, had been the one to rub Maringani in wallaby fat and bring water to her lips when first they arrived here. She'd been cold — so cold on the inside like she was just bones.

There is smoke coming from Guvner's chimney and Sal waves her hand towards it. Guvner back.

Together they speak in that third way. Not Palawa. Not Ngarrindjeri. But in the short quick falling stones of the men, yet not quite. More

252

like stones falling into water — they'd made something new.

Guvner had been gone for some time. Down at Nepean Bay along with Munro and Piebald, William said, trading his wares — skins, vegetables, wheat — with the hookers, the small vessels passing through. When Guv was gone his wives and the little boy stayed down at camp, scared of the wind through the cracks in the hut, and the snake that got in one day and could not get out again. But sometimes, Maringani thought, those wives looked at her cold. Spoke Palawa only. They were back in the hut now, making tea from swamp ti-tree, grinding wheat for damper.

She puts down her weaving, smoothing the sweep of rushes that stick out and are yet to be woven in. Standing, she stretches out the back of her knees, and sees William in the garden, making those melons so sweet. She waves to him and he calls her over. One of the dogs follows, licking her hand as she walks along the track to the garden, and then barks wildly as they pass the penned-in hogs.

Guvner's back. And Piebald.

She nods. He puts his hand at the small of her back and even through the fine sealskin, she feels the scar from his burning. Knows it's there, and turns into it, taking his hand to her lips and holding it there. He tastes of the earth. Scorched earth. And she knows just how completely he can set her aflame.

We'll take 'im something. An offering, he says, looking towards the hut, there'll be a feast tonight. William curls his hand around the back of Mari's neck. She folds into his chest.

Tiyawi, she thinks. And then says, Iguano. She frees herself from William to get the brugi, the fire, the coals going. She'll cook it sweet. With ant eggs and waikeries. The children run past in a flock, shrieking, and setting off the kukaki, the kookaburras laughing.

King George Beach (Sandy)

In the heart of Diana's newly built room — shell room — there is a pot-belly stove with a fire burning, orange flames licking the glass brightly. They're new flames. Just lit. Not yet the deep warmth of coals. Diana kneels before the door of the stove. The room is round but just before it makes a complete circle it widens out to a small passageway, more of an opening, and begins to loop around again. The beginnings of a spiral. She stands and walks to the entranceway, pushing open the wooden door, stepping over the woven mats as she crosses the threshold. Her hand rests on the little shelf made into the wall for a candle. Outside the air is wet on her cheeks. The grasses on the dune pressed flat in the wind. She turns towards the alcove and lights the tea candle, dropping it down into its glass holder. Uncle Jim died yesterday. Diana walks the perimeter of the stone room, the light so washed out it could be dusk but it's only morning. Every stone for the building was found here on the island and placed carefully by hand. Uncle had worked with Joe and Nico and the girls to find the stones — helping out whenever he visited the island. It had taken more than a year to collect all the pieces. It's a kind of cairn, she thinks, this shelter. Diana wraps her shawl tightly and takes the path down the dune. She should have more clothes on, but she's not turning back now. Stooping against the wind she weaves down the hill, the path so familiar her feet know just what to do. The beach is wind-tossed. Driftwood scattered along its length. Spinifex uprooted and spinning along the sand. Seaweed banked up in a series of mounds at the highest watermark makes it look messy. She sinks into the scratchy dampness of the seaweed. Jim once told her he'd slept in one of these pillowy seaweed channels. Just for an afternoon, he said, winking. Best nap I've ever had with the sun beaming down on me and the sea singing lullabies.

Diana first met Uncle Jim when she and Nell had gone to stay at the Ngarrindjeri Cultural Centre, in the Coorong. Nell insisted. David had just left Diana and she wasn't coping. Nell said it would give her some time out. Their dormitory was sparse and utilitarian. Diana had lain awake all night, swatting at fat, slow mosquitoes, listening to Nell snoring, and to the wind whipping eerily around the concrete building. In the morning, they were up early for a strong, sugary cup of tea and workshops: fabric marbling, weaving, a bush foods walk. Diana had been fascinated watching the barefoot children that ran together in a clump right to the edges of a weedy paddock, or in and out of cabins under construction. As a child, she'd always wished for a gang, a clan, to carry her along. Her childhood had been lonely. But her first memory of Uncle Jim was him telling off a little girl who'd used the wrong bathroom — the boys' instead of the girls'. Diana had looked to Nell. There are strict rules for boys and for girls, Nell explained simply.

Diana tucks up her hair and wraps the shawl around her ears. Her fringe is going to dry funny now, and the wind makes the bones of her face ache. She's ploughed a track through the seaweed — a little trench of water ribboning in her wake. Diana's not quite sure what she's looking for. She'll know when she sees it.

At that first visit to the Cultural Centre, Diana smoked almost as much as Uncle, so she'd spent many hours beside him sitting on crates by the outside wall, stubbing their butts into a bucket, while Nell made silk scarves with the women inside. Diana, Diana, Diana, he said, what can we do for you? Nothing, Uncle. I'm just taking a break from everything. He nodded. Do you have your mother's island thing — interest? I guess, she said. But she didn't really. To her, the island was always its same old self — beautiful and stifling. She couldn't have imagined, then, ever moving back.

In the cultural museum, she'd sensed something she couldn't explain. The artefacts were not lying mutely; they were not like the dusty relics she'd gawped at on school excursions. Diana spent hours in the hushed half-lit room, leaving Nell to her socialising, and she began to notice, to pay attention. The artistry in the fish traps, the spears, the baskets, the shields, the clubs, an archive of knowledge that she could only glimpse at. It overwhelmed her. The graceful curve of the plonggi, the fighting stick, perfectly honed to be held comfortably in the hand, and the weavings, all made on slow time, and created for protecting, transporting and carrying. This was art not separate from its utility.

Diana squats at the edge of a pool and a pelican lands in the distance; it bobs on the choppy water. That gullet, she thinks. Perfectly suited to its needs. The end of her shawl drops into the pool and she whisks it out. Christ! Diana straightens, her hands on her hips, and another pelican joins the first and then another. She looks on, incredulous.

Near the end of their stay at the Coorong, Uncle and Nell had been yarning, yunnan, and Diana remembers Jim talking about ruwe, country, lands and waters and all living things. And ruwar, body and spirit. Ruwe and ruwar are those overlapping words at the centre of the Ngarrindjeri concept of wellbeing. All things assessed as being healthy and lawful according to Ruwe. Everything is connected, he said. His body got sick because his country was sick. Like so many Elders, he was exhausted caring for country. The Murray River is dying, he had said then. We need whitefellas, like your Nell, to come on board with us. Protect our spiritual waters. Diana had been too caught up in her own lonely situation to realise the significance of the conversation then. To realise she was part of something much bigger than herself.

Caroline told her yesterday that Uncle's heart just stopped. He was working at his computer and his heart just gave out, she said. Pelicans were his ngatji, his totem. There are six of them now, gathering at the water's edge. Diana walks towards them, going slowly over the jagged rocks. In her pocket is her seal brother letter. Her hand closes around it. The pelicans all face the same direction, sitting on the water, drifting.

★   ★   ★

Diana places the pelican feather on the hearth of the fire and hopes it will dry out. After the whole mob of pelicans had shaken themselves out and swung into the sky, flown away, one feather remained, caught in the dry seaweed.

She studies it now to understand its design. She wonders whether the white part will brighten when it dries. On the opposite wall Nell's last painting hangs like a promise. It is finished now — the blue at the edges all filled in. Through the bay window facing the ocean, the light spills suddenly and everything gleams — the scrub, the sky, the crests of the waves. Diana stokes the fire and puts in another log. It makes a ticking noise as it catches. A curl of smoke drifts past the side window, and beyond the haze, the main house nestles squatly in the dunes. Further on, Marian and Red's outside light is still on. When the daughters aren't around, Diana rarely makes it back over to Nell's house from the shell room. It's too cold to make the walk across. And the space is so small it holds heat right to its edges when the fire's been on all day. Sometimes she sleeps on the wooden bench under the window, or by the fire right on top of her feather quilt. She's beginning to understand this place. So wet and clean and stunning.

Diana lights another candle and sets it in the middle of the table. She turns on the stereo. She needs music when she's working. The letter had come benignly with a stack of bills. Now, she takes it from her pocket and smooths it out. She'd opened it unknowingly when it arrived, but that was in the weeks after Nell's death — almost two years ago. She'd scanned her eyes down the page, and everything took on new startling definition. It was as though she'd stepped out from a cave she'd been sheltering in. Hiding in. She walked out into a crescendo of sound and sensation as the words on the page dropped into place. She remembers thinking, Why is it that some days are just ordinary days, and others, you find out you have a brother, or your mother dies, or your child is born, or your beloved cat drowns. Why is it that some days, the fabric of your world tears open and you fall into the fissures, changed forever — bruised and transformed all at once. Lucy wept and gripped on to a stony-faced Pearl — just like when they were little — after Diana showed them the letter. Nell's grief belonged, now, to all of them.

This letter she will not burn. Not ever. Not like the others. She tears it into three clean pieces.

Being Nell's next of kin meant the request had come to her. The son, her brother, had been notified of his birth mother's death. The son, her brother, wanted to make contact.

She places the first strip carefully onto the archive paper. This will be the first of the triad. She hadn't thought to work in the image of a pelican feather before. Maybe for the last in the series, she thinks. Yes, for the last. For this first one she'll sketch the fine hairs of sealskin: the pelt like the flattened grasses on the dune — so many colours when you look up close.

On the day they were to meet — just months after the letter came — she'd spent hours beforehand in the art gallery on the mainland trying to still her nerves. This was her solace; this was to galvanise her. She'd spoken to him on the phone. They'd emailed. But she was so nervous about seeing him in person. Would she be able to handle it if he looked like Nell? Or if he didn't? What if he looked like Diana? And so there she was in the gallery. The emerald walls, the parquet floor, all the creative endeavours fully realised and on display were long ago witnesses to a kind of awakening in Diana, and so she needed them again. She stood in front of the Ngarrindjeri sister basket, woven from sedge, and admired its perfect circles, its long neat handles, and tried with her eyes to follow the spiral of the weaving. It was so clear and so unfathomable. During that first visit to Camp Coorong with Nell, it was in the learning to weave with the women, the aunties, that her sorrow over David began to unfurl. They sat around a big table with the rushes of varying lengths in the middle. The women spoke in low, gentle voices and she had never felt so welcome, so accepted with all her failings. Aunty Ellen sat up close beside her and got her started on the weaving. You're making a spiral — begin in the centre, like this. She showed her how to bend the rushes over and stitch them together to form the heart of the weaving. The hardest part is getting started, she said. And later, We need fresh water for our rushes. When the land salts up our rushes die. The council has been growing us big ones. Great big long rushes we use for weaving kondoli and pondi. Diana remembers that each time she brought in a new reed to the weaving more tears would come and the women kept talking, or laughing like a song, or they were quiet, and all together they were a held circle for that moment in time. Even Nell was gentle then.

And so that day, before meeting her brother, Aunty Ellen's basket in the gallery was a touchstone. You keep adding the sedges like family, Aunty says. All at different stages, all connected. The blood was thumping in her ears, her heart was muscling so fast.

Diana would have been kinder to Nell if she'd known. If only she'd known. She always imagined that the brother in Nell's selkie story was hers. And, she supposes now, he was. Seal brother.

The second in the triad will have a weaving pattern as its backdrop. She already knows how she'll use the different edges of the charcoal to show its warp and weft. But first, something else. The words she'd torn up yesterday — strips of paper like fallen petals in the fruit bowl. Diana takes one curl of paper and uncrumples it with the edge of her hand.

Regarding our recent discussions about your current situation I am offering the following legal information below for you to consider.

The Aboriginal Ordinance Act 1918 places restrictions on Aboriginal people's rights to marry whom they choose; namely, legal permission is required. While the law is particular to the Northern Territory, in your daughter's case, there are certainly ways to obstruct the marriage, if you so desire.

She is hot at the back of her neck as if great angry roses bloom on her skin. Then she scrubs at the words with her nails, tearing the paper, until the words have no meaning at all. Diana incises the paper as the words once incised Nell. She rips them up. They are just drifts of torn snow. They are just drifts of torn snow that flurry and settle. Second triad.

mar ry

obstruct

ghts

part

de

sire

Diana kneels by the fire again and opens the door of the potbelly. The heat of the fire flaring against her cheeks makes her forget, even momentarily, how long she ached for that brother. For Samuel. The ache is still there even though she's found him. Nell would have loved his hands. Just like Nell's own. And that funny crease at the bridge of Nell's nose — he has that too.

She takes from the mantle the package of letters tied up in a ribbon. All week, she's been looking at them. Today is the right day. The scene with the pelicans earlier. Jim. Yes, now is the right time. She unties the package and spreads out the notes. Diana wonders why her grandmother held on to them, yet went to such lengths to keep them hidden.

Pearl and Lucy will never know exactly why Diana finally decided not to sell the house. It's their own fault, though, she thinks. Diana had been the one to scrupulously go through everything, even while they criticised her. She'd been the one to make painstaking piles: for keeping, for the op-shop, for throwing away, for Pearl, for Lucy, for Diana, for the children, for the museum. She'd been the one to pack up an entire life, and so this was her reward. She'd been the one to find Sol's letters in her grandmother's recipe book — wrapped up in newspaper and folded into the back lining. They belong to her now. She won't ever tell the others about the letters. Let me be the one to finally understand Nell, she consoles herself. Let me have this Nell. My mother. I am greedy for her.

Each note catches quickly, the yellow paper brittle with age. Tinder. And they flare brightly before blackening. Carbon. What good are these words now, Diana thinks, if Nell never saw them? And if she did see them, well it was all too late. Nell, she whispers, I am sorry. Sol. Samuel. Dad. Dad, god I miss you. Diana had found out all

she could about Sol's whereabouts. He'd
enlisted. She wonders how cold it was in Sol's
bones in El Alamein — the desert at night, cold
as diamonds, and as pure. The tears run into her
mouth.

Nell

I want to tell you this. Last night there was a light that kept me awake. It came through the rip in the curtain and it made the whole room bright. The humps of the others sleeping were sharp at the edges like big rocks under the moon. You see, it was the moon. I saw it sliding past the curtains. But it was not the moon I'm used to, the gentle one. It was yelling wake up wake up wake up. My whole body was twitching. Bursting out of my skin. I wanted to run outside climb up the iron shed. Shout your name across the paddock. But I stayed where I was. Aunty's been ill. Sleeping lightly. Not yet snoring. I didn't want to wake her and start her up coughing again. Then the little ones would start up too. But Nell all I could think of was you. Your hair on the pillow. We have the same moon. Did it wake you up too? We have the same moon, same paddock, same wind. Same trees stringing between us. I stared into the rip in the curtain and wanted you.

★ ★ ★

It will be soon. I'm chucking my hat in the air. Clicking my heels. You better watch out Nell. I'm coming to check the hives Tuesday for your mum. Hettie is getting better. Thanks for asking she says and she says very keen on that ginger you mentioned please. It was a fever that went to her chest like you thought. She says she swam, chasing after the little ones who were very naughty to go in the water — before the dandelion flowers had properly died off. before the Muntjingarr, what you call Seven Sisters, were moving on a bit. Water still in chill. Brings sickness. We are not allowed to swim for a couple more weeks. If I don't get to talk to you much on Tuesday know this. I would plait your hair every night if I could. Your Sol. Don't swim.

★   ★   ★

Nell, I got your note. I will meet you by the grass tree. The one with two stems. I'm worried to know you're sad. I aint going nowhere, Nell. I'll be waiting for you. Tomorrow night and always. S

★   ★   ★

Nell darling, Hettie says we must get married. It's the only way to make your folks okay with this whole thing. And so we can be together every day, always talking, always touching, never going our separate ways home like you said. Hettie heard me sneaking out last night and was waiting up for me when I come home. At first, I was gonna lie she looked that grim, but she kept saying tell me the truth boy or

267

forever hold your tongue. I told her everything about us. Except that we been finding ways to meet long before now. I played it down a bit. But she knew we met up last night. She's clever that way but I couldn't wipe the smile off my face so it probably wasn't too hard to tell. She likes you, Nell. Not quite as much as I do, mind you. Hettie says it will all work out. I'm jumping for joy. Clicking my heels. Honey harvest in 2 weeks, so I can see a lot of you then. Official! Hettie says we shouldn't meet in secret anymore so we don't mess everything up. I'll have to speak to your father. What do you think, Nell my girl? I love unplaiting your hair too! Your loving Sol xx

⋆   ⋆   ⋆

Next time I see you, I'll go down on my knees, I promise. I've upset you. I haven't heard nothing from you. You okay? I could feel you across the table. The more I tried not to think about all that space between us, the more I couldn't bear it. Makes me jingle and jangle. And the sting, I'm alright y'know. It's just I was thinking about what I was gonna say to your father bout us getting married and wallop I was stung. It was like a hot wire pincing. Couldn't think straight. I am reading too much into it. I've noticed I'm doing that lately. When I see you, I know everything is good between us. The best things could be. But when I don't see you, I have mad ideas. Too long apart. Let me know how you are. What you've been up to.

* * *

Nell where have you gone where have you
GONE.

* * *

Nelly! Nell. Hettie and I was that worried we
came to see you and you weren't there. I'm
still putting these notes in our spot. Hoping
you'll find them. Not giving up.

* * *

Nell. Honey. I hope this letter finds you. I've
writ you that many. Where are you? Please let
me know everything's okay. Is it my fault Nell?
Your mum says your staying with cousins in
Adelaide and helping out in a button shop.
You never said anything about cousins. Or buttons. Not ever! Your mum's so sick of me
badgerin her that she says I'm not to work for
her anymore. It don't bother me. It wasn't that
kinda work — she didn't pay me and I thought
we was all friends. Neighbours. You see Nell it
was all about you. And the bees, they brought
us together, don't you think? That's why I was
always comin' around. And Aunty said I had to
help your mum with your dad sick and no
brothers. So that's how it was and I liked
things the way they were. If I'd known you was
going, I'd of kissed you more. Told you more
things.
     Your mother was real sad when last clapped

269

eyes. I think she misses you. But I worry for you Nell. She's a tough bird that one. She's gonna turn that sadness into something real hard. It scares me. I know she thinks I'm not good enough. I could be. You used to think so too.

Your old man wrote down this address and told me not to breathe a word to your mother or anyone. Which is further proof your mum don't approve of me. Please write. Please talk to me. I'll wait. Remember last summer when I sat all night outside your bedroom window? I slept with my back to the wall. And you never came. Your dad was in a fever and you were helping your mum. Well I'm waiting like that now. Back to the wall. Geranium perfume tickling my nose. And through the cold. You know how I hate the cold. How it gets in my bones and won't leave. But I'm waiting. Nell, I'm waiting this out.

★　★　★

Still nothing back from you, I'm breaking. I'm never gonna be the same. Sorry Nell. I upped sticks and came here for yaccaring. Antechamber Bay. What else is there for me to do? The yaccas are nice and close to the road here, so's I don't need my own transport. Just an axe and a hook and a pile of jute bags. Hettie's gonna lose the farm, and so I got no other prospects now. Nothing to offer you. It's no wonder you've turned away.

By the end of the day, I'm coated in red dust

head to foot like I'm ochred up for ceremony. And the sweat runs down like rivers through the red dust of me. Like tears. I'm just a body now, and I can put it to work — yaccaring, laying roads, farm jobbing, eucalypting. I like being with the yaccas, your grass trees best. I think you know why. And I can turn these bags of gum into food on the table just by flexing my muscles. I can put in the effort. Keep my reaping hook sharp. I'm just dragging this body through sunup to sundown. Trying not to think of you.

It's a small camp near the old sealers hut at Chapman River. Just me and a couple other fellas sharing a tent made of hessian. Dirt floor. Cooking up potatoes and onions for dinner. Yarning by the fire at night. Especially with Tiger Simpson — he's a character alright. He says he's camped on every three-quarter mile of road in the Dudley district and I believe him. Tiger's got everything we need out here piled up in his old wheelbarrow including a banjo and we sing at night. In the day we strip the gum from the trees with our axes. It's my job to keep moving the boat around the trunk — that's the little tray that catches the fibres and the gum. When it's full I tip it out onto the canvas spread round the bottom and then I tie it all up in a bundle and haul it over to the jigger for sifting. The damn thing gets shaken by hand and that arm shuddering job falls to yours truly. But the gum's fine as sugar once it's gone through the sieve. All set to be sent off overseas for explosives. Isn't that a thing!

271

Nell, you should see what happens when you set fire to the trees. I wish you could see.

Last night Tiger showed me how you can nibble on the spear of the grass tree. It's like sugared almonds, Nell. The only sweet thing out here in this dusty place. And then he got me thinking about something that's like glass in my foot now. I can't forget it. Every move I make, wham, it hurts.

Do you remember last year when little Lizzy my cousin wasn't allowed to be the fairy in the school concert? She cried and she cried those pretty brown eyes of hers. And we couldn't understand why she wasn't picked? She was the smallest and cutest. And she was the lightest one to fly through the starry sky we all helped paint. But that great lump Amelia was picked. They couldn't even get her off the ground. Well, Tiger says it's because Lizzy got black in her. I suppose I knew this was why all along, but I didn't want to know it if you get my meaning. It got my 'Tassie up' as Tiger likes to say. Tiger says I gotta be more proud, like him. Flaunt it, he says. You're a blackfella he says. And don't you go getting cold-footed, he says. He says I should enlist. Tiger's the proudest Anzac I know, Nell. He never misses the parade down in Adelaide. So I guess I'm considering it even with this glass in my foot. And it seems you won't have me now.

I've been thinking a lot out here about everything and I can't be stripping gum trees my whole life. And you? Will you be selling buttons forever? I imagined something different for

us. But Tiger's calling me now. We're tying
some bits of old tin together. Rain coming. I
just wanted you to know where I am. So I'm
giving you these words Nell — it's everything
I've got now.
   Love,
   Your Solomon of the bees

1849
Lubra Creek, Antechamber Bay

Maringani likes the way everything is hushed in
the creek bed. The in and out breath of the
ocean, muffled and regular, and the shade so
thick, the women sleep here in the heat of the
afternoon. She will not go near the tree where
Poll was lashed. That tree is very sad now. But
this is a women's place and they protect it so
that it will take care of them in return.
Maringani and Betty and Minnie and Mary of
Blackfellows in Hog Bay, and Waub, too, and the
older children, are talking fire. They've been
camping out, waiting for the winds to be right,
the spirit to be ready. Tomorrow, in the cool of
the morning they will spread out from here and
light spot fires in the grass. They will walk
barefoot, fanning and coaxing the flames. Cold
fires. The light of the fire bringing life, and the
smoke, the spirit, will cleanse. Fire is at the heart
of all things, Maringani knows. It is kin. In the
hearts of grass trees, even, there is fire. Without
fire, the grass trees cannot regenerate.
   But it is difficult now, burn grass time, with all

the fences and the land carved up, so it takes more planning, more discussing. Especially after the trouble Sal and Suke got into with the settlers. They're in hiding now. Maringani fingers the shells around her neck Sal had given her when they'd all cleared out from Three Wells River. She thinks of the shells as little ocean songs, the way they trick the light, and are blue and green and like the moon and the sea all at once.

Betty pulls her red knitted cap down low and rests against the trunk of mallee, her chin sinking into the folds of her neck. It is not because Betty is tired, but because she does not agree with Waub, and so she shuts her eyes. Waub is a loner. No kin. Just herself and the stone wall she built overlooking the gully. And so, Betty decides Waub has no say — she doesn't have a farm or Nat Thomas's reputation at stake. Anyway, Bet is the queen around here with her lovely Freshfields, a house just like the settlers'. She found a bar of gold, too — struck lucky! Waub thinks it's time for a hot fire, to burst open the hearts of the trees, but Maringani knows that even though Waub is right, it is too dangerous. She will go along with Bet for now. Minnie is there, too, and tiny, with her long stick-like arms and legs and a shock of wiry, white hair, which the children like to decorate with combs and flower-chains and shiny bits of shell. Maringani holds the glass scraping tool and runs its cool edge along her thigh. Whenever she is apart from William, it reminds her of him. And of Emue, of course.

Chapman River, Antechamber Bay

William thinks that in being here at the river again, there's a sort of beautiful endless return, not quite a circle, like Maringani's weaving that grows out and out from the centre, ever-widening. He is digging for kuti, and like Maringani's country, across the way there is freshwater and saltwater mixing here. There is sand dune and grass country. There is spinifex. William loves to be between the river and the sea listening to the sea grass whisper and croon. Place of crossing over. If he cranes his neck towards the south-east he can just make out the Sturt Light that he helped her build — that lighthouse that made his shoulders strong and his cough so ragged. The lighthouse that trapped his breath, so thinks Maringani. Behind the river, he has cleared a space for water-melons and vegetables, though they don't grow so well here as at Wallen's, and he's added onto the remains of the sealers' hut, making the back outer wall an inner wall, keeping the original hearth.

There's four of them living here now — Minnie, still in her wurlie on the other side of the river — William, Maringani, and their youngest, Beatrice. Emma, the only one born at Three Wells, lives in Hog Bay now with her husband and the little'uns, Jack, Silvie and Hettie. And Samuel stayed with the Wallens all that time ago, and was god knows where now. William sends little arrows of hope and light his way whenever he thinks of him, though he's not to mention his name. Firstborn. He'd be a man

275

now — older than William was when he'd become his father. To William, Samuel is a lurch in his chest that is something between worry and longing and surrender. He wonders if Mari ever thinks of him. He doesn't think so.

In the shallows a black-winged stingray steals gracefully along the sandy bottom, and William straightens to follow it with his gaze. A small cloud, he thinks, in a fathomless sky, and he wonders how long he and Mari can hold fast here. He worries about burn grass time now — they're already attracting too much attention from the settlers, and he'd tried to be so very quiet, just tending his own little patch. Everything was changing. When the boats started coming in one after the other, thick as sap, the island grew heavy and weary with footprints that would not disappear.

King George Beach (Sandy)

On the threshold of a hive, thinks Diana, preparing the smoker, and acknowledging this small ritual she has come to understand. It is the first day of the new year. She tests the bellows and the smoke is gentle as whisper. Not too hot. Bees have a tenderness for the colour blue, Diana read in Nell's falling-apart copy of Maeterlinck's *The Life of the Bee* that now sits on her mantle, so she'd painted the boxes blue. I have a tenderness for blue too. She fingers the lapis lazuli pendant she bought to mark her shift to the island and hopes this keeping of bees is a somehow fitting way to acknowledge Nell's hexagon-holed story. And Sol's. And Nell's mother's, too. She has an inexplicable sorrow for that grandmother, knowing how easily one can be placed on the outside of children — even their own. Especially their own. Diana marvels at the baffling industry inside the box. The slow drone. Every bee playing its small perfect part. Each time she waves the smoke in large slow gestures, it is not that the bees are under attack, but that they submit to a force, something like a natural catastrophe, and they dip themselves in honey, ready to build a new refuge should they need to flee the ancient one — the first one. She loves the drama of this. The passion — the higher purpose. *Fleeing*. She hovers at the hive like the bees are her wily charge. She knows them at their noisiest, knows their shivering darkness. Knows their honey to be a beautiful golden thing. Sweet nourishment. Belonging, now, to the island like so many have before. The bees and Diana. The wounds passed down from her mother are staunched — a little. She might come to understand them yet. Understanding is only ever first a listening. The bees huddle together like they're listening. And, of course, they always know just what to do.

Nell

Sol, my streak of blue — once awakened, I could only burn; burn away all that was before and burn in the inmost heart of me where you reached right in, setting us aflame, burning down the tinder of your burning world and mine; our fire leaves a wake that burns us to the bone — guts this house of love my love — but turns us to burning burnished gold too my love. What can we salvage but our own charred remains? Let me love you long and burning light light light.

Sol, my sun. Samuel, my lonely stranded moon.

near *Lubra Creek*

Maringani is almost as light as air. She knows there is nothing much to earth her now. The fire is warm, but the heat goes right through her, as if she is evaporating. She has walked and walked and walked. For a whole week, since Weellum died, she has walked, and that was the beginning of her disappearing. She has been cutting out kinyeris from the grass trees with Emue's scraper. The hearts of grass trees to keep her alive, but with her own heart breaking, this one will be her last. William was right — this was a place you couldn't hold on to. Always slipping through. She knows this is because it's land of the dead, Kukakun, entrance way to the Sky World. But the country here has been good to her. Ngurungani. Kangaroo Island. She'd been gentle with its body and it showed her things. She was sorry she could no longer take care of it. No more burn grass. Their bodies were all hurting now. Choking.

Maringani rubs the scar she made for Emue just below her hairline. Where the rock had split the skin raggedly. Where the blood had gushed and dripped into her eyes, changing how everything looked. And there's the other scar too, tight on her belly, where the rock had not got rid of the boy growing inside.

She chews the kinyeri slowly. It is fibrous in her mouth, like she's eating a weaving. From behind Waubs Wall, she watches the grass tree burn, its heart set free to grow again. The flames bright and loud curl around and around and spiral upwards as if the spirit of the tree flies out, and Mari wants to go with it. She thinks of Ngurunderi's wives bound up in the stem of the grass tree. Maringani runs her hands over the neatly interlocking stones of the wall and marvels at Waub's strength. Good place, this one. Maringani lies down with her back pressed to the wall and her knees curled in protectively. Weellum always said her bones were filled with air, like the bones of birds. But it was he who made her light. And remembering the spiced honey smell of him makes her even lighter still. Light as fire. The scraper falls from her hand and when it catches the sun, it gloams like black water.

near Antechamber Bay

The scruffy limbs of the mallee turn gold at dusk, glowing almost, and reddening as the sun drifts lower — the last burning ember. Pearl wonders whether they've crossed some kind of threshold turning down the track that runs past Nell's childhood creek, everything's so drenched in other-wordly light. Small kangaroos silhouette the hills, their alert ears and humped backs making perfect outlines against the empty sky. They turn their noses towards the car, and Pearl leans out the window to better glimpse their little marsupial faces as they pass. So many of them. A gathering. The light gentle for them now after the burning rag of day. Nico slows the car to a stop.

I've never seen so many kangaroos at once, he says.

I know — so strange.

Shall we keep going? Do you know where to go?

Just a little further along.

But they sit in the car and don't move. The ocean in the distance is flat and shiny. Mirror silver. And the grasses in the foreground are catching the light now. The hairs on Nico's arms hold the sun. Eventually, Nico turns the car and they continue along the track. Pearl points to

282

where he should pull in near the empty creek that is just a memory of water now. There is more than one grass tree, and they wander between them, lifting up the sharp leaves and checking the black flanks. Almost like inspecting cattle for brandings. But the trees are so very quiet and stationary and give nothing away.

Nell, which one? Pearl whispers.

She scans the curve of creek and wonders where the best place to lie down would be. There is a small mound, a clearing. And there's a grass tree beside it. Pearl crouches before the tree, placing her hands on its sides. It has two stems, jutting upwards, leaning slightly towards each other. They pin the sky. I wonder if two stems means it has two hearts, Pearl thinks.

Nico squats beside her. Is this it?

Not sure. Could be.

Nico crawls around the tree, running his hands up and down its rough stubby length, peering closely. Pearl rests her forehead against it. Her blood thumps in her ears and the grass tree's own vascular system carries water and minerals from one part of the tree to another. Slow metabolism.

Nup. Can't see anything. Could be grown over?

Maybe.

Pearl remembers Nico for a moment stretched out vulnerably after they'd made love near the inlet following Nell's wake, and she cupping his penis and everything of him in the whole of her hand, the sun glaring down on his chest and the side of her face, and his skin so white and so bare. But he shone. And the scrimshaw shone, like some other kind of matter. Not dirt, or leaf, or plywood, or desiccated bees. This was polished bone, not the weathered bones of fallen animals. Sea bone. Out of place there, and strangely cool. Nico had fingered the yellowing surface and the etched lines of a woman's face. They'd marvelled at it and then he'd smoothed it over her cheeks and lips and in the dip of her collarbone. She thinks of it now as some kind of talisman of fertility. She is pregnant.

Nico puts his arm around Pearl and leans his forehead against the back of her neck. They stay there a long while, the tree imprinting its rough pattern on Pearl's skin.

This is the one, she says.

Nico stands and unpacks the box of implements they've brought. He begins sweeping the dirt in a methodical perimeter around the grass tree, clearing debris. Pearl takes out the long matches and the newspaper and the kerosene. Nico uncaps the jerry can and pours water on the dirt around the tree. Dampening. Together they stuff the screwed-up newspaper in the tree's secret places, parting the protective leaves lovingly. They are careful with the kerosene, not to get it on their hands, and dab it on the little bundles of newspaper. Nico had wanted to use firelighters — safer. Pearl thought it somehow cheating, though now she wonders whether Nico had, in fact, been right. The element of fire, not to be reckoned with. And this plan, slightly mad, she knows.

You should be the one to light it, he says.

It catches easily. Flames spreading in quick dancing steps and then wrapping, spiralling around the tree like a dervish. The leaves are oily. They spit and snarl and resist. Pearl and Nico step back and the tree roars at them. In the middle of searing brightness and the smoke, Pearl sees in flashes the silhouette of the tree, the heart, the bones, its crooked naked outline. Pearl cries and it is not for Nell, not even for herself, but it's some other bodily response that she surrenders to. Something primal. Nico stamps at the spot fires and wields the second jerry can of water heroically on the nearby shrubs.

When the fire is just a gentle crackling and the smoke whips to follow them wherever they stand, they step back to the clearing and sort of crumple. Together, they watch the whole thing burn. Release it from the heart place where it grew — Nell's love, her own grief, and all the ways we are connected to each other. Connective tissue of the universe. Her tears sting as they dry. Nico's hand is strangely cold on her shoulder — adrenaline, she thinks.

There is something about that place — its expansiveness, its wind-rush, and its sea-howl that makes everything she holds tight just fall away. Her mind turns to all those before Nell who have on the island known the thrum of the sea in their ears, the wind beating around their shelters, or shaking the windows, and the damp smell of salt in the midnight air. And the sand. Everywhere sand. In the bed, under fingernails, in the hollow at the base of the neck and sand with every mouthful of food.

In the last of the light, the smoke is a shroud, monochrome over the sculptural lines of the tree. Its shape revealed. A chiaroscuro. Two stems charred and hopeful in the way they stand so straight and sure together. The letters gouged into its skin long blistered over — healed and bumpy with scar tissue. All the names are gone now and in the deep of the tree. Disturbed by the smoke, a bee drifts above, its wings glinting.

Lubra Creek

there is nothing that says you were here,
the mallee continues to grow in a tangle
with its gold-tipped crowns of green
and messy bark hanging down like scrolls,
that I wish I knew how to read

there is nothing that says you were here,
it is cool and muted as it was
the creek curving to a breathing sea
out   and   in
the mainland beckoning like a mirage

there is nothing that says you were here,
even though you were tied and lashed
for trying to escape across Backstairs Pas-
     sage,
flesh sliced from your buttocks like a
     seal's —
the blood is all gone now

there is nothing that says you were here
but the minka bird — messenger of death,
who wails overhead as its ancestors did
     before.

Author's Note

Set into the hill that faces the mainland and overlooking Penneshaw Beach, Kangaroo Island, is the Contemplation Seat: a memorial to the Tasmanian and mainland Australian Aboriginal women (including Ngarrindjeri, Kaurna, Peramangk and Ramindjeri nations) brought to Kangaroo Island by sealers prior to official settlement in 1836. Engraved on each concrete step leading to the seat are the names of women (the ones we know about from both public and anecdotal records) who contributed to the history of Kangaroo Island. Some of the women's names can be made out, but most of them are starting to wear away because of the weather. They are disappearing. Some names never made it onto the steps.

More often than not, the women were forced into these relationships on the sealers' terms. They were stolen from their homelands and brutalised. In some cases, however, the partnerships over time became more equitable than they seem at first glance. The relationships between the Aboriginal women and the sealers were complex. And in these relationships there was the opportunity for cross-cultural exchange and for a shared space to develop, where the two cultures became inextricably tied to one another. My aim in writing this story was to show a nuanced perspective on the relationships between sealer men and Aboriginal women. I was both inspired and informed by the work of Lynette Russell in her *Roving Mariners: Australian Aboriginal Whalers and Sealers in the Southern Oceans, 1790–1870*, where she highlights the complexity and transformative power of these relationships.

While this is a work of fiction, I have drawn upon a range of primary and secondary sources. I would like to acknowledge those anthropologists, historians, scholars, authors and early colonial writers whose research and writings have helped shape my understanding of Kangaroo Island's past, as well as my knowledge of aspects of Ngarrindjeri culture. These include Norman Tindale, H.J. Finnis, W.H. Leigh, John Wrathall Bull, Alexander Tolmer, Rev. G. Taplin, Jean Nunn, Wynnis J. Ruediger, J.S. Cumpston, Rebe Taylor, David Unaipon, Lester Irabinna Rigney, Deborah Bird Rose, Stephen Muecke and, especially, Diane Bell.

I owe much to Richard Hosking's body of work on Kangaroo Island; particularly, his introduction of William Cawthorne — educator, diarist, columnist, author, artist and occasional preacher of the new colony of South Australia. Cawthorne's novella, *The Kangaroo Islanders*, depicts the lives of sealers and their Aboriginal 'wives' in the first literary representation of Kangaroo Island's early history. Cawthorne's novella gives an insight into the sealers' lingo and patterns of speech, but it also describes the landscape and climate of Kangaroo Island in exquisite detail. It also references 'A Kangaroo

Island Dinner', where the heart of a grass tree, 'a queer-looking vegetable' is eaten as a delicacy.

Nell's Seal Brother story is adapted from Duncan Williamson's story of the same name in *Tales of the Seal People*.

The lines from on pages 203 and 230 are taken from 2:14 and 8:6-7 of *The Song of Songs: A New Translation and Commentary* by Ariel Bloch and Chana Bloch. Thank you, George Borchardt, Inc, for permission to reproduce this.

The poem 'Lubra Creek' was first published in *Rewired: Friendly Street Poets 32*. Thank you, Maggie Emmett.

While this is a work of fiction, I have identified individual Ngarrindjeri people with whom I worked, such as Aunty Ellen and Uncle Tom Trevorrow at Camp Coorong. I have also retained the names of key individuals whose lives are documented in the historical records such as Nat Thomas, Piebald — one of the names given to the well-known figure of 'Fireball Bates' — Governor Henry Wallen and Tiger Simpson. These men are all Kangaroo Island personalities about whom information is easily available. In the naming of other characters, I sought names that reflected the time period and sensibility of the story; for example, Maringani. By coincidence, 'Nell' and 'Pearl' were also the names of sisters born at the mission at Point McLeay (Raukkan). The 'Nell' and 'Pearl' of *Heart of the Grass Tree* are fictional and not based on the Cameron sisters of Point McLeay. The characters of Anderson and Emue are sketched from records found in N.J.B. Plomley's *Friendly Mission: The Tasmanian Journals and Papers of George Augustus Robinson, 1829–1834*, and his *Weep in Silence: A History of the Flinders Island Aboriginal Settlement, with the Flinders Island Journal of George Augustus Robinson 1835–1839*. I also used Luise Hercus and Jane Simpson's *History in Portraits: Biographies of Nineteenth Century South Australian Aboriginal People* to help imagine my characters from two hundred years ago into being.

The black glass scraping tool that belongs to Emue and Maringani in the story was found on Kangaroo Island by textile archaeologist Keryn James, and is described in detail in her thesis, 'Wife or Slave'. Thank you, Keryn, for illuminating the minutiae of life for the islander women in the 1800s. I would also like to thank Andy Gilfillan of Antechamber Bay, who showed me the location of Lubra Creek and Waubs Wall, and allowed me to spend a magical afternoon at those places, gestating ideas for this story. And thanks, too, to Christine Walker and the late Karno Walker for the chats at Murray Lagoon, and for the notes you both put together regarding Kangaroo Island history.

The glossary of Ngarrindjeri terms at the beginning of the novel has been put together using the *Ngarrindjeri Picture Dictionary*, compiled by Mary-Anne Gale and Dorothy French with the Ngarrindjeri Elders, *Ngarrindjeri for Smarties*, compiled by Mary-Anne Gale and Phyllis Williams and Diane Bell's *Ngarrindjeri Wurruwarrin: A World That Is, Was, and*

Will Be. It was also compiled from conversations with the late Uncle Neville Gollan of Camp Coorong, who generously shared Ngarrindjeri words — their meanings and pronunciation. And without the guidance of the late Uncle Tom Trevorrow and his wise counsel in regard to Ngarrindjeri culture, protocol and sensibility, this book would not have been possible. Uncle Tom knew the importance of meaningful dialogue, across and between cultures. Yarning with him was a gift. Any errors are my own. And thank you, especially, Aunty Ellen Trevorrow, for making the conversations with Uncle Tom possible, and for your generosity and friendship along the journey of *Heart*.

Acknowledgements

The making of this book would not have been possible without the support of the following dear people.

My children, Saskia and Jachimo, who have lived gracefully with this book for a long time now and, in many ways, were its inspiration. I write for you. My parents, Sally and Alan, who nurtured my imagination always. My sister, Roxy, who is the loveliest person I know. My grandmothers — their stories. Thank you, Michael Collister, for your insights and your hospitality, and Geoff Wallbridge, for advice on all things weather and Kangaroo Island. Thanks so much, Jula Bulire. Jacqueline Kohler, thanks for the champagne and chats and for always checking in. Also, Catherine, Emma, Tess and Cin — lovely gals.

My gratitude to early readers of the novel, and tinker-sisters, Melinda Graefe and Threasa Meads. And to Jeri Kroll, who was there with this story when it was just a seedling. Thank you, Giselle Bastin, Janie Conway-Herron, the late Syd Harrex, Mark O'Flynn, Catherine Milne and especially Jaqueline Blanchard, for seeing the potential. Thank you, too, Flinders University and the Document Delivery Service.

Thank you to the absolutely lovely Pippa Masson and all at Curtis Brown Australia for looking after me so very well. Thank you, Lisa

Babalis and Kate Cooper at Curtis Brown UK. Hannah Kent — beautiful writer and mentor — thank you! You know why. Also, dear word-weavers, Alex Miller, Rebekah Clarkson and Julia Cameron, thank you for showing the path.

The gorgeous staff and friends at Matilda Bookshop, Kim, Sarah, Fran, Heloise and especially Joanna, wonderful reader of books, and Gavin — for encouraging me to find ways for *Heart Tree* to be in the world, and then supporting it so beautifully. Thank you!

My dearest publisher Meredith Curnow and editor Elena Gomez, whose fine insights helped grow *Heart Tree* to fruition — you've been amazing and such a pleasure to work with. Thanks to the whole team at Penguin Random House Australia, especially Anyez Lindop, Bella Arnott-Hoare, Louisa Maggio, Lou Ryan, Clive Jackson, and all the sales reps. Lex Hirst, thank you.

Jelina Haines and Diane Bell, I am grateful for your insights and conversation and advice. Thank you for being so generous.

This book has been supported by a residency fellowship from Varuna, The Writers House. My residency there saw the beginning of this book coming to fruit.

Andrew — my fire. Without you, there is no heart tree. Darling thank you. All-ways.

Finally, thank you, dear readers. Release it from the heart place where it grew.

We do hope that you have enjoyed reading this large print book.

Did you know that all of our titles are available for purchase?

We publish a wide range of high quality large print books including:
Romances, Mysteries, Classics
General Fiction
Non Fiction and Westerns

Special interest titles available in large print are:
The Little Oxford Dictionary
Music Book
Song Book
Hymn Book
Service Book

Also available from us courtesy of Oxford University Press:
Young Readers' Dictionary
(large print edition)
Young Readers' Thesaurus
(large print edition)

For further information or a free brochure, please contact us at:
Ulverscroft Large Print Books Ltd.,
The Green, Bradgate Road, Anstey,
Leicester, LE7 7FU, England.
Tel: (00 44) 0116 236 4325
Fax: (00 44) 0116 234 0205